Elsie stuck the end of the candy cane into her mouth and stepped into Santa's workshop.

She took in racks of wood, a pegboard of tools, and makeshift tables covered with toys. A wooden train, carved but not sanded or painted, half-filled with wild animals. A stable with horses and a partially finished bull that were sized for action figures or fashion dolls. Maybe for a toy rodeo. Rocking horses and toddler-size rocking chairs. And that was with a quick glance.

"Levi!" She pulled the candy from her mouth and pointed with it. "This is amazing!" He could go nationwide with a website. Other Amish had them for their businesses. If she could take a few pictures with her phone and talk to an *Englisch* girlfriend who designed websites…He'd object, of course, but it'd be for his own good.

"I'd forgotten how you always smell of peppermint," he said, his voice strangled. "It makes me want…" He shook his head.

He wanted peppermint? She broke off the curved end, still in the wrapper, and held it out.

After a moment's hesitation, he took the end she'd sucked the color from.

"It makes me want to kiss you. But this will have to suffice." And he stuck the candy in his mouth.

The
AMISH
CHRISTMAS
GIFT

ALSO BY LAURA V. HILTON

The Hidden Springs Series

The Amish Wedding Promise

The
AMISH
CHRISTMAS
GIFT

A Hidden Springs Novel

Laura V. Hilton

FOREVER

NEW YORK   BOSTON

Copyright © 2020 by Laura V. Hilton

Cover design and illustration by Elizabeth Turner Stokes
Cover photography by Shirley Green
Cover copyright © 2020 by Hachette Book Group, Inc.

Forever
Hachette Book Group
1290 Avenue of the Americas, New York, NY 10104
read-forever.com
twitter.com/readforeverpub

First Edition: October 2020

Forever is an imprint of Grand Central Publishing. The Forever name and logo are trademarks of Hachette Book Group, Inc.

The publisher is not responsible for websites (or their content) that are not owned by the publisher.

All Scripture quotations are taken from the King James Version of the Holy Bible.

ISBN: 978-1-5387-0068-6 (mass market), 978-1-5387-0069-3 (ebook)

Printed in the United States of America

OPM

10 9 8 7 6 5 4 3 2 1

ATTENTION CORPORATIONS AND ORGANIZATIONS:
Most Hachette Book Group books are available at quantity discounts with bulk purchase for educational, business, or sales promotional use. For information, please call or write:

Special Markets Department, Hachette Book Group
1290 Avenue of the Americas, New York, NY 10104
Telephone: 1-800-222-6747 Fax: 1-800-477-5925

*To the God who loved me enough to
die for me because He loved me first
To Loundy: my favorite song
To Michael: my adventurous one
To Kristin: my darling daughter
To Jenna: my sunshine
To Kaeli: my shower of blessing*

ACKNOWLEDGMENTS

Thanks to Marilyn Ridgway for information about the Amish in Arthur, Illinois, buggy snapshots taken with her cell phone, and answering questions. I've been there a zillion times, but you were an excellent resource.

Thanks to Jenna, Candee, Lynne, Linda, Heidi, Marie, Christy, Kathy, Julie, and Marilyn for your parts in critiques, advice, and/or brainstorming. Also to my street team for promoting and brainstorming. Candee, this story would not be what it is without you.

Thanks to Jenna for taking on the bulk of the cooking while I was on deadline.

Thanks to Hachette Book Group (Forever) for taking a chance on me and to Tamela Hancock Murray for representing me.

The
AMISH
CHRISTMAS
GIFT

CHAPTER 1

There he stood. Levi. The man of her longtime dreams. The man she once believed she would marry. The one she'd still marry in a heartbeat if...

If.

She shooed the thought away. No point going there. Water under the bridge and all that.

He leaned over the counter saying something to the *Englisch* man on the other side. The *Englisch* man laughed as a sudden burst of wind caught a paper on the counter. The paper blew off. Neither man appeared to notice, but she gave chase, stalling its progress with her foot.

It was the size and shape of a folded check. Definitely important. Levi would be looking for it, upset that he lost it.

She'd been a victim of his skill at losing things too many times to count. Like the time he misplaced her during a date.

Elsie Miller still hadn't figured out how that was possible, but she carried the receipt for the bus ticket home in her wallet as a tangible reminder.

Levi Wyse was nothing but trouble. Too bad he was so handsome. And too bad her heart had major problems remembering that he was trouble. Which was why she resorted to spying to avoid getting her feelings hurt when he would inevitably reject her and walk away...But she just couldn't help but stare, long, wish, dream, and regret the way things had ended.

She peeked around the edge of the endcap at the handsome man now scrabbling for something on the floor in front of the register. Why was Levi in town on a Monday anyway? He hadn't made a purchase, not that she knew of anyway, but had carried in a huge cardboard box full of something that rattled and had the *Englisch* clerk oohing and aahing and gushing nonsense about how "this year Santa Claus will be bringing lions and tigers and bears, oh my!" Then, all in a dither, the clerk had called for the store owner, who came out of his office, talked quietly for a bit, then handed Levi a piece of paper. The one that he'd already lost. Though to be fair, it had been caught by a gust of wind that blew in with a customer, so it wasn't entirely his fault.

Elsie knew exactly where it was, too. Under her foot. And she desperately wanted to know what the paper was. But finding out would involve leaving her hiding place, approaching Levi, and exchanging enough pleasantries to find out what the box held and what the owner had given him in exchange. And since he would rather run than talk to her, that was an open invitation for heartbreak. This was as close as she'd be able to get to Levi. The heartbreak was ever present.

Of course, she could unfold and look at the paper, before returning it to the clerk, while pretending Elsie didn't know who Levi was. The same clerk who refused to give her a job application, stating very firmly that they weren't hiring. A lie, because she'd given an application to another girl.

Elsie would rather give the paper to Levi. Just for the opportunity to share oxygen with him one last time before she left the Amish for good.

And that was assuming he would even speak to her, since the last time they'd had words—eighteen months ago—he'd accused her of lashing out irrationally. Her! Irrational! He was the one who'd lost her.

But since then, whenever he saw her coming, he turned and walked in the other direction.

As if she were the one in the wrong.

"Elsie Miller, as I live and breathe," a voice boomed from behind her.

Elsie wanted to shush the man, but it was too late for that. Besides, George Beiler knew only one volume. Loud.

Levi shot to his feet so fast he whammed his head on the edge of the counter. He said something in a low rumble to the *Englisch* clerk and strode for the door.

Elsie gave him points for not running. But even so, he was getting away.

She bent and grabbed the edge of the folded paper. It flapped open enough to reveal that it was a check with a row of numbers that factored into a huge amount of money. Now curiosity really burned. She murmured her excuses to George, who was telling her—and everyone else in the store—about the ant farm he was buying for the school. As if anyone cared.

He cupped his ear and leaned near. "Speak up, missy," he shouted.

Elsie smiled brightly, waved the check at George, and dashed after Levi. Well, sort of dashed, because a tourist bus chose that inopportune moment to grind to a stop, and the passengers making a mass exodus into the gift store blocked Elsie's exit.

"Levi!"

He continued his fast trot toward the hitching post. If he heard her, he ignored her.

A tall man wearing a black Stetson passing on the sidewalk stopped, turned, and gave a loud, piercing whistle. "Yo, Levi!"

Levi stopped. Turned. And with unfailing accuracy, his gaze connected with hers.

Her heart stuttered.

* * *

Levi's foot tapped impatiently as he tried not to watch Elsie Miller maneuver her way through the crowd outside the touristy gift shop. One of several on the strip: gift shops, antiques shops and a thrift store, plus a small ice cream and sandwich shop. He'd been headed to the corner crosswalk so he wouldn't get in trouble with the local police for jaywalking. Even now an officer sat in his cruiser, keeping an eye on traffic. Besides, *Daed* always used to scold him for that. Lesson learned when he was almost hit by a bus as a boy.

His gaze kept returning to Elsie like the homing pigeons his *daed* used to raise back before... well, before.

Before his life turned into tattered shreds, not even vaguely resembling its former glory.

Elsie's strawberry-blond hair shone like rose-tinted gold in the early December sunshine, and the green dress she wore accented her pale-green eyes. A shade of mint today. She always wore some shade of green, at least ever since he'd mentioned how it brought her eyes to life and made them sparkle like homemade limeade Popsicles when the sun hit the ice crystals just right.

He should've commented on how cranberry-colored dresses would highlight the natural shades of juicy strawberry pink in her hair.

Actually, he should've kept his mouth shut and not said anything at all. It seemed as if she wore green to torment him and remind him of everything he'd had and somehow lost. Which included...everything.

And *jah*, it made him more than a little envious when he noticed her with another man, but since he quit attending singings and youth frolics eighteen months ago, that was at a minimum.

His gaze shifted to the *Englisch* wannabe cowboy now trotting beside Elsie, with the black Stetson, skinny jeans, and a loud Hawaiian-print button-down shirt, not tucked in. Worn cowboy boots completed the picture. The man looked like a thrift store full of discarded cast-offs exploded on fill-your-bag-for-fifty-cents day.

He shouldn't judge, but it was hard not to when the wannabe cowboy swaggered nearer to Elsie and shouted, "When you get tired of the pilgrim, babe, look me up."

Pilgrim? Really?

Elsie graced Wannabe Cowboy with a tight smile that still somehow brightened the world and continued toward Levi. Cowboy froze in position and watched. Levi tried not to smirk, because he was really in the same position.

Elsie was the forbidden fruit—and oh, he craved her like cold water on a hot day.

Really, he had better things to do than watch temptation herself stroll through the burgeoning crowd toward him, though what they were escaped his memory. He forced himself to look away and pulled out his cell phone to check the time.

The bank closed in fifteen minutes and he needed to hurry—oh shoot. That's right. He'd lost the check inside the store before he'd even gotten a good look at it. He'd counted on the money to pay toward his sister's medical bills and to buy a few groceries so they could eat.

The phone buzzed in his hands with an incoming message from Luke Zook the furniture maker, a man he worked for occasionally. Not a job Levi preferred, but he couldn't afford to be choosy. He turned away and opened the message.

> Orders backed up. Need help winterizing house and getting wood in.

The furniture maker had kind of adopted Levi since he lost his only child in a tornado a year ago, and Levi had lost pretty much everything, but since the man already had one full-time employee, it seemed he thought Levi should work for pennies on the dollar. But still. He *owed* Luke.

> On my way.

Traffic opened up and Levi dashed across the road to where his horse, Trouble, and buggy waited. The small town of Hidden Springs didn't generally have that much traffic, but there was some sort of festival going on and tourists were bused in from who knows where.

Trouble nickered as Levi unhitched her, and he rubbed her nose. "I'll give you a carrot stick when we get home." If they had any carrots, which was doubtful. He needed a personal grocery shopper. And the money to pay for one.

He really needed the check he'd lost. At least the store owner had promised to send it when he found it. Or issue a new check.

Levi climbed into the buggy, signaled, and merged into traffic. And then he noticed Elsie standing beside the road, waving something and her mouth moving. She shouted something. Not that he heard her, since someone laid on the horn.

Oh. Shoot. She'd wanted to talk to him.

The horn blared again. Not to mention he had a job waiting.

Since he wasn't sure what else to do, he waved back and drove on.

* * *

After Elsie finished her errands—aka an unfruitful job hunt—in town, she drove out to the small house where Levi and his sister, Abigail, lived. She had to drive past their place on her way home anyway so it was no trouble, except for the heart-wrenching possibility of seeing Levi. She still couldn't believe the man just walked off and left her in town, and after she made a spectacle of herself in front of a busload of tourists and the man who made a point of following her around town, calling her "babe" and not so politely reminding her that the "Quaker dude" didn't want her.

She was smart enough to figure that out on her own. She certainly didn't need his help. But Levi needed his check, even if it meant she faced another rejection. Still, maybe she could sneak in and out without actually running into him. Or his sister.

Levi's buggy wasn't parked in its spot when she drove in, so maybe he'd had other errands. Relief warred with disappointment, but really she wouldn't be brave enough to stop if he were obviously home. Most Amish in Hidden Springs left their doors unlocked, so even if no one was home, she'd be able to leave the check on the table and hopefully he could get it deposited before he lost it again. Elsie could leave a note to explain that was why she'd been trying to talk to him in town. The only reason.

She parked several feet away from the back porch wheelchair ramp and was halfway up when the door opened.

"Elsie?" Abigail peered out from her perch in the wheelchair. "What brings you by?"

Elsie smiled at her seventeen-year-old sister Mandy's former best friend, and her friend, too, since all the girls used to hang out together. "Levi lost his check." She pulled it from her pocket and held it out. "I brought it by. Can you give it to him?"

Ugh, that sounded rather formal. And stilted, but really, this was awkward. She hadn't stopped at this house in... well, ever. The former one, a rambling farm-house, had been blown away in a gas explosion close to two years ago, killing everyone inside except Abigail, who survived but might never walk again. Levi hadn't been at home. Maybe. She wasn't sure where else he would've been. Details were sketchy, and he'd refused to talk about it, though they'd continued to court for a time. And then they'd broken up soon after he lost her on a date.

Broken up, when she'd been expecting a proposal.

But he was the one who'd misplaced her on a date to an out-of-state wedding.

He was the one who'd accused her of lashing out irrationally when she'd confronted him about it.

Irrationally! When he'd offered no explanation about why he'd left her, lost her, or forgotten her. Okay, maybe she'd been a bit harsh, especially since he'd had a lot on his mind at the time, but still—

"Do you want to come in?" Abigail pushed the wood door open wider and opened the screen door.

"Um." Elsie glanced toward the road. Was that a horse and buggy stirring up dust in the distance? "No, I have groc—"

"Please." Abigail sounded close to tears. "I can't lift the iron skillet down from the high shelf and Levi isn't home yet. I was praying for help."

Oh. She'd never been the answer to anyone's prayers before. Usually they begged the Almighty for her departure, not her arrival. Hence her unfruitful job hunt today. She just wanted to be useful somewhere and to contribute money to her family's needs instead of being a burden before she left forever…especially since her marriage prospects were as slim as her job search.

Organizational skills were her gift—but they no longer

paid the bills. Not since the tornado blew the dentist office she'd worked for far away.

She shook her head. She wouldn't think about that. She'd focus on the positive. "How can I help?"

Abigail wheeled back and shut the door as Elsie entered the kitchen. She laid Levi's check on the table, set the almost empty sugar bowl on top. For a moment, she was tempted to cross to the woodstove and hold out her hands. It hadn't been all that cold when she left home, but a cold front had arrived as her *daadi*'s aches and pains predicted, and she was caught totally unprepared. She should learn to listen to him and his pain-level forecasts.

"The skillet is up there." Abigail pointed to an upper cabinet. "Levi was doing cleanup the other night and he just puts things wherever, which is so not helpful."

Elsie opened the cabinet door and lifted the heavy iron skillet down. "What's for supper?" She asked to be polite and because she didn't know what else to say. Should she put the skillet on the table or the stove?

"Cabbage and sausage. It's the last of the food except a little oatmeal for breakfast. I hope Levi got paid and remembered to buy food." Abigail still sounded close to tears.

Elsie sat the skillet down on the stove and swung around. Her gaze went from the check on the table to the buggy parked outside the window where her family's groceries waited. Her thoughts wandered to the full pantry shelves from all the canning they had done this past summer. Her family wouldn't go without if she left the food she purchased here and shopped again tomorrow. Except, she'd only bought things they didn't raise themselves, so the contents of her bags were probably worthless to Abigail. Flour, sugar, baking powder, cocoa—well, she could make a chocolate cake. If she had the other ingredients.

It would be the nice thing to do. It also might help make up for the fact that Levi thought she was irrational. And maybe *Gott* would take notice and give her a job.

"I'll be right back." Elsie dashed for the door and went outside. A gust of wind blew her dress up around her knees and she hugged herself. The temperature must've dropped ten degrees while she was inside.

She grabbed the bags of food, hurried back into the house, and deposited them on the table.

"What's that?" Abigail paused in chopping cabbage.

"Just a few things I picked up at the store." Should she offer to bring more tomorrow? Probably she should talk to her family first.

"For us?" Abigail's eyes widened.

No...not really, but maybe. Elsie pulled in a deep breath. "*Jah.*"

Abigail set down the knife as Elsie unloaded the bags. She reached for the cocoa powder as if it were a rare and valuable treasure. "Oh, I've been praying for chocolate. *Gott* is so good."

That was almost enough to make Elsie cry. "If you have butter, eggs, and milk, we could make a cake." We. Implying she'd stay. She cringed. "I should've said you."

"No butter, about a cup of milk, and exactly one egg."

Barely enough milk for a cup of hot cocoa. But Levi would surely milk the cow when he got home.

"He sold the cow." As if Abigail read her mind. She glanced out the window at the barn.

Elsie followed her gaze. The barn door was open now. She needed to hurry and get out of here before Levi walked in.

Oh, this poor family. Why hadn't the community been made aware of the need? Or had Levi simply failed to mention it because he worked from sunup to sundown and...

Speaking of which, where was all that money going? *Daed* had mentioned last church Sunday that Levi must have a padded bank account.

Abigail adjusted the position of her wheelchair.

Right. Funeral expenses. Medical bills. And Abigail's ongoing therapy.

Elsie's gaze went to the table, to the check waiting. There were multiple numbers. Then she glanced at Abigail, still cradling the cocoa powder, a bright smile on her face.

Was the community not helping with the medical bills or were they unaware of that need, too?

Elsie pulled in a quick breath. "Do you need help with anything else before I go?" She needed to be gone before Levi arrived.

Abigail returned the cocoa to the table and picked up the knife to finish slicing the cabbage. "No. *Danki* so much for what you did. And *danki* for stopping by."

Elsie nodded, biting her tongue to keep from promising more food tomorrow, though she was certain her parents would agree. "I'll try to come back sometime and help you organize the kitchen better. Don't forget to mention the check to Levi."

She sucked in a breath to try to prepare for the frigid cold and opened the door.

The screen door blew out of her grasp, almost slamming into Levi, who was standing there out of the wind, cell phone to his ear.

His gray eyes widened and he held up a finger, telling her to wait, but she dashed past with an exaggerated shiver.

They had nothing to say to each other anyway.

CHAPTER 2

Levi half listened as the employer he'd meet Tuesday morning—tomorrow—detailed what exactly he was contracting Levi to build, but mostly he watched the sway of Elsie's body as she speed walked to the buggy. Her skirts whipped around her legs, giving tantalizing glimpses of skin. He wanted to put down the phone and race after her to discover what she'd wanted in town, and why she'd stopped by to deliver the message personally.

Well, personally to Abigail, anyway.

It probably was about some women's frolic Abigail wouldn't be able to attend, because she couldn't get into a buggy without being lifted in and out, and he couldn't afford a driver all that often.

Whatever it was, it didn't concern him, because she hadn't even bothered to give him a simple greeting. He was the one who'd avoided her in town, though, until that wannabe cowboy so rudely caught Levi's attention. And then he stood there tapping his feet while waiting for Elsie to catch up. But then he'd gotten sidetracked and raced off to a job instead of remembering that Elsie had called out to him. He was the one who was willing to forgo the check he'd dropped for an undisclosed amount just to avoid seeing her... and breaking his heart. Again.

Sins had consequences. And he was the worst of sinners.

Mostly, he wanted to gaze into her beautiful green eyes and dream about what might've been. Back when she loved him. Liked him. Well, at least tolerated him. He didn't want the cold, sharp shards of green glass he'd looked into after his sister fell during her extended stay at the hospital. After he accidentally forgot he'd taken Elsie to an out-of-state wedding and had rushed back to Illinois to be with his sister. Of course, she might've understood if he'd explained, but she lashed out and broke up with him before he could and after that the reason was unimportant. She no longer needed to know.

Elsie scampered into the buggy and drove away as the man on the other end of the phone started repeating himself. Levi might be only half listening, but he was sure of that. Obviously, the *Englischer* sat in a warm place and wasn't standing outside in the cold wind. Abigail probably wouldn't tell, though, if he broke the district's no-phone-calls-in-the-house rule, due to the circumstances.

He watched Elsie make the turn onto the dirt road to head home, swallowed his disappointment on how things were, and turned his full attention back to the *Englischer*, who sounded like he was wrapping things up. Finally. Levi cleared his throat. "Okay. I'll see you tomorrow, Mr. Fletcher."

He ended the call, turned the sound to vibrate, and went inside.

Abigail sat at the kitchen table in her wheelchair, chopping cabbage and humming.

She looked up as Levi came in, grinned, and pointed the sharp end of the knife at something on the table.

Plastic grocery bags, baking supplies—where'd they come from? But that reminded him: He had a few groceries he'd bought with the money he'd earned from Luke, and he needed to bring them in. He turned around, dashed out to the buggy parked in the barn, and grabbed the bags.

Abigail was no longer smiling when he came in. She glowered as he dropped the full bags on the table.

He held out his hands in an unspoken apology, red and chafed from his labor in the cold. "What? I stopped at Zooks' Salvage Grocery and got food. Milk, carrots, eggs—"

"I was talking to you," she said.

He didn't remember her saying anything, just pointing to the baking supplies. But ouch. Maybe he needed to slow down and actually focus on the people in his life instead of not listening and driving wedges into his relationships.

Starting now with his sister.

"I'm sorry." He took his boots off and set them by the door, added a log to the fire in the woodstove, then sat at the table and looked at Abigail. "What were you saying? Someone brought the flour and sugar...?"

Abigail's frown deepened.

He wanted to do something to ease her frown and make her smile again. She hadn't smiled often since the accident—until she'd pointed at the supplies.

"Elsie brought your check."

Levi blinked at her. "Check? Oh, from...She found it?" He looked around but didn't see it. "Why didn't she give it to me?" And then he knew. While he was avoiding her, ignoring her calling out his name, and then forgetting her when he got sidetracked, she'd been trying to return his check. "It was nice of her to bring it by," he added rather inanely. "Along with the flour and stuff? You told her *danki*, right?"

"I did." Abigail leaned forward and picked up a folded piece of paper. She held it out. "And you need to, as well."

He took the check, opened it, then stared. Four digits in front of the decimal, but the first two were large. It was enough to pay the balance he still owed for Abigail's medical care. It'd be so nice to have that burden lifted. Enough to maybe hire an occasional personal shopper since he forgot to grocery shop so often.

And then he noticed the note on the memo line.

To Santa Claus for the carvings.

Despite the store owner's excitement, Levi hadn't expected things to sell, but still, he'd agreed to a commission.

To Santa...

His thoughts wandered to his cluttered workshop and disorganized office. The way he hunted for hours to find anything. His gaze landed on his seventeen-year-old sister, who, at least for now, lived in a wheelchair. There was so much she needed help with.

To Santa...

And he remembered the huge order the gift shop had made when they saw the circus train toy he'd brought in today. Complete with lions, and tigers, and bears...

To Santa...

"Maybe I could hire an elf."

Abigail smiled. "I know just the person."

* * *

The next day, Tuesday, just after noon, Elsie hitched up her horse, Dart, and headed for Thomas Zook's Amish-owned salvage grocery store. Her younger brother, nineteen-year-old Noah, had mentioned during breakfast that he'd heard they were hiring and desperate for help. That sounded promising. Unless news of her ineptness preceded her. But how much damage could she do at a salvage store, where almost everything was bent and dented already? There wouldn't be any unruly scholars to try to teach—which had prematurely ended her promising teaching job. She had the not-so-great honor of being the only teacher fired. And after only two weeks!

There was no hot coffee to pour on unsuspecting customers' laps—who knew it was so hard to talk and pour at the same time? No fragile figurines to break, no books to sidetrack her from doing her job...

Jah, she had a well-rounded employment history. Just no longevity. It seemed that quick turnover was a deficit. Especially since she couldn't even pretend interest in the hated jobs. She did like interacting with the people, though.

The owner, Thomas Zook, was just opening the door after their closed lunch hour and turning the gaslights on as Elsie pulled in. She parked at the red hitching post, pulled her heavy black sweater tighter against the cold wind, and hurried into the store. If she'd known they were hiring yesterday, she could've saved herself the cold ride today.

That would be a benefit to leaving the Amish. Heated vehicles. Too bad she didn't know when she was going. That all depended on...

Thomas Zook looked up from loading the cash drawer into the register. He smiled. "Elsie Miller. Weren't you just here yesterday? What brings you by again today? Did you hear about the fine sale we have on baloney?"

She hadn't but didn't want to admit to not reading their flyers, which were delivered with the weekly market-place news. "I heard you need someone to work for you. Stocking shelves and stuff. It just so happens that I need a job and I'm good at lots of things. Especially customer service." She couldn't remember exactly what her brother said the store owner needed. She aimed what she hoped was a bright smile at Thomas Zook, but it faltered as his lips flatlined and his eyes turned to steel.

"Why do you think you'd be a good fit for Zooks' Salvage Grocery?"

Oh. She hated this question. And the correct answer wasn't *You need someone to give money to in exchange for showing up. Why not me?*

"I shop here a lot. I know the layout." An embar-rassed giggle escaped, which only made things worse. Could she possibly act any more immature? She set her jaw, determined to get this interview going in the right direction.

"You do shop here a lot, and I appreciate that."

Thomas Zook closed the register, leaned his elbows on the counter, and surveyed her. "But I know your employment history. The only job you kept was for that *Englisch* dental office until it blew away. You're a screwup who spends more time talking than working. Why should I take a chance on you?"

Of course he knew. Elsie restrained a huff. "Customer service is important. And I wouldn't be dumping hot coffee on people, hiding in dusty corners reading books, or trying to teach thirty scholars of assorted ages, none of which know the meanings of 'sit' or 'quiet.' And, no offense, but there's nothing in this store I could damage much worse than it is." She cringed. And there went her chances of getting hired here.

Thomas Zook slowly straightened. He stared at her, silent, one hand tugging at his salt-and-pepper-colored beard. Then he cleared his throat. "I do carry honey and homemade jams and jellies in glass jars."

Oh.

"Pickled eggs, chowchow, and relishes, too."

Elsie pulled in a deep breath and forced a smile. "I help with canning at home. I haven't broken any jars. Well, not that many, anyway."

Thomas Zook chuckled. "I appreciate your honesty. When can you start?"

Elsie blinked. "You'll hire me?"

"Step into my office," he said, coming out from behind the counter. "We'll get the paperwork squared away, then put you to work."

Elsie tugged her sweater off as she followed him down the wide aisle to a swinging, canvas-style door at the back. He pushed through the heavy material and on the other side immediately took a left into a doorless room with a cluttered desk, overflowing file cabinets, and chairs piled high with boxes.

She'd love to get her hands on this room and clean it up. Organize it. Her fingers twitched. She tried to hide them in the folds of the oversize black sweater draped over her left arm. She wasn't sure of her job description but was pretty sure it wasn't office manager. She'd loved working for the dentist though her official title there was receptionist. She did the filing and helped out in other ways as needed.

Thomas Zook rummaged through a file cabinet. Papers fell out and landed on the floor, only to be stepped on and crinkled. "My daughter will pick them up when she cleans," he said. "I'll refile them later."

Elsie bit her lip. By the look of things, later never came.

"Ah, here it is." He pulled out a paper. "You know how to operate a cash register?"

She nodded, accepting the paper he held out.

"Good. You'll be cashier, stock person, and generally whatever is needed." He lifted another sheet of paper from the desk and handed it to her.

She looked at the boxes stuffed full of papers. The messy desk. And smiled.

He frowned. "The office is my domain. You stay out unless I call you in."

Too bad. She could work wonders in here. But she nodded, determined to keep the job long enough to actually start.

"Fill out the papers, then come find me. There's a table you can use in the storage room." He led the way out of the room, pointed to a table, and walked away.

Elsie pulled a black-ink pen out of her purse, pulled out a rusty metal folding chair, hung her sweater on the back, and put the papers on the sticky table. What appeared to be jam was smeared on it.

She picked up a balled wet rag at the other end of the table and wiped it clean, then sat on the chair. It wobbled.

Even though she was already hired, she filled out the application for employment, as well as the form for taxes, then gathered her things and went to find Thomas Zook. She didn't want to lose the job by not doing exactly what he said.

He stood at the front of the store, talking to a man whose back was to her, but she recognized his stance. Levi. What was he doing here? She froze, not wanting to interrupt and very tempted to run and hide. Was he following her? Though, why would he when he'd gone out of his way to avoid her? No. That didn't make sense.

She started to back around the endcap of the aisle, but Levi palmed his hat and turned, his gray eyes connecting with hers. His eyes widened as if he were surprised to see her there. She forced a weak smile and stepped forward. No point in hiding now.

"Elsie." Levi gripped his hat with both hands. "I was going to stop by your home after work tonight, but this will save time. *Danki* for bringing the check and groceries by yesterday. I appreciate them both more than you know."

That reminded her—she needed to buy more to replace what she'd given.

Levi kind of grimaced. "And I—"

"Elsie is a brand-new employee here," Thomas Zook said.

Levi sagged. "Congratulations," he muttered. "I hope you'll have a good, uh..." He frowned and pressed his lips together.

What had he been about to say? A good long employment? Probably not. Even though they'd been apart for eighteen months, he knew she hadn't been able to keep a job—other than the one at the dentist office—for longer than two weeks. He probably wondered what was wrong with her and counted it among his blessings that he escaped marrying such a failure.

Oh, that hurt.

Levi dipped his head as he handed Thomas Zook cash for whatever he'd purchased before Elsie came out. Then he cleared his throat and glanced at Elsie. A hint of disappointment darkened his gray eyes. "*Danki*. Abigail and I appreciate what you've done." He accepted his change, lifted the plastic bag, and walked out.

Elsie watched him go. A strange desire to chase after him and find out what he'd wanted to say filled her.

But bygone romances were best left undisturbed.

Especially since her time as an Amish woman was measured in weeks and days.

* * *

Levi felt strangely disquieted as he drove away from Zooks'. He hadn't exactly been excited about Abigail's insistence that he should hire Elsie as his elf, but now that she was unavailable, he was disappointed. And he didn't have the foggiest of ideas why. It seemed he should be happy, because he and Elsie had history— then again, she'd kept him organized. She'd been the one to call their relationship quits, and he'd readily agreed, just so they could say it was a mutual decision. But in reality, he'd *loved* her, and if she'd stopped her scolding long enough for him to formulate his thoughts to find the words to explain, maybe they'd still be together. They would have even been married by now. It was just that her mind worked faster or something, because she could spit out what seemed like a thousand words to his ten.

Not that he was stupid. He'd scored at the top of the class during school and could work math problems lickety-split, but when it came to expressing himself verbally, he needed to think.

That wasn't her problem. She spoke first and thought later. And usually had to do some damage control. Good thing she never ran out of words.

Levi drove through Hidden Springs, stopping at the small branch bank to deposit his checks. Then he drove past the turnoff for Arthur toward another town closer to the highway. He passed an old factory then turned into the driveway for his afternoon job.

As he parked, he glanced down and realized he'd forgotten to eat the lunch he'd stopped by Zooks' to purchase. Instead, he'd spent the drive time thinking of Elsie and what might have been. A dangerous pastime.

Too late now. The man he was working for approached the buggy.

Levi ignored the grumbling of his stomach and pushed the memories of Elsie aside.

He needed to focus on his job now.

He'd ask Abigail for recommendations for a new elf later since Elsie was off the market.

CHAPTER 3

Elsie straightened what seemed like every aisle in the first half of the store, making sure the grocery items were at the front of the shelves where customers could reach them and everything was where it belonged.

Then she unpacked and shelved endless numbers of cans from dusty boxes that sometimes had icky, sticky black stuff in them from cans that had burst. She recorded the spoilage, discarded them in a container, and cleaned the mess.

She was thankful she had a place to work. Really. But accidentally setting a microwave on fire during her short-lived job as nanny to an *Englisch* family had been infinitely more exciting. The parents hadn't been so happy to learn that an entire kitchen wall had gone up in flames, but the fire department had responded and she'd herded the two children outside to watch. Elsie had been scared—terrified, actually—but being Amish, she hadn't known she couldn't heat certain things in a microwave. She still wasn't clear on that. But no matter. She'd been fired and no *Englisch* family would consider her for a nanny position.

Black tennis shoes appeared in her peripheral vision, and she paused, clutching a badly dented can of off-brand cream of celery soup in her hand. She looked up from her crouched position in front of the bottom shelf and met Thomas Zook's gaze. He bounced an apple in his hand. His mouth was set in a slight frown. Oh dear, had she done something wrong already?

"I hate to do this on your first day, but my wife has a doctor's appointment. Keep an eye out for customers, watch the register, and oh, I'm expecting an ice cream delivery from a factory outside of Chicago that's going out of business. Sign for it, but make sure they don't try to push some overly strange flavor on us. Use your best judgment. If you think it'll sell, accept it. If you don't think it will, reject it."

Elsie grinned. "I can do that. You can trust me." If there was one thing she was an expert on, it was ice cream.

Thomas Zook's expression didn't ease, but he nodded, palmed the apple, and walked out.

Elsie finished fronting the bottom shelf, then moved to the stool behind the register as an Amish family from another district came in. She'd seen them before but didn't know them.

They were new friends by the time they reached the checkout. Elsie had just finished ringing up their large order when a bunch of schoolchildren came in. "Hi, Teacher Elsie."

As they flocked around the candy aisle, Elsie cringed.

How could they call her teacher when she'd taught them nothing? She'd tried, really, but the usually well-behaved children had turned into monsters when she'd accepted the job. Either that or they got her talking about something totally unrelated to the lesson. The current teacher hadn't had a bit of trouble since she took over. So unfair. At least the bishop was kind about it. He'd said Elsie's voice was soft and sweet, but she lacked authority.

Levi would probably disagree with that assessment, since he'd accused her of lashing out irrationally. She could still see the shock on his face. The horror. And then the slow shaking of his head. *Jah*, a year and a half later and it still stung. Especially since she killed the chance of marriage to her one true love.

She checked out the noisy bunch of children— hopefully she wouldn't get into trouble for ruining their appetites—and breathed a sigh of relief as they banged their way through the doorway with their bags of leftover Halloween candy Zooks' sold at a steep discount.

She could handle this job. She could. She took a moment to bask in the swell of success.

Fifteen minutes later, the ice cream delivery truck rumbled into the parking lot.

"Zook here?" a burly man asked, sticking his head through the doorway.

Elsie turned toward him. "No—"

"Unload the truck!" the man shouted.

Elsie tried to remember Thomas Zook's instructions as flats piled high with boxes were wheeled into the store. At least they knew where to take it. She hadn't known there was a walk-in freezer they could leave the flats in. And the amount! Did Zooks' really sell so much ice cream? She started toward the back to find out the flavors but was interrupted by a customer with an overfilled cart who needed Elsie's listening ears.

Finally, one of the men slapped a paper down on the counter. "Sign here. We're in a hurry to get back to Chicago. The weatherman is predicting an ice storm."

"I'm supposed to look over the packing list." She signed her name.

"Yeah, lady." The man snatched up the signed sheet and slapped another paper down.

The truck rumbled away as she scanned the list.

Twenty flats of dill pickle ice cream?

She frowned, her heart sinking. She'd been taken advantage of.

Dill pickle ice cream. Really?

It was kind of a pregnant woman cliché, but maybe it would sell.

Maybe.

Probably not.

Ice cream had just murdered her job, for sure and certain.

*   *   *

Levi wasn't late, but the day had seemed to stretch on forever. He was glad to finally be home. He trudged up the porch steps, tired, discouraged, and in serious need of a shower. He also faced a long evening working on toy orders. What did late to bed and early to rise make a man? Other than exhausted? Sometimes it seemed he never had a chance to truly rest. Especially since his sleep was often interrupted by nightmares.

A delicious scent of fresh baked bread mixed with something chocolatey and another smell he couldn't identify. He needed to eat on the run, though. Hopefully, Abigail wouldn't be peeved at him for ruining her plans for supper.

The predicted ice storm still hadn't arrived, but traffic was terrible and Levi heard that everyone was stocking up on necessities. He needed to ask Abigail what the necessities were and whether they needed any, but he'd probably forget before he got to the store. Or lose the list. He had so many stresses and concerns since the gas explosion it was a wonder he didn't lose himself.

Or maybe his mind was the first to go.

He paused long enough to take off his work boots. Considering what they'd waded through, they needed to stay outside. He opened the back door and stepped into the warm kitchen. Abigail sat at the table frosting a batch of chocolate cupcakes. She hummed as she worked, a happy smile on her face. Behind her, something simmered on the stove. His stomach rumbled.

Abigail looked up, her smile turning upside down as she stared. Gawked, really. He winced. He must look and smell worse than he thought.

"What happened to you?" *Jah*, there was buggy loads of shock in her voice.

He grimaced. "I'll explain later. Let me shower first, okay?"

She wrinkled her nose. "You need to. Go on, now. And use the mudroom entrance so you don't track through the house."

Levi hurried around the house, went through the mudroom door, grabbed a clean set of clothes from his pile, and went into the shared bathroom. He dropped his clothes into the laundry basket Abigail left in there and, without waiting for the water to warm, stepped into the spray.

Once he was clean and dressed, he took the basket full of dirty laundry to the mudroom and dumped the contents right into the gas-powered machine. He started the load, then returned to the kitchen. Abigail had rolled her wheelchair closer to the stove and now stood on wobbly legs, stirring whatever was in the kettle.

"How can I help?" He peered over her shoulders. Carrots, celery, onion, bits of chicken, and noodles. Chicken noodle soup. "Oh, that looks good. Do you want to dish it out here or should I carry the kettle to the table?"

"Dish it out here. I need to slice a loaf of bread." She carefully lowered herself into the wheelchair. "Did you ask Elsie to be your elf?"

"Ah, no. I stopped at Zooks' for some baloney, cheese, and bread for my lunch and Thomas told me she was his newest hire. It seemed pointless to ask after that. And besides, I was a little too filthy to go calling on Elsie after work. Especially to offer her a job."

Abigail snorted. "A little?"

He wrinkled his nose at her, then grabbed a couple of soup bowls. Soup was quick. He'd slurp it down and head out to the workshop to do the job he loved instead of remodeling or home maintenance or construction jobs. He should rename his *daed*'s business from Wyse and Sons Construction to Levi's Honey-Do Business. Except, he was no longer anyone's honey.

Oh, Elsie . . .

"What happened to you at work anyway?" Abigail's voice yanked him back to the present.

"I was hired to help someone finish their basement. But the homeowner didn't know what he was doing and knocked a hole in a pipe when my back was turned. Unfortunately, I was standing under it and got a sewage shower. He needs to hire a plumber to fix it before I return." Hopefully, someone else would clean it up, too. That wasn't in his job description. *Ugh.*

"Ewww. Not appropriate supper conversation."

"Hey. You asked." Levi carried the filled bowls to the table. "Do you have any other ideas for an elf?"

"No. But let me think about it. I really wanted Elsie. She would've been perfect."

Jah, she was perfect. Except, he'd have to arrange her hours so they never saw each other.

Perfect. Except, he would know she'd been in his home, handling his things.

Perfect. Except, she'd be always on his mind.

Perfect. Just perfect.

* * *

Fired. On the same day she was hired. That had to be a first.

Tears burned Elsie's eyes and clouded her vision as she clutched the bags of replacement groceries in one hand and her purse, containing the day's wages in cash, in the other.

She'd be embarrassed to slip that small wad of cash into *Daed*'s hand from her purse.

She'd never eat ice cream again.

Okay, maybe that was a little overdramatic. She'd never eat dill pickle ice cream again.

Not that she would've eaten it in the first place. It even sounded disgusting. Who came up with such flavors? And why?

But that aside, where could she go to be alone so she could mourn in private? She placed her shopping bags and purse on the buggy floorboard next to three cardboard boxes from home and untied the reins from the hitching post.

Home was out of the question. There were too many people with grandparents, parents, brothers, and sisters all clustered in one five-bedroom house. There was no privacy anywhere.

It was way too cold to go to a park or to the hidden springs. She'd have privacy there, though, thanks to the frigid temperatures.

Best thing to do would be to pretend that nothing bad had happened and to take the home-canned foods *Mamm* said she could give to Abigail and Levi to their house.

Levi. Hopefully, he wouldn't be home yet. He had been nice enough at Zooks', thanking her for bringing his check by, but she wasn't prepared to risk seeing him twice in one day. Not that he was ever mean. He'd practiced avoidance skills so much he about had them mastered. Still, if he was home, she'd drive past. But if he wasn't home, she would stop.

Abigail wouldn't say anything if Elsie looked a bit stressed. They were friends, but not that close. Probably the best thing to do would be to pretend she was fine, deliver the home-canned goods, and maybe by the time she finished and went home she'd have her emotions under control.

She climbed into the buggy, unwrapped one of her

candy canes from last Christmas that she'd purchased at Zooks', and drove away, blinking back tears. But really, getting fired over ice cream seemed so unfair. The *Englisch* men from Chicago had taken advantage of her. Thomas Zook even admitted the truth of it, but he fired her just the same.

She'd never get a job around these parts. The best thing she could do would be to continue with her oldest brother Sam's offer to move with him to the city—Chicago, a *big* one where she wasn't known—and work as a nanny-housekeeper-cook for Sam while she studied for her GED and he went to college. He needed her to care for his son since his wife died in childbirth. The idea of moving excited her more than it probably should. The only bad thing was she didn't want to leave these parts. If she did, she'd be shunned. Her friends and family were here. And so was Levi. Not that they'd ever be a couple again. Not after she'd been the one to break up with him.

Worst mistake of her life. But she didn't know how to fix it. How did she apologize for being a complete and total fool?

She sighed. She couldn't. Leaving was her best option. Her only option.

She swiped her knuckles across her eyes and paused on the side of the road by the Wyse mailbox. The barn was closed, so she couldn't see if Levi's buggy was there or not. But because he usually left the barn doors open when he was home since his woodworking shop was out there, that meant he wasn't home.

Elsie parked near the wheelchair ramp and stared for a moment at the work boots set near the screen door. She could leave the boxes and not stay to talk, but if Abigail heard a noise, she might try to carry the boxes in on her lap in the wheelchair and might fall or drop a box full of glass jars.

Elsie glanced again at the closed barn doors. Levi wouldn't have done his evening chores yet. He probably wore a different pair of shoes. Besides, it was not yet five. Didn't he normally work until five?

Satisfied that Abigail was alone, Elsie set the brakes and got out of the buggy. She lifted out one heavy box full of home-canned vegetables, carried it up to the door, and kick-knocked.

The door swung open, and Levi stood there. For a brief second, he stared; then he took the box from her. His mouth worked, but nothing came out.

Behind him, Abigail wheeled her way closer. "Elsie! Welcome. We were just about to sit down for supper. Would you like to warm up with a nice bowl of chicken noodle soup?"

"No, *danki*. I have a couple more boxes in the buggy." Despite herself, her voice cracked.

Levi blinked, put the box on the floor, and stepped forward. "Come in out of the cold. Might as well join us since you're here. I'll get the boxes." He shoved his feet in a pair of black tennis shoes but didn't bother to tie them.

"Please, join us." Abigail clasped her hands together.

Elsie's bottom lip quivered. "I really don't think—"

Levi's hand landed, warm and familiar, on her shoulder. Tingles raced through her. He jerked away as if he'd been burnt. "Then don't think. It's been a while." His voice was husky. Raw. "Please stay."

Said the man who'd been avoiding her?

"Besides, you look like you need a friend," he said gruffly.

She wasn't sure she'd define their relationship as friends. Still, tears beaded on her lashes. She tried to blink them away. "There are two more boxes. I'll get the smaller one."

"You moving in?" Levi asked, going past her. "I'll get both. You talk to Abigail."

Oh. He meant Abigail was her friend. Not him.

Anger flared. At least it dried up the tears. "No, I'm not moving in. They're full of food for you and Abigail. *Honestly.*"

He grunted and shut the door behind him.

"You brought us food?" Abigail frowned. "Why? Actually, never mind why. *Danki.* We *really* appreciate it. But supper is getting cold. You simply must join us. I insist. Besides, Levi is right. It's been *forever.* Sit."

"But... Levi... Well, I..." Why did words have to fail her now?

Abigail giggled. "*Jah.* He feels the same. Besides, aren't you the one who told me that chocolate fixes everything? I have chocolate." She pointed to the cupcakes.

"I was wrong. It can't fix this. I was hired and fired on the same day. From Zooks'! And he was desperate for help." Elsie's voice hitched.

Abigail smiled. Smiled—as if getting fired was something to smile about! "Stay for supper. I guarantee chocolate can fix this."

CHAPTER 4

He was ten times the fool, that's all. Levi kicked at a rock and then wanted to howl when his toes took the brunt of it. His fault. Both for kicking a hard object and for seconding Abigail's supper invitation. But the pain in Elsie's eyes about did him in. He didn't know what had gone wrong in her life, and all things considered, he probably shouldn't care, but he did. He also wanted to fix the problem. And not just this one, but all of them.

He breathed in a lungful of frigid air that somehow seemed tinted with the scent of peppermint, which smelled infinitely better than his stinky work boots beside the door. Elsie always smelled like the red-and-white candy. She'd tasted of it back when he used to kiss her.

Ugh. He groaned. His thoughts *had* to go there. But abandoned on the buggy seat was a partially unwrapped candy cane, the end white from her sucking the red coloring off like she always had for as long as he'd known her. For about a half second he was tempted to taste the candy. But how would she react if she knew he'd candy-cane-kissed her?

Okay, that bordered on creepy. Obsessed. He forced his attention away from the candy and to the boxes stacked on the back seat of the buggy. He'd only been half joking when he teasingly mentioned her moving in, but he liked the idea. Too much.

Wow. His thoughts were wandering down rabbit trails they had no business traveling. And just because of Elsie's beyond sad expression—and Abigail's supper invitation.

Time to focus. They'd broken up. Were history. No chance of reconciliation. He hefted the boxes into his arms. What was his ex-girlfriend delivering anyway? He turned and almost dropped the boxes when he nearly ran into Elsie. Despite his earlier objections, she lifted the smaller, top box from his arms. And even though fabric covered his skin, he burned from her light, fleeting touch.

"They're heavy. I'll take one," she said.

"Don't you think I'm man enough to handle it?" His voice was husky.

Her face flamed red. She dipped her head as she turned away. "I know you are," she whispered.

He pressed his lips together to smother a groan and gripped the box tighter to keep from reaching for her. It was a good thing Elsie had a job at Zooks' because he would go literally insane if she worked for him.

He'd be tempted to do ever so much more than candy-cane-kiss.

* * *

Elsie was way too conscious of the handsome man following her into his house. She still remembered the way his brown hair curled at his neck and around his ears. His always-serious gray eyes that used to darken with desire when he wanted to kiss her. Not a good thing to think about eighteen months after they broke up.

The screen door squeaked on its hinges as Abigail held the door open. She watched them as they approached, a secretive smile playing on her lips as if she alone knew something tantalizingly delicious. Elsie couldn't imagine what it might be. Except, the hot soup she'd promised was getting cold and Elsie had a good excuse not to go home quite yet.

Elsie walked past Abigail and placed her box on top of the one Levi had set down earlier. Then she moved out of his way, glancing at the table. Three soup bowls waited, two of them already filled. A loaf of homemade bread was partially sliced, and a plastic tub of butter waited in the center of the table.

"How can I help?" she asked.

"If you aren't moving in, what's in the boxes?" Levi asked at the same time.

"I told you already." Elsie turned.

"I must've forgotten. Either that or I didn't hear you." Levi stared at her; his mouth flatlined. He rarely, if ever, smiled anymore. Not since his family died. His two brothers, a sister, his *grossdaadi*, and his parents. It hurt Elsie's heart. But there was nothing she could do to ease his grief or his burdens.

"Food," she said. "From our over-full pantry.

Vegetables are in the bottom box, fruits are in the top one, and meats, pickled eggs, salsas, chowchow, and jams and jellies are in the middle."

He blinked at her. "Why? I mean, why now? Actually, why at all? We're nobody to you. At least, now we are." A touch of bitterness colored his voice. A hardness in his expression.

"Levi!" Abigail hissed.

The food gift wasn't welcome? Elsie stared at him. What did he mean why? Should she offer to take the food back home?

"Well, it's true," he said. His gaze landed on his sister. His expression softened. "You and I both know that the church and community abandoned us when the rest of our family died. When Elsie and I broke up."

Ouch. It hurt to know what he thought. But come to think of it, it was true. Or not, because Elsie had seen men in the district approach Levi on multiple occasions and he'd practiced his avoidance skills on them, too. And how many times had Bishop Nathan asked her *daed* and both of her grandfathers to pray with him about how to best reach Levi? Maybe he'd lost his ability to welcome expressions of care and concern from their church district.

She opened her mouth to tell him just that but then caught the sheen of tears in Abigail's eyes. Elsie snapped her lips together. *Daed* was trying to encourage her to think before she spoke. To keep harsh words unsaid. Something she should've done instead of breaking up with the only man she'd ever loved.

The man she'd reconcile with in a heartbeat.

The man she'd never have. She needed to focus on her plan—well, her oldest brother's plan. Her future.

Levi sighed, his focus shifting to Elsie. "*Danki*. We appreciate it."

The words were right, and the tone nice enough, but there was a note of insincerity as if he was just saying them because it was the polite thing to do.

Abigail huffed and glared at her brother.

Okay, then. And on that note...Elsie forced a smile. "Well, *danki* for inviting me for supper, but I really must be going. It's been a long day and—"

"You. Are. Staying." Abigail's glare transferred to Elsie. "I have chocolate and..." She sniffled. The glare faded and the sheen of tears returned. "And please stay even though the soup is no longer hot."

"Please," Levi echoed, sounding more sincere than he had before.

Elsie stifled a sigh. Abigail was probably lonely. And it wasn't her fault Elsie interrupted supper. "Okay."

"I'll reheat the soup." Abigail reached for a full bowl.

"I'll reheat the soup," Elsie offered. It'd be awkward for Abigail to carry full bowls of soup on her lap in a wheelchair, and she needed to be helpful. Elsie carried the bowls over. "It is brutally cold out there and the ice cream delivery guys said something about an ice storm being predicted." *Ugh*, that sounded stilted.

"It's in the extended forecast. The *Englisch* men I worked for today mentioned it. Also something about a blizzard following it," Levi said as he belatedly shut the door.

The ice cream guys had sounded like it was for that evening. But men who would defraud a store owner probably could easily lie about a storm, too.

Elsie took her sweater off and hung it on the hook

next to Levi's jacket, then placed her bonnet over it. She hurried over to the stove to reheat the soup—including what had already been dished out—while Levi carried each of the three boxes over to the pantry. Abigail unpacked them and placed them on the almost-empty shelves, exclaiming over each jar. Elsie felt better about the gift being welcomed. It also was nice to make sure they had food to eat.

But standing in Levi Wyse's kitchen while he and Abigail puttered and Elsie warmed supper made it almost seem as if they were a family and she was part of it.

Dangerous thoughts when she was still in love with the man.

Even more dangerous when she planned to leave.

* * *

Levi could get used to this. His sister and his Elsie—who wasn't truly his—working in the same kitchen. But watching Abigail so carefully unpack each jar from the box and acting as if they were Christmas gifts hurt. *Jah*, he was a terrible shopper. He usually lost the lists she so carefully wrote out and just went on memory—when he remembered to go—so he was more miss than hit when he brought groceries home. Hopefully, Abigail would have another idea who to ask to work for them. Maybe a couple of ideas in case the first person said no.

Or in case the first person got any silly ideas in her head about marrying him.

In the first place, he was off the market. His heart belonged to—and always would belong to—Elsie Miller. When she broke up with him, it was proof positive that he'd never marry. In the second place, he couldn't wed anyone, because he'd killed his family. Accidentally, to be sure, but he'd murdered them just the same. And murder—according to Levi's understanding of the story of Cain and Abel in Genesis—made Levi an outcast, undeserving of a family. It cursed him to eternity in hell.

Not that anyone blamed him, but the bishop and the preachers didn't know he'd discovered the strong odor of gas in the air and had gone out to work in the barn anyway instead of telling his family to turn off all the gas appliances. If he would've backtracked and told *Daed*...But he hadn't, thinking someone else would notice. Or maybe that the gas company had spilled some since the odor came only from the tank area outside. He hadn't even thought of it until it was too late.

And because he hadn't...He glanced at his sister, sitting in the wheelchair. His only surviving family member.

His fault.

He gulped at the stubborn lump clogging his airways and forced his mind away from those disturbing thoughts. They usually filled his night hours because he tried to stay too busy to think during the day.

"Soup's hot," Elsie sang.

He turned toward the table. *Jah*, it was good Elsie had a job because if she were his elf, he'd go stark raving mad.

And he'd rekindle the impossibility of a hoped-for and much-desired relationship.

Best to leave things as they were.

CHAPTER 5

Elsie peeled the paper liner from the chocolatey goodness waiting for her. Chocolate might not fix her problems, but it might help to minimize the despair weighing down on her. *Daed* expected her to help carry her portion of the family finances and that meant having a job and handing her earnings over to him to work into the household budget.

A budget that was strained with her current inability to find and keep a job.

Beside her, Abigail moaned as she bit into her cupcake. "This is heaven. *Danki* for thinking to buy us cocoa, Elsie."

Levi grunted. The only sound he'd made during the entire meal. Other than "Let's pray" and "Amen." Abigail had carried the bulk of the conversation, chattering about everything and nothing. He removed the paper liner from his cupcake and ate half of it in one bite.

"It is good," Elsie agreed after taking a nibble. "You're a good baker."

Abigail shrugged, something melancholy filling her expression.

Levi shoved the rest of his cupcake into his mouth. "Excuse me," he muttered, getting to his feet.

"Sit down. We need to talk." Abigail pointed to his chair.

"I have chores," he said. "And toy orders to fill."

"Elsie was fired from Zooks'," Abigail blurted.

Elsie winced.

Levi paled and plopped back into his chair. His mouth gaped as he stared at Elsie. "How did you manage that?"

"Isn't it wonderful?" Abigail said at the same time. She beamed.

Elsie closed her eyes and wished the floor would open up and swallow her. How could Abigail call it wonderful? It was awful. Beyond awful. Terrible. Horrible. And to just blurt it out to Levi... She couldn't imagine what he thought of her. He probably was counting his blessings that he hadn't married her. She opened her eyes and peeked up to see his nonverbal reaction.

"Seriously? What on earth did you do? He just hired you today!" And with those words, Levi snapped his mouth shut. He just looked at her, silent a minute or two, then turned to his spluttering sister. "You! How did you manage this?"

Huh? Elsie blinked. He blamed Abigail? Why?

Abigail giggled. "I prayed. I wanted Elsie. She's perfect."

"Hardly perfect, but what are you talking about?" Elsie stared at Abigail. "You prayed I'd get fired?"

"Santa Claus needs an elf." Abigail beamed as if that explained everything.

It didn't. Not even remotely.

"Perfect," Levi murmured. "Just perfect." He bowed his head and shut his eyes as if he were praying. Then he flexed his hands.

Elsie was familiar with the fancy, jolly, big, red man, but as a rule most Amish didn't celebrate him. Maybe some of the more liberal districts gave him a nod. Maybe. So what did Santa needing an elf have to do with her? Even if the hired Santas seen at stores or malls needed an elf, there was no way the church leaders would be okay with her donning a green tunic, tights, and shoes with curled-up toes.

"My *daed* would never allow me to dress up as an elf," she said. "And even if he did, I'd feel too self-conscious. But *danki* for thinking of me."

Levi snorted.

Abigail giggled again. "No. You misunderstand. Tell her, Levi."

Levi fell silent, fisting and unclenching his big hands. His eyes turned to Abigail, a helpless, lost expression appearing on his face.

Abigail waited a beat or two as if hoping Levi would say something before she looked at Elsie. "The *Englischer*s in town call Levi 'Santa' because he makes toys. He needs an elf."

Elsie frowned. That still didn't make any sense. "So...?" But wait. That's what was in the box? Toys? That explained the memo line on the check, too. *To Santa*...

"Abigail wants you. I...uh, *we*...want you." Levi's troubled gaze turned to Elsie.

"*Daed* still won't let me wear an elf costume."

Levi's gray eyes darkened as he gave her a slow perusal, possibly imagining her in said costume. Then they rose and caught hers. Held them.

Her body heated at the unbridled desire she saw in his eyes. Her lips tingled, heart pounded, and she caught her breath. Maybe he didn't hate her after all. Maybe there might be hope for them. Hope for a future together. If she didn't keep her promise to go with Sam to Chicago. And that ripped at her—promises versus her heart's desire, a job in an office versus being a wife and mother. If she were *Englisch*, she could have it all. As an Amish woman, not so much.

Levi tore his gaze away and the heat left, leaving her chilled. Rejected. But she could think again. What were they talking about? Right, elves and toys. "And I don't make toys." Her voice came out breathless.

Abigail looked back and forth between them. "*Jah*, we want you," she whispered. Then she cleared her throat. "What we need is an office manager, someone who gets and keeps Levi organized, a housekeeper who helps me, and someone to do the grocery shopping."

"And we'll pay you," Levi croaked.

"Basically, a, um, wife. Except one who goes home at night," Abigail chirped.

Elsie's face burned. "A wife?"

* * *

"A wife?" Levi spluttered. "You had to go there?" He looked toward Elsie, hoping she understood what he couldn't say about the impossibility of marriage. "We need an office manager and housekeeper. Not a wife. We—you and I—will never see each other. *Never.* Abigail will hand over your wages. If you take the job, that is." He stood, walked around the table, then strode over to the door and shoved his feet into his shoes. Then he stilled, hand on the knob, and bowed his head, praying for grace, for mercy, for... help.

Maybe for divine intervention. If *Gott* cared enough to help him out of this mess.

"So you want me to organize Levi," Elsie said, as if he'd already left the room.

He stiffened. But organization. *Jah*, he needed that. It might help him keep his head above water, instead of worrying about when the next hit would come. Wondering if he'd made a payment on all the outstanding medical bills or if he'd forgotten one. Worrying about the state stepping in and taking Abigail from him even though she was seventeen and he was her sole remaining relative.

"He loses everything. He can't even find an eraser when he needs one," Abigail confided.

Truth, but it still hurt. Although Abigail had no idea about the stress he was constantly under. Or that he was literally burning the candle at both ends.

"Don't I know it. He lost *me* before."

Levi sucked in a breath. The reason for their breakup. But she didn't sound bitter. And he hadn't realized she'd felt "lost" just like an eraser or his shopping list. As if she didn't matter enough to him.

Abigail giggled. "Do tell."

"It's his story to tell." Elsie's voice held a strange note. One he couldn't identify.

And she didn't know the story because he'd never

told her. But she didn't need to know since they were no longer a couple. He turned his head. Abigail's back was to him.

Elsie met his gaze. "I'll take the job," she said, a hint of challenge in her eyes.

Fantastic. He swallowed. He needed her. And Abigail was right. Elsie was perfect. He nodded. "You can start tomorrow if it's okay."

Abigail startled. "I thought you left." She swung the wheelchair in a tight semicircle. "You can take her on a quick tour. So she knows where to start tomorrow. And we never did discuss her hours and wages."

Levi coughed to cover up a groan. But his office was in the second-floor loft and Abigail couldn't go up there. His workshop was in the barn and she rarely ventured out there.

"Follow me," he muttered. He led the way through the living room, with its one end table and a recliner, to a short hallway that led to the two bedrooms. He stopped at the entrance. "Abigail's room is on the left, mine is on the right. Bathroom is at the end of the hall."

Elsie continued down the hall and peeked into the rooms as he turned to head back. He didn't want to see her standing in his bedroom doorway. That would be pure torture. He waited at the foot of the steep, ladderlike loft stairway in the living room, built against the side of the outside wall.

She finally joined him.

"Be careful. I'd hate for you to fall." He motioned for her to go first.

She gave him a look and scampered up. Of course, because she was raised on a farm and her family barn had a loft. He tried not to focus on her climbing to his private domain.

Tried but failed. Oh, what she did to him…

He took a breath and followed her up.

She reached the top, stepped into the room, and gasped.

He stopped on the top rung and peered past her.

Somehow, the mess seemed worse than he remembered.

Haphazard stacks of papers were piled on the floor and covered the surface of the desk, and he didn't need to look to know the file cabinet was empty.

She had her job cut out for her.

Oh! And there on the floor under the desk was his missing eraser.

* * *

This was unreal. A nightmare. It had to be. How could Levi get any work done in such an environment?

"Excuse me," he said.

She moved out of his way as he stepped up on the loft floor. He headed straight for his desk, got down on his knees, and reached to retrieve something.

"My missing eraser." He turned to sit cross-legged on the floor and held the object up, then set it on the desk. "Have a seat on the chair. We'll have a brief chat before I show you the wood shop."

She sat, silent, still overwhelmed by the magnitude of the mess. Where would she even start? And his use of the word *chat*? So unusual for him. Was that on purpose?

He clasped and unclasped his hands, staring down at them. "I know how awkward this is and tongues will wag. But I obviously need the help and so does Abigail. Not to mention you need a job. So, I will hire you part-time, starting about ten in the morning until around three in the afternoon, Monday through Friday. We won't see each other. It's just best this way."

In other words, he was still avoiding her—and using the gossips as an excuse.

But he was right. With their history, and her lingering feelings for him, it was best this way.

He still didn't look up. "I can't afford to pay much. Not what you're worth. I just finished paying off one of Abigail's hospital bills today, but she has ongoing therapy and doctor visits, plus a social worker has been coming by from time to time, making sure I am taking care of her adequately, I guess." He sighed and named an amount. "I understand if you want to change your mind."

"That's fine. *Daed* will just be glad I'm bringing money in and he'll understand." She'd be happy to work for Levi and Abigail for free. And to organize this mess and lift the burden from Levi's shoulders. To be a partner of sorts to make his life a little easier even if he didn't want her in it...though that would hurt. But given enough time and proximity, maybe Elsie would have a chance to make amends. Maybe she and Levi would stop avoiding each other. To start communicating. To become temporary friends again. Though she wouldn't count on that. She was leaving after all...

Levi gave a curt nod, rose to his feet, and started down the ladder steps. "Okay, then. I'll show you the workshop. But other than an occasional cleanup, that isn't your job."

She followed him down the ladder. "I'm anxious to

see it. I'm curious about those lions and tigers and bears that clerk raved about yesterday."

He grunted.

What was it with some men communicating in grunts?

Abigail wasn't anywhere in sight when Elsie peeked into the kitchen to say goodbye. Levi headed out the door so Elsie grabbed her sweater and bonnet, tugged them on, and followed him.

Darkness had fallen, but she could still see clearly from the *Englisch* neighbors' floodlights.

He was halfway to the barn by the time she stepped outside. Wow, those boots stunk. How had she not noticed them before? She stopped at her buggy long enough to grab her candy cane—hopefully, the taste would eliminate the stench—then she ran to catch up with him. He tugged open the barn doors, flipped on the gaslights, and stepped into what seemed an unnaturally quiet building. And then she remembered Abigail mentioning that they'd sold the cow. Probably the chickens, too, since Elsie didn't hear any clucking. No dog came to investigate.

There was only the whinny of a lone horse.

The barn smelled of sawdust, and Elsie smothered a sneeze. It emerged as a squeak.

"Bless you," Levi said. He opened another door, turned that light on, and moved aside.

Elsie stuck the end of the candy cane into her mouth and stepped into Santa's workshop.

She took in racks of wood, a pegboard of tools, and makeshift tables covered with toys. A wooden train, carved but not sanded or painted, half-filled with wild animals. A stable with horses and a partially finished bull that were sized for action figures or fashion dolls.

Maybe for a toy rodeo. Rocking horses and toddler-size rocking chairs. And that was with a quick glance.

"Levi!" She pulled the candy from her mouth and pointed with it. "This is amazing!" He could go nation-wide with a website. Other Amish had them for their businesses. If she could take a few pictures with her phone and talk to an *Englisch* girlfriend who designed websites…He'd object, of course, but it'd be for his own good.

"I'd forgotten how you always smell of peppermint," he said, his voice strangled. "It makes me want…" He shook his head.

He wanted peppermint? She broke off the curved end, still in the wrapper, and held it out.

After a moment's hesitation, he took the end she'd sucked the color from.

"It makes me want to kiss you. But this will have to suffice." And he stuck the candy in his mouth.

CHAPTER 6

The workshop walls threatened to close in around Levi. He avoided Elsie's shocked gaze. His face burned, and he muttered some sort of excuse—he had no idea what he actually said—and fled. Why did he say and do something so incredibly stupid as admitting he wanted to kiss her? Admitting that peppermint made him think of kissing her? And then he'd deliberately taken the piece her mouth had touched. All he knew was that *this* time he couldn't control himself—seeing her in his home, his office, his workshop, hearing her words of praise, the scent of peppermint filling his senses and thoughts...Now Elsie knew beyond a shadow of a doubt that he'd never gotten over her.

Not like it mattered, though. She was clearly over him, and even if she weren't, his other reason for never marrying held fast. He was still a cursed man. A murderer.

And if he didn't get away from her tantalizing presence

right that instant, he would sweep her into his arms and kiss her until he was senseless, mindlessly confessing all and then begging her to leave his heart, his home, his town, his state, and let him live his hopeless, loveless life without any chance of forgiveness.

All the while he'd be silently pleading for her to stay.

A wail rose in his throat. Choking him. He coughed it into submission.

Levi hightailed it through the barn and out through the old cow doors. But he tasted the sweet mint in his mouth and couldn't escape his thoughts of her so easily.

A blast of cold air hit him and he silently cursed himself for forgetting to grab his jacket. No matter. He wouldn't be found—or show up—until Elsie Miller was long gone. And he'd be very careful—and intentional— in avoiding her in the future.

Really, even though she was custom-made—and *jah*, perfect—for his elf position, she was the last person he should've considered hiring due to their history and his continued affection for her. And when Abigail suggested her, he should've flat out told her no. Unfortunately, he would do *almost* anything to make his sister happy.

Almost. Including hiring Elsie. Excluding courting Elsie again.

But the thought of Elsie in an elf outfit—*whoa*. His body heated to the point where a jacket probably wasn't necessary. Combined with the taste of peppermint in his mouth and the knowledge of what he'd said and done…

Levi groaned.

He stumbled through the out-of-control weeds growing on the uneven ground behind the barn—weeds he hadn't taken the time to bother with since the explosion. They seemed so unimportant when, at age twenty-three, he was suddenly solely responsible for Abigail. For everything.

Almost two years later, the weeds were still unimportant.

So many other responsibilities weighed him down.

Adulting was not easy.

Not at all.

Levi gulped at the lump that clogged his throat, swiped at the tears burning his eyes, and froze as somewhere behind him, Elsie's sweet voice called out for him.

The adult thing would be to turn around and face her and make some sort of believable plea for temporary insanity.

He had nothing. Believable or otherwise.

So he did the immature thing. Dropped down in the tall weeds and prayed for invisibility. At least the darkness worked in his favor.

* * *

Elsie took advantage of Levi's absence and snapped photos of about ten handcrafted toys, including a wooden farm animal puzzle for toddlers. The *Englischer*s who shopped online would just eat this up. That'd help Levi and Abigail, though he might have to hire someone to do the computer work. She wasn't sure how to set up or maintain a website. Though that would change if she eventually took business classes in Chicago. For the first time, a burst of excitement filled her. She'd be able to help small Amish businesses everywhere.

Minutes ticked by, and Levi didn't return. He wasn't going to, of course. She should've guessed. He was a master at avoiding her.

But she couldn't let Levi just disappear into thin air after his confession. If his desire to avoid her during working hours wasn't personal aversion, dislike, or only for the gossips but because he was too tempted to wish for or want things he couldn't have, maybe she could change his mind, apologize for her hurtful words, and give them a second chance...

At friendship, of course. The romance was dead. Mostly dead. It was only alive in her dreams. And she needed to let those die.

Unfortunately, it seemed he was able to disappear. She couldn't find him anywhere in the barn and when she glanced out the wide-open back cow door, all she saw was a weedy pasture. Not a man in sight.

He'd probably headed for the house and was even now hiding in his bedroom or the loft office.

She sighed and started to close the cow doors but then stopped. She scanned the lit-up fence line, but no one skulked along the barbed wire looking for escape.

She'd return to the house to find Abigail, say good-bye, and thank her for the job, then head home, but if Levi thought he could avoid her forever, he had another think coming.

As *Mammi* Pearl always said, "A wise woman knows when to be foolish."

It was time to do whatever it took to get Levi's attention because he'd made it very clear he was hers for the taking. Okay, sort of clear. He wanted to kiss her. That was a step in the right direction to winning back his heart. Maybe.

At least until she left.

She'd take that chance. She'd let him go once. She wouldn't lose him again—make that she wouldn't let him lose her again. Levi was hands down the best man she'd ever dated or been courted by. The only one she'd ever wanted to marry. Somehow she *had* to get his attention.

As friends.

For now. Temporarily.

Elsie started to close the barn doors again, but this time a buzzing sound and a light in the flattened weeds near the exit caught her attention. Was that a shoe sticking out? The lace dangled untied and the hem of a pair of pants brushed the heel.

She caught her breath but was too realistic to seriously consider the possibility of a suspense novel coming to life in the Wyses' overgrown pasture. No, those pants and shoes belonged to one very-much-alive man engaging in a childish game of hide-and-seek. For a second she was tempted to utter the very true words, "Ready or not, here I come." Or maybe he was currently thinking as her nephew did when he was naughty and covered his eyes: *I can't see you so you can't see me.* Whatever. It didn't work. Not for her nephew and certainly not for Levi.

But she didn't know what to say to the man-child. Declaring her intentions to rewin his heart would get her fired and getting fired twice in one day was a feat she didn't want to accomplish.

She took several steps forward and nudged his foot with hers, just enough to let him know his hiding place was found. "*Danki* for the job, Levi. I really appreciate it and I'll try not to let you or Abigail down."

The foot moved. "You're welcome," he said. Then he sat, his face probably turning beet red as he looked at her. Though, to his credit, he didn't offer a lame excuse. He also didn't reach for the still-buzzing, lit-up cell phone that had given his location away.

"I'll say goodbye to Abigail."

"Hiring you was her idea, you know. I never would've done it," he blurted, but pain filled his voice.

She winced. He never would've hired her?

Did his stomach ache the way hers did after saying unkind things? When she said hurtful things, it didn't feel so good. In fact, if felt terrible, like it had for weeks after their breakup fight.

He stood and sucked in air, then exhaled noisily. "I'd appreciate you never mentioning my foolish words and actions."

"Of course," she murmured. She missed the Levi who was slow to speak and slow to anger. Had she done this to him? Had she taught him how to lash out irrationally?

"I have no intentions to act on them," he said formally as he pocketed his still-buzzing phone. "You and I are history and—"

"I am well aware of what we are." Elsie backed away. He didn't need to know that she did intend to act on them. Eventually. Not yet. As soon as he got over hating her. Not that he said he did, but he must. Otherwise he wouldn't have said that they were history and he never would have hired her.

He nodded. "Of course."

"No worries, Levi. I'll see you tomorrow."

"No, you won't," he stated. "We can't—"

She growled, though she tried to muffle it. Her eyes

burned even though she recognized the defense mechanism for what it was. Rejection still stung. And he didn't want to hire her? It wasn't about the gossips. It was about his loathing?

Elsie blinked back the tears. A simple conversation would settle this, but she was too upset to talk rationally, and apparently he was, too. They'd have another ugly fight.

Except he wouldn't talk otherwise.

She opened her mouth, then shut it.

A wise woman knows when to be foolish...

She'd take the foolish first step. She didn't have to stay where she wasn't wanted. She stepped into the darkness of the cow barn and shut the door.

Hopefully, he'd take the wise, rational next step and follow her so they could talk it out.

And there was one way to make sure he would...

* * *

Levi waited long enough to be semisure Elsie had headed to the house, then reached to open the barn door. It wouldn't budge. He sighed. She must have locked it, adding insult to injury. With her attitude, maybe his, too, her employment probably wouldn't last long. She'd quit in frustration. Firing wouldn't be necessary. Though truthfully, he probably shouldn't have said any of those hurtful words. He'd wished them all back immediately. This was why it was better to be slow to speak as *Daed* always said.

He pulled out his cell phone, lit the flashlight, and trudged through the darkness to the front of the barn.

Her horse and buggy still waited, spotlighted by the neighbors' floodlights. Something he'd never thought he'd be thankful for. He'd actually resented them at first.

Instead of proceeding to the warm house, he went into the front of the barn to his still-lit workshop that somehow still smelled of peppermint and opened the voicemail to listen to whatever the recent caller had to say. It'd better be important after helping him appear to be an idiot in front of Elsie. Hiding like a child. And then mouthing off...

He was an idiot. His face burned with shame. Next time, he'd act like an adult.

If there was a next time.

He pressed in his voicemail code—the date he'd accidentally killed his family. An ongoing source of regret. But they would always be remembered. He didn't dare forget. Didn't a president or someone equally important once say, "Those who don't remember the past are doomed to repeat it"? He definitely didn't want to repeat the horrible event. Ever.

"Hey, Santa. This is Mark at the gift shop. I thought you'd like to know that we sold the circus train already and have orders for two more. Give me a call as soon as you can." A number followed.

An order for two more circus trains filled with animals? Levi looked around the workshop. There was a partially finished train, but only a few animals. He'd need to stay out here and work for a few hours tonight and, if that *Englischer* who'd given him a sewage shower today hadn't gotten a plumber yet, stay home and start work on filling the orders tomorrow. These toys weren't made in a day. Generally, not even in a week.

In fact, *Daed* always called it a hobby, one to enjoy after the real job.

But the check he'd gotten yesterday proved it could pay—and pay well.

At least around the holidays. Christmas was only a few weeks away.

Stress weighed down on him. How could he...? Did he dare follow the money or should he be honest and tell Mark he asked the impossible?

He needed the money for Abigail's ongoing medical bills and so many other things.

But *Daed* always warned against letting greed rule.

Was it greed if it would all go toward caring for Abigail?

There were two sides to this coin, though. He'd work super hard and for long hours to make the order and get the money. But it also seemed to be better-paying work than the home improvement and honey-do jobs that he and *Daed* did for income during the fall and winter. It would also let him pursue his passion for part of the year in a way that could truly support his sister without any sewer showers or low-paying guilt jobs for Luke. Now that the biggest hospital debt was paid, he could potentially settle into a "saner" pace of work.

Should he continue Wyse and Sons Construction or close it down and open Santa's Workshop for business?

The hobby versus the real job...

Think about it, son. Use the brains Gott *gave you.* *Daed*'s voice played in Levi's memory.

Levi wandered over to look at the partially finished train to try to decide on the best course of action.

And there on the flatbed car was the half candy cane Elsie had broken off for him.

A blatant reminder that Elsie was back in his life.

Not that he was in any danger of forgetting.

She was another necessary step in taking care of Abigail to the best of his ability.

He needed the money to pay her wages. And paying Elsie was taking care of her, too. Just as he would if she were his wife.

He groaned.

Oh, good Lord. I'm following the money.

It was a prayer, though he wasn't sure how *Gott* would answer. Maybe it was a confession.

If only he could talk to *Daed* and ask his advice. Other than to think about it. Would *Daed* still call it a hobby if he'd seen the check Levi deposited? And talking to *Daed* would mean Levi could apologize for his bout of stupidity not warning the family about the gas leak. If only he could do it over…

Would *Daed* hear if Levi prayed to him? Or maybe would *Gott* relay the message?

Gott, I need help. Wisdom. I need wisdom. I need to talk to Daed. *I need—*

"Levi!"

The scream interrupted his pitiful attempt at a prayer.

Abigail. Had she fallen? Again? *Gott, help.*

Levi dropped the cell phone down on a workbench and ran.

He burst through the doorway to the house, expecting to find Abigail on the floor.

She sat in her wheelchair at the table, staring at a chocolate cupcake, tears running down her face.

"What's wrong?" He gasped for breath.

"Elsie. She quit."

That was a quick answer to prayer. At least the Elsie part. He wouldn't be adding Elsie-induced insanity to the mix. And then it registered that her horse and buggy were gone. She'd left.

Something must have shown on his face because now his sister looked truly disappointed, lonely, devastated, like someone had handed her that cupcake and then stole it before she could take a bite.

"She said you don't want to hire her. Not really," Abigail accused him, swiping at her face.

She was right. And to his shame, he'd told her so.

"You have to talk to her." More tears beaded on Abigail's lashes. "We agreed that she was perfect."

"She would be." But—

"Talk to her."

Seriously? Well, he needed to apologize for his unkind words anyway. "Tomorrow." He sighed. "Abigail, I thought something was wrong."

Abigail blinked at the tears. A clear sign that this hurt her. "Something is! Aren't you listening? Elsie quit!"

"Right. There are others—"

"Not for us. You need to talk to her. Tonight. Go to her, Levi."

He stared at his sister. Silent. Then he glanced at the clock. If he didn't loiter, he wouldn't be too late. "Fine. I'll go now." He took down his jacket. So much for getting a jump start on the train order.

Except, he didn't know how to do damage control. Elsie was the expert on that.

And hopefully, he wouldn't regret this.

CHAPTER 7

Elsie stabled Dart, wiped him down, and gave him fresh water. Her shoulders sagged as she went into the house with the bags of replacement groceries from Zooks'. Her family was just sitting down for a late supper of chicken and dumplings. It smelled beyond delicious, but she'd just eaten with Levi and Abigail. She could use a hot drink, though, to help warm up. She set the bags and her purse on the nearest counter and removed her sweater and bonnet, hanging them on a hook by the door.

"Were Zooks' hiring?" Noah asked from his seat between their two grandfathers.

Elsie sighed as she opened her purse and withdrew the small wad of cash. So much for keeping it quiet until later or maybe telling *Daed* privately. "And firing." She handed the bills to *Daed*. Her large family—all thirteen members present; her young nephew was at his other grandparents' house—gawked even as *Daed* accepted the money. He silently counted it, putting the bills all facing the same direction and by denomination, the way he always did.

"At least you earned fifty dollars," he said. "*Danki*. We appreciate it."

"He must've overpaid. Either that or added severance pay." Elsie poured a mug of hot tea and sat in an empty chair between two of her sisters. "Some ice cream factory delivered innumerable flats of dill pickle ice cream. They were going out of business. I was fired for checking out a customer and not refusing the ice cream." Seriously, though, what had Thomas Zook expected her to do? And he'd refused to listen to her explanations.

"Dill pickle ice cream," *Mammi* Janice said, shaking her head. "Explains why they were going out of business."

Mammi Pearl cackled. "You said it."

At least both her maternal and paternal grandparents got along. But they sort of had to when they lived in the same house.

"Death by ice cream," Noah said with an impish smirk. "Only you, Elle."

Levi used to call her Elle, too, back when he courted her. The memory hit with the force of a flash flood, reminiscent of the time about five years earlier when she was sixteen and all the low-water bridges were flooded and impassable, and she was forced to stay at a friend's house for several days. Not a hardship, since Gracie had some good-looking brothers—not that any of them were interested in her, and not that she was looking. Ever since she was a fourteen-year-old, her heart had belonged to Levi.

"You'll never be able to get and keep a job here, Elsie," her twenty-five-year-old brother Sam said. He gave her a pointed look but said no more. Leaving could not be discussed openly. She'd have to just disappear in the dark of night.

"You're so encouraging." Elsie's vision blurred. And due to her sudden foolish move, she couldn't even claim to have a job working for Levi as Santa's elf. She'd kind of hoped Levi would chase after her, tell her that he didn't mean his hurtful words, and beg her to please come back to work for him.

No, that foolish move hadn't paid off, because even though she made the horse walk as slowly as possible, Levi hadn't followed.

What had she expected anyway? That he'd upgrade the job offer to a marriage proposal? Levi getting down on one knee, telling her that he'd never forgotten her despite the overwhelming evidence to the contrary and asking her to please, please, please marry him?

Of course, she'd accept.

After she made him stew a little.

And in that stewing, make him explain why she'd been forced to take a bus home from the wedding a year and a half ago after he'd left her there. The laughing-stock of a crowd of strangers. It was his second or third cousin who was getting married, after all. And everyone stared at her, a strange judgmental look in their eyes as they made fake pitying sounds with their pursed lips.

It still hurt. Big-time.

A bowl filled with yummy dumplings thumped on the table in front of her. A spoon clattered beside it.

Elsie looked up and met *Mamm*'s frown.

And then she realized the room was silent. Both sets of grandparents, her parents, and all seven brothers and sisters stared at her.

"What?" she asked.

"You should forgive him," *Daed* said quietly. "But explain yourself. Working for Levi as Santa's elf? What does that even mean? Is he masquerading as Santa?"

Had she blurted all that out loud? Judging by *Daed*'s comments and her family's expressions, she had. All that including how she'd accept his proposal and how she'd driven slowly and how humiliating it had been to be left? Her eyes swept over the mixture of grins, shocked eyes, giggles. Wow, Levi's blurt-it-out condition must be catching. Good thing everything but the elf business shouldn't have been too much of a surprise. Still, her face burned and she tried to think how to word her explanation.

"Someone just drove in." *Mamm* peered out the window, then glanced at Elsie. A small smile played on her lips. "I wonder who would come by at this hour?"

The thumping of shoes sounded on the back porch followed by a knock on the door. "Obviously, a man," seventeen-year-old Mandy whispered.

So why didn't anyone get up and answer? Why were they looking at Elsie? Was it suddenly her responsibility to answer the door? Or did they think the male caller was for her?

Sudden hope surged. Was it Levi? Doubtful. He'd made it abundantly clear he'd never chase after her. Even waving his check hadn't been enough to make him come. In fact, he'd still avoided her—to the point of hiding in a field of weeds.

What would it take for her to win Levi's heart again?

She confused herself. Her plan in the barn had been to stick around and eventually make her move; then he'd said something true and she'd quit. How could she win his heart if there was no reason to accidentally run into him or to at least get Abigail on her side and singing her praises? And the man truly did need help with that mess of an office.

She shouldn't have quit.

And even if she never did win his heart, they needed to part as friends when she moved to Chicago. She'd feel better about it if they did.

Whatever strategy she used, it had to start with an apology, even if he wouldn't believe she meant it eighteen months after the fact.

She was genuinely sorry, though. She'd handled the situation poorly.

Although, if he started with an apology of his own for leaving her, it might be easier to get past the pride and humiliation clogging her throat. But still...

The knock came again. Harder.

And still, no one moved.

"What if it's your one and only?" Mandy breathed.

She read too many sappy romance novels. But Elsie read and enjoyed them, too.

"Oh, so dramatic." Elsie stood and stomped past her three giggling sisters. *Daed*'s eyebrows shot up. She flung open the door. And then stared into Levi's too-serious gray eyes.

Her breath hitched. It *was* her one and only.

"You came." It probably sounded too damsel-in-distress-ish.

He blinked. "*Jah*, I came."

But the sudden shutter that darkened his eyes—his expression—clearly stated, *Not because I wanted to.*

* * *

This was beyond awkward. Levi shuffled his feet in the doorway, heat burning his cheeks. He avoided the curious gazes of the large family staring at him from behind Elsie. He focused on Elsie's forehead. "Um, can we talk?"

"Do you want to come in?" Elsie stepped out of his way.

No. No, he didn't. "I was hoping for a little privacy," he muttered. He nodded toward the porch. They'd be alone, and thanks to the bitter cold, no lingering. He'd state his mission, Lord willing she'd refuse, and he'd go his way. Relieved and disappointed at the same time.

Her breath caught and two fingers rose, aimed straight at his eyes. Then back at hers. "Look at me. Right here."

He'd rather not. Eyes were the window to the soul and she might see what he'd rather she didn't. But despite himself his gaze latched on hers. Hungrily. He gulped and stepped inside. She shut the door. Shut the cold out and him in.

And brought him into the warmth of home, hearth, and family.

A family that boisterously greeted him and probably stared when he didn't respond, but he couldn't look away from Elsie long enough to find out.

Her pink lips moved, but what she said didn't register.

Instead, she turned and walked away, and like a numb-skull, he followed.

Through the kitchen, into the living room—and away from the curious members of her family. Up the stairs, to her bedroom, where there were two bunk beds built into opposite walls. She flopped down on a bottom bunk. He stumbled to a stop just inside the open doorway.

Something in his head started roaring, and he stared at her, taking in the soft-looking quilt in shades of blue and green. The plump pillow.

The woman reclining on the bed…

Oh, merciful Lord…

Her mouth moved again and her hand flapped toward the bottom bunk of the bed on the opposite wall.

Um, no. He gulped again. He was *not* getting on some-body's bed in her bedroom. Not even her bed, though the thought interested him way more than it should.

Elsie sat up, swung her legs off the bed, and scowled at him.

That shook some sense into him. He leaned against the doorjamb. "All my life, I envied those who can think things and say them on the spot, without putting hours of thought into the words. Sure, you have to do occasional damage control, but you can think on your feet. I wanted that skill."

She opened her mouth.

He held up a hand. "I did it today with you. And I discovered it's not all that I cracked it up to be. I hated the person I became. Unkind. Vicious. I'm sorry. I should've kept my mouth shut and followed my *daed*'s advice: 'If you can't say something nice, don't say any-thing at all.' Abigail is right. You would be the perfect elf. Our history shouldn't factor into it. If you could forgive me and reconsider working for me and Abigail, we'd appreciate it."

"So you do want me?" Elsie's voice was whisper-thin.

More than you'll ever know. He couldn't—shouldn't—say that, so he simply nodded instead. "We both do. Please reconsider working for us. I promise to keep any unkind or insensitive or..." He hesitated, looking for the right word. "Sexist comments unsaid." He wasn't sure *sexist* was the right word, but it was all he could think of. He hadn't planned out this part of the conversation on the drive over. Hopefully, he wouldn't have to do more damage control after this.

"Okay. I'll work for you and Abigail."

Levi sagged as relief filled him. "Good. *Danki.*"

"See you tomorrow. And thank you."

He wouldn't reiterate that they wouldn't see each other, because they might. Especially if he stayed home in the morning to work on the order. "One last thing. No peppermint is allowed on the property."

Her lips twitched, drawing his attention. "We'll see about that." She sounded as if she was teasing.

And he suddenly wanted to kiss her the way he used to back when they were a couple. He backed away before he did something he'd regret. "Good night." His voice was too husky. Too filled with desire. He cleared his throat. "See that you don't."

She flopped back on the bed.

His body burned, so he did the only thing he could. He fled, taking the stairs two at a time. He rounded the corner into the kitchen and almost ran into Elsie's *daed*, Stephen.

"How are you doing, Levi? It's been a while since we've seen you darken our door." Her *daed* put his hand on Levi's shoulder and guided him into the living room. "Take your jacket and hat off and stay awhile. Have a seat."

Levi left his jacket on because he *couldn't* stay long, removed his hat to be polite, and sat on the edge of the sofa. Staying to shoot the breeze, or worse, declare his intentions with Elsie, wasn't on his agenda. Not today, not ever. "This isn't a social call. I came to reoffer Elsie a job."

"Reoffer? She said something about being an elf for Santa." Stephen's gaze narrowed. "Are you Santa?"

"I'm not dressing up like Santa. It's kind of a joke, I think. The *Englischer*s call me that because I make toys for them to sell." The words came out in a rush.

"In addition to your regular construction job and the secondary odd jobs you take on?"

"*Jah*. We have a lot of medical debt." Had. Still had some, but at least the hospital bill was paid. Finally. Although why he felt the urge to explain, he didn't know.

"What do you need an elf for? What would Elsie be doing?"

Ah. This was about whether Stephen would allow Levi to hire Elsie.

Levi pulled in a breath. He hadn't expected to be interviewed. But Stephen was a wise father. "Mainly helping Abigail and grocery shopping. Plus being an office manager for me. Making sure bills are paid, billing customers, keeping the office clean and organized, and of course, tax season is coming."

"You used to court Elsie…"

And that was a loaded question—even though it trailed off and didn't end with a question mark.

"There's nothing between us now." At least on her side. "And I'll make sure we rarely see each other so the gossips won't assume anything."

"That won't stop a gossip," Stephen said.

"True." Levi clasped his hands together and leaned forward. He had nothing to say to counter that truth. But he did have a question he wanted to ask *Daed* and Stephen was a *daed*. Just not his. "I'll let you decide whether you will allow Elsie to work for Abigail and me. But that got me thinking. I wanted to ask my *daed* a question, and, well, obviously, I can't. But maybe you might have some words of wisdom for me."

Stephen's brow rose. "Regarding my daughter?"

His mind would go there. Didn't he believe Levi when he said there was nothing between them? *Jah*, he was a wise man...

"No. Well, only indirectly. You see, I got an order for two very detailed toys that normally take months to make, and the *Englischer*s want them both by Christmas. I need the money to take care of Abigail—and that includes hiring Elsie—but *Daed* always said don't be greedy. Should I follow the money and take the job even though I will be working constantly to get it done? Or should I tell the buyer that I can't do it even though it will hurt us financially if I don't?"

"Tough question. Do toys really sell that well?"

"I think the store raises the prices because they're made by an Amish craftsman. So, *jah*." He named a price.

Stephen's brows rose as he whistled. "Hmm. What are you thinking? What is your conscience telling you?"

"That *Gott* is providing. That He won't bring me to something He won't take me through. But at the same time, this guy is asking the impossible and I'm setting myself up for failure, which would reflect badly on me and my business in the long term."

"There's your answer. Tell him the truth. It may be that he will work with you and your schedule for delivery. Then, with the predicted ice storm and blizzard, this opportunity would give you a job at home where you're near Abigail if she needs you. If all the factors are in *Gott*'s will."

"*Danki.*" Levi pushed to his feet, feeling a little peace. He could almost imagine his own *daed* recommending the same path. He nodded with relief. Now it was time to go, get home, perhaps call the man tonight or get a start on at least organizing what he'd need…

"And regarding my daughter, you'll find that she's custom-made for this job. I've always been sorry you two broke up." Stephen stood as well.

Jah, Levi, too. But, "I can never marry."

* * *

Elsie stumbled halfway down the steps, catching herself on the railing. *I can never marry.* What on earth was that supposed to mean? Amish encouraged marriage and family. There wasn't any reason she could think of for Levi not to be allowed to marry. And knowing Levi as she did, his use of the word *can* was intentional. He could've said "I will never marry" or "I don't want to ever marry," but no. He said, "I *can* never marry."

Judging by *Daed*'s "hmm," he'd picked up on it, too.

"You don't need to tell the bishop." There was a touch of alarm in Levi's voice. "There's nothing wrong with me and I have nothing to confess…" He trailed off as if he was suddenly unsure and maybe he *did* actually have something to confess.

A sudden, irrational fear worked through her. *Daed* would get to the bottom of this. But what on earth was Levi hiding? An affair with a married woman? An *Englischer*?

Elsie wasn't sure she wanted to know. Her stomach churned in dread. But still, she lowered herself to sit on the stairs—where she could eavesdrop in ease. And not accidentally bang into the railing or wall and give away her presence.

"Why can you never marry?" *Daed* asked.

There was a long silence; then Levi cleared his throat. "I need to get home to Abigail. She'll be worried. If you decide not to let Elsie work for me, I understand."

What? He was leaving her employment up to *Daed*?

"Elsie makes up her own mind. But I admit to some worry. What is going on with you, Levi?"

There was another long silence. "Nothing to concern yourself with. Let's just say that Abigail is my responsibility and I intend to take care of her."

"Commendable." *Daed* made some sort of grunt—one that usually warned he was about to disagree with what was said. An unspoken *but*. "Levi, your *daed* was one of my closest friends. He would've wanted me to reach out to you—which is why I have, multiple times. He would've done the same for my family."

Truth. Levi's *daed* used to stop by all the time to visit with her *daed*. Elsie scooted down two steps. A board creaked and she froze.

"Please, let me help you. Don't keep pushing me away. If nothing else, like tonight, I can listen to your worries or troubles and advise you."

More silence. Then, "*Danki*. I appreciate that. And I'll keep it in mind."

"But you won't talk to me now?"

"Abigail is waiting. She'll worry."

Daed sighed. "You know where to find me."

Levi took a step, moving into view. He glanced up the stairs and met Elsie's eyes. His jaw flexed. A muscle jumped, then he plopped his hat on and looked away—toward the living room where *Daed* must be. "Did Elsie put you up to this?"

CHAPTER 8

Did Elsie put you up to this? Levi felt ten times the fool as soon as the words left his mouth. How could Elsie have put Stephen up to it if she didn't even know he was coming? And why would she? He sighed. Simply put, she hadn't and she wouldn't. It was far better to keep his mouth shut and have people believe he was an idiot than to open it and remove all doubt.

He tried to avoid looking at Elsie again but failed. His gaze was drawn to her. Her lips were shiny as if she'd just added lip gloss. The scent of peppermint teased his senses, and despite the presence of her *daed* mere feet away and probably unaware that his daughter was there listening, Levi fought the urge to pull her into his arms and kiss her until she clung to him, wanting him every bit as much as he wanted her.

Inappropriate thoughts and actions, all things considered.

He gazed at her with every bit of longing apparently visible because her lips softened, parting. Her eyes glistened. Her hands rose as if she wanted to reach for him, but she hesitated.

Levi took an involuntary step toward her, his lips tingling. His arms ached to hold her. It'd been so long. Too long.

She whimpered.

A hand clapped him on the shoulder. Stephen. "*Jah.* I see how it is."

Just like that the moment was gone. Forever.

"No. No, it's not like you think," Levi said gruffly, despite the fact that it probably was every bit what Stephen thought, if not more. It was just that there was no way Levi would allow—could allow—himself to act on it. None. Zilch. He shook his head, turned his back, and strode away.

It was the hardest thing he ever did.

No. It wasn't. Having to bury his entire family, minus one, was much harder.

A sudden lump clogged his throat. His vision blurred. His ears hurt. He gulped and rushed past the rest of the family still gathered around the kitchen table.

Someone called to him, but the words swam, unrecognizable. He dashed outside, untethered Trouble, and lifted a leg to vault into the buggy.

Except the scent of peppermint surrounded him. A hand landed on his arm. Sparks shot through him. And with a groan, he turned and tugged her—his Elsie—into his arms, pressed her against his chest, and kissed her like a half-crazed man.

Not exactly his proudest moment. Especially when he

realized that she'd stiffened. Her hands pressed against his chest, pushing as if trying to get away. And her lips didn't respond. *Ugh.*

He started to release her, embarrassment and shame burning. And after he'd assured Stephen there was nothing between him and Elsie. At least she demonstrated her lack of interest very clearly.

And then, wonder of wonders, her hands slid under his jacket and up his chest. They lingered there a bit, then she pulled her hands free of his jacket and her arms looped around his neck, and she kissed him back just as desperately. As if she was as starved for him as he was for her.

His hat fell off and her fingers tangled in his hair. He groaned and deepened the kiss.

Jah. I see how it is. Stephen's words replayed. Mocked. It was as effective as a sudden, unexpected cold shower.

Elsie must've sensed his withdrawal because she moaned, a sound that made him want more and more and still more...

And even though he didn't want to, he untangled himself from the snare of her arms and stepped away.

* * *

It took Elsie a moment or three to go from Levi's toe-curling, knee-buckling kisses to the emotional disconnect that hit when he wrenched himself away, physically moving three or four feet back. And even though it was dark, she could feel his gaze on her, probably wondering what all that was about.

But, dash it all, he started it.

Or maybe she had with peppermint-flavored lip gloss and a cotton ball doused in peppermint essential oil on her pulse points.

He'd admitted that peppermint made him want to kiss her.

She was the one who'd liberally applied it, wanting to tease and tempt him beyond the level of his control. She just hadn't expected him to grab her like a half-starved man.

She reeled, fighting for her balance, fighting the...definitely not shame, no; it was more on the level of acute desire...that engulfed her.

And then the despair when she realized exactly what she'd done.

"I'm fired, aren't I?" And oh, that hurt to ask, especially knowing the answer.

He jerked. Violently. And then a word she'd never before heard Levi utter crossed his lips.

She dipped her head, ashamed she'd driven him to swear.

"Fired. *Jah.* You are. Fired. I mean, no. Not fired. I mean, Abigail. Oh bother." And then that same word he'd said before—twice—the second time much louder.

Did that mean she was—or wasn't?

"Levi Matthew Wyse," *Daed* scolded.

Wait. *Daed*? He'd witnessed their passionate embrace?

"Somehow, I think Abigail wouldn't mind if she knew Levi kissed Elle," another voice said. Noah?

Elsie jerked her head to the side, but both men were shrouded by shadows on the porch. Bright windows shone behind them and how many others might have seen? And what else had she expected rushing through the kitchen to follow him out here?

Still. How would Noah know? How would any of her brothers know?

"It was an accident. I didn't mean to," Levi blurted. "She...I mean, I know there are objections, but it...I mean..."

Elsie couldn't think of any objections. But he wasn't making any sense.

"Your *daed* would be ashamed of you using such language," *Daed* continued.

Levi spluttered to a stop and bowed his head. After a moment, he bent, picked up his hat, replaced it, then looked up. "I'm sorry," he said, "I didn't mean to do it. Either one of them, actually. But I need to go. Come or not tomorrow, Elsie. Makes no difference. You won't see me."

"But we need to talk." Elsie held her hands out in a pleading way.

"There's nothing left to say. Except I'm sorry. So sorry. For so many things." And, shoulders slumped, he trudged to his buggy, muttering something about making a mess out of a simple errand.

"Wait."

Elsie took a step after him, but *Daed* stopped her with a hand on her shoulder. "Let him go, daughter. There will be time enough for talking when the job is done."

Huh? What job? Mine? His? Elsie frowned. *Let him go?*

And with those words of veiled wisdom, *Daed* and Noah turned to go inside. Trouble pulled the buggy holding Levi out to the road. And Elsie was left standing all alone in the freezing-cold darkness trying to make sense out of the past hour.

And failing.

Except for the searing reminder that Levi still wanted her.

* * *

"I'm sorry," Levi said partially to the horse and partially to *Gott*—if He was listening. "I should've known the conversation would go places I hadn't prepared for. *Daed* always said to expect the best but prepare for the worst. He was so wise. I prepared for the best." He sighed. "Abigail wants Elsie. I agree that she is perfect for the job, and blast it all, I still love her."

The horse bobbed her head.

Levi snorted. "Nothing will come of it, though." He couldn't fail another person. Just couldn't.

Trouble made some sort of quiet nicker in response, but whether the horse was agreeing or disagreeing, Levi had no clue.

"But how am I supposed to keep my hands off of her, knowing that she welcomed my kiss?"

Trouble turned her head as if to look at Levi, but the darkness kept him from seeing if the horse rolled her eyes. Really, it was better not to know. If an animal rolled her eyes at him, then Levi really must be every bit as pathetic as he felt.

Especially since he suspected from the strength of the scent that Elsie had perhaps done it on purpose. He shouldn't have mentioned the "no peppermint" rule in her room, because it seemed to only have put ideas in her head. Now he really needed to avoid being alone with her.

Despite the beyond-cold temperatures, Abigail sat on the porch with a quilt draped awkwardly over her body when Levi arrived home. "Well?" she hollered as he drove past.

He gave her a thumbs-up, and with a grin she bundled the quilt in her lap and rolled backward as if heading inside. Levi continued into the barn. Abigail had accepted the thumbs-up as an answer, but truthfully, Levi had no idea what the gesture meant other than acknowledging the other person.

Because *jah*, he'd talked to Elsie and reoffered the job, but he had only the vaguest inkling of what Elsie would do. Her outstretched hands and plaintive "we need to talk" strongly indicated she'd show up with "talking" on the agenda. Something he wasn't good at, unless he had a memorized script—complete with possible questions, comments, and answers.

Elsie followed no script. He couldn't even begin to venture a guess where her mind would go or what would pop out of her mouth. Like when she accused him of losing her at the wedding. He hadn't lost her. It was just with his panic over Abigail's potentially serious fall so soon on the heels of the deaths of the rest of his family, he'd forgotten he'd taken Elsie to the wedding.

And while she usually was patient with him as he searched for words, that time she wasn't. She'd refused to hear him, breaking up instead of giving him a chance to explain.

Although maybe he was wrong to accuse her of lashing out irrationally. He'd been so proud of the words at the time. To his mind, they'd sounded so Elsie-ish. But no. They'd only fueled her anger to the clichéd redheaded boiling point. And cost him—almost—as much as the gas explosion.

After that, they'd reached the point of no return. He had no words. Just like now. If he saw her in the morning, what would he say?

He paused at the door to the barn, shivering in the cold, and realized that Trouble was in the stall. When did that happen? Somehow, he'd unhitched the buggy and stabled and cared for Trouble while his thoughts were wandering. He stopped and stared, then turned off the lights, shut the barn, and stumbled to the house to attempt to answer Abigail's questions. At least she tended to be patient with him, giving him time to think out his answers.

But he couldn't mention his loss of control, kissing Elsie as he had.

Abigail would believe that he and Elsie were a *thing*, on their way to happily ever after.

There was no happily ever after. Not for him. The sting of tears burned his eyes. He blinked them away.

The kitchen was warm and welcoming, and mugs of hot cocoa with a sprinkling of mini marshmallows waited on the table along with two chocolate cupcakes.

Nothing like going to bed with a burst of sugar-induced energy. But at least Abigail would be happy.

Maybe.

Unless she read between the lines some nuance of the conversation that he'd missed. And that was very likely.

Abigail rolled her chair to the table and angled it toward him. "Have a seat and tell me about it. And don't leave anything out. Will she be here tomorrow?"

"I'll be surprised if she doesn't show up tonight." Levi

kicked his shoes off, hooked his jacket and hat beside the door, then plopped down in the chair. And caught a whiff of peppermint coming from the cocoa.

His sister's eyebrows arched. "Why would she—"

"I kissed her, okay?"

Abigail's eyes widened and her mouth gaped.

Levi's face flamed, and abandoning his cocoa and cupcake, he fled to the solitary confines of his loft office.

Curse his runaway tongue! Admitting that to Abigail. What had he done?

It was all the fault of the peppermint. It muddled his senses. Had to be.

CHAPTER 9

Elsie tossed and turned all night, replaying every word out of Levi's mouth and reliving each second of his embrace. And still the big question remained. If she took the job working for Levi Wyse, was she setting herself up for heartbreak or for happily ever after?

Probably heartbreak, because every romance she'd read had a devastating black moment when all was lost. She'd already survived one black moment starring Levi Wyse. She wouldn't survive another.

And after that kiss, any hope of friendship was gone.

But still, they *had* to talk. Argue, probably, unless he remained stoically quiet, letting her rant, and then he'd turn and walk away, leaving her to dissolve in a puddle of tears—and the situation unresolved.

No. She couldn't go through that again.

However, peppermint had unleashed his tongue. And his hands. Not to mention his lips.

She shivered. She *could* go through that part again. With pleasure.

Considerable pleasure.

Okay, that settled it. She'd liberally douse herself in peppermint oil and stop at Zooks' for a bag of peppermint candy for good measure.

Except, he'd forbidden her to bring peppermint on the property.

Bring. He hadn't mentioned wearing it. And maybe she could smuggle some white chocolate candies with crushed peppermint in to use in baking Christmas cookies. Abigail would love that. And Elsie could argue that it was technically white chocolate.

Technically. Not officially.

And maybe some peppermint-flavored baking chips.

Jah, there were ways around his directive, and even if they didn't *see* each other, there were still ways to communicate. A note here, a card there, an occasional small gift... not to mention being the best elf ever.

Wasn't there a fairy tale about a shoemaker and an elf? It'd been a while since she'd read it, so she wasn't sure of the details, but if she remembered it right, the shoemaker got to the point where he was desperate to thank the elf.

Of course, there wasn't a very happy ending—for the shoemaker. She frowned, rolled over, and stared at the dark form of her sister Mandy asleep on the bottom bunk across from her. The top bunks were filled with her two other sisters, Leah and Carrie. How could they sleep at a time like this? She needed a plan.

It was a good thing these beds were built into the wall. It kept her tossing and turning from disturbing her sisters.

Elsie slipped out of bed, dressed in the dark, then went downstairs to the kitchen. She lit a lantern, brewed a mug of peppermint tea—her favorite—and found a notebook and a red-ink pen.

An index card waited at her place at the table. "Elsie" was written in *Daed*'s masculine script. Elsie pushed it aside. No distractions.

While the tea steeped, she tapped the cap of the pen against the open page of the notebook. What to write? "The Plan," which she had initially thought, now sounded rather blah. But it was three a.m. on Wednesday morning.

Oh! A brilliant title came to her. Perfection!

With a flourish she wrote:

The Christmas Challenge

1. *Organize Levi's office*—that would be vital to winning his affection.
2. *Help Abigail with household chores*—the reason she was hired.
3. *Befriend Abigail*—important to get her support.
4. *Decorate for Christmas*—as much as allowed and to make his house a home.
5. *Do lots of Christmas baking*—after all, the way to a man's heart is through his stomach.
6. *Do random surprise acts of kindness*—just to keep them guessing.

She removed the tea bag, took a sip of tea, and studied her list.

Wait. Were *random* and *surprise* the same? She raised the pen to cross out one of the words but then hesitated. She was pretty sure there was a slight difference in definitions. Elsie rose to check the dictionary, but the thick volume had disappeared from its place on the living room bookshelf. Her oldest brother, Samuel, was working on his GED and planning on going to college. He also teased about memorizing the whole dictionary, but since the book was gone he probably had been serious. *Daed* hadn't said a whole lot about it, but there were furrows of worry in his brow when he looked at Sam.

Elsie admired his bravery. But at the same time, it hadn't been a step she'd planned to take. At least not until Sam approached her and asked her to come to help him and his two-year-old son, Sammy. He promised to help her obtain a business certificate if she did. He'd also reminded her she'd probably never get the job she wanted in their Amish community.

He was right.

And she'd agreed. With no job and no boyfriend, it seemed like a bright hope for a promising future.

But they weren't going yet. Sam liked all his ducks in a row. Elsie had no ducks and no neat rows. She had squirrels and they were everywhere.

And *Daed* wasn't looking at her with the same worried expression he looked at Sam with. Either he didn't care whether she left the Amish or not, or she and Sam were doing a fantastic job keeping it quiet that she was going to jump the fence, too.

She preferred to believe they didn't know.

She returned to the kitchen and reclaimed her seat.

Unless that was what the index card was about. She reached for it. Flipped it over. And smiled.

On the other hand, *Daed* had been leaving Bible verses everywhere. Like this one. Hebrews 11:1: *Now faith is the substance of things hoped for, the evidence of things not seen.* She stared at it. Read it over a few times. Drew a border of red hearts around the edge of the card. Shaded them in.

And that brought her back to her current dilemma: Was Levi's job offer a heartbreaker or a happily ever after? Or was that a directive to go, help Sam achieve what he hoped for...and then pursue a business degree for herself?

There was only one way to find out.

But there was the potential for so much to go wrong that it scared her.

She took another sip of the rapidly cooling peppermint tea.

Wasn't there a verse in the Bible about *Gott* directing paths?

Jah, there was. She was sure of it. She closed her eyes. *Think. Daed* had written it on another index card on Sunday. He gave each of his children a verse to memorize every week.

And then it came to her. Proverbs 3:5–6: *Trust in the Lord with all thine heart; and lean not unto thine own understanding. In all thy ways acknowledge him, and he shall direct thy paths.*

Elsie bowed her head. *Lord, what should I do? Please lead me in the direction I should go.*

Levi had come looking for her. Something he'd never done.

It had to be a *Gott* thing. Had to be.

On the other hand, Sam had asked her to help...but then that wasn't uncommon.

But Levi...

She closed the notebook, slid the index card under the cover, and left it on the table while she finished the tea, pulled her shoes on and her coat, then went out to feed the chickens. It was early, way early, but she was too excited to sleep.

She'd be working for Levi Wyse.

And prematurely thinking she *could* become his bride. *Faith is the substance of things hoped for...*

If everything worked out right.

* * *

Levi hid in his loft office until long after Abigail went to bed that night, not wanting to see her knowing smirk and answer her questions about whether he and Elsie were a couple or not. They were not. Nor would they ever be, despite his inability to control himself around her. Avoiding her worked ever so much better. He'd need to be diligent in putting it into practice.

He finally fell into a restless sleep and overslept, waking with a headache.

Abigail sang a chorus that *Mamm* used to sing while she sorted laundry, so Levi took advantage of her preoccupation to go out to the barn to care for his horse. He would have to face his sister eventually, but maybe he'd have figured out what to say by then. If he tarried long enough.

The cold air sucked the breath from his lungs with a whoosh, brought tears to his eyes, and burned his nostrils. Maybe he'd be fortunate and Elsie would decide it was too cold to venture out.

But no. That would go against her determined nature. And her "we need to talk" had sounded pretty determined.

Mental note: *Avoid Elsie at all costs.*

For today, his only hope was that job he'd started yesterday with the inept homeowner. And if he were going, he needed to grab a quick breakfast and hit the road. With that in mind, he checked the time. Seven forty-five. Probably not too early to call the guy who'd dumped sewage all over Levi to find out if he contacted a plumber yet.

Better yet, maybe the plumber had made an emergency evening call to fix the broken pipe. Best case would be if the toxic waste cleaners had come and were already finished sanitizing the mess.

Levi sighed. Honestly, probably nothing had changed, but he'd make the call anyway.

He pressed in the numbers. "Mr. Smythe, this is Levi Wyse with Wyse Construction. Were you able to reach a plumber—"

"No, not yet, but you need to be aware that I talked to my neighbor and I will be contacting my lawyer and suing you for malpractice."

Malpractice? Levi's breath stalled for a moment. Shock waves worked through him. The guy had done it to himself. How could he be so dishonest?

But hold on a moment. Levi was almost positive malpractice was medical. And if there was such a thing as construction malpractice, Levi had proof the owner had done it himself. If his part-time apprentice would testify on Levi's behalf. And since Benji was Amish and trying to learn a trade... *Jah*, Levi was covered.

He cleared his throat. "Mr. Smythe, I have a witness that you broke the pipe yourself. If you sue me on false charges, no Amish construction business will ever work for you again," Levi stated calmly.

"Well, now, I didn't mean... Of course, I wouldn't," the guy said, backtracking in a hurry.

But he still needed to hire a plumber.

And clean up the mess.

Levi would be working at home today.

He called Benji and left a message saying he wouldn't be needed, then called Mark and left another message saying he'd love to make two circus trains, but...

Mark picked up his phone on the *but*. "You can't say no. I already promised the customer you'd deliver."

Levi pressed two fingers of his free hand against the bridge of his nose. This wasn't going according to script. "But..."

"Ah, you know you need the money for that sister of yours," Mark said.

True, but...

"How about I just tell him you'll try?"

That was pretty much what Levi had planned to say. "No promises, no commitment, but I'll try."

"Great! I'll tell the customer. He wants a December twenty-fourth delivery date, but the store will close early so you'll need to have them here by noon..." Mark continued chattering.

Levi's head pounded. He had a bad feeling about this. Like he'd just been taken advantage of.

Come right down to it, he had been tricked into following the money.

Lord Gott, *help this to be provision, not a disaster.*

His stomach lurched as he ended the call, but then his belly rumbled, so he hurried through the morning chores. Heavy, gray clouds hung in the sky to the west. The approaching storm? He'd heard in town yesterday that the system had stalled in the Dakotas and would be delayed, but it was still predicted.

He found Abigail in the kitchen slicing a banana. The room was warm and smelled delicious, like oatmeal cookies.

She looked up. "I made baked oatmeal." Her voice held a measure of firmness that meant he was in trouble.

And since baked oatmeal was his favorite...He tensed, wondering what she had planned. Discussing the kiss? Not happening. Or talking about the way he fled last night, leaving her alone during her weakest hours? He deserved to be scolded for that. "Sounds good," he said, trying to sound upbeat. "I need to wash up. I'll be right back."

She nodded. "And then we need to talk." She gave him a pointed look.

Jah, he was in trouble. His head hurt worse. He tried not to move it. "I'm sorry, Abigail."

She studied him. "For what?"

For what? This was worse than he'd thought. He pulled in a deep, calming breath. "We'll talk when I return." He tried to keep his voice even.

Asking what he did wrong would only put Abigail on the defensive, so he'd need to put some thought into this.

He plodded to the bathroom, trying to think of what all he was sorry for. He was sorry for speaking out of turn and almost letting their elf help get away. Sorry for running last night and not helping her. And sorry for not following up on the groceries so many times...

Maybe he could distract her with a focus on his relationship mistakes where she was concerned and lead her away from their peppermint-scented helper.

He swallowed a headache pill and then scrubbed his arms, hands, and face before he made his way back to the kitchen.

Abigail had pulled the square baking dish from the oven and dished out three servings of the delicious-smelling...

Wait. His breath hitched. Elsie was here so early? "Three?"

"Four." Abigail motioned toward the window, a soft blush coloring her cheeks as she reached for a fourth plate.

Odd. Levi turned to jerk open the door. Elsie and her brother Noah climbed out of the buggy.

Levi tried to avoid focusing on Elsie. Instead, he focused on her brother. "Noah?" Was he there because he witnessed *the kiss*? Chaperoning? Or worse, to find out what Levi's intentions were regarding Elsie?

This was going from bad to worse. At least his scolding from Abigail had been delayed. But he'd rather face his sister's wrath than Elsie after their kiss.

Levi's stomach knotted, and for about three seconds, he was tempted to grab his outerwear—again—and sneak out the side door to hide in the barn. But that would be the coward's way out and he had already played the coward three times yesterday. Enough was enough. He was done running from his problems and needed to face them head-on even though it terrified him.

Jah, it terrified him.

Gott, if you hear me, help me to think on my feet, even though I have no idea how the conversation will go. Please?

"Good morning," Elsie said as she climbed the porch steps. Her smile was too bright, as if she was nervous.

He gulped and stepped backward as Elsie passed him with a bulging plastic grocery bag and a whiff of peppermint. No candy in sight. Was she wearing the stuff?

"Morning." Noah followed her in. "Hey, Abby."

Abby? Abigail had been known by her full name ever since she was born, and there were four girls with the same name born at the same time in their district. Noah should know that. Levi opened his mouth to say so, but Abigail giggled. Levi gawked. His sister had a crush on Elsie's brother? Their relationship was as doomed as his and Elsie's but for different reasons.

But that might explain why she pushed so hard for Elsie to work for them. It hadn't been about him after all, but about her and Noah.

And maybe that had been why Abigail wanted to talk to him this morning...no. The pointed look and the tone of her voice indicated he'd been in trouble.

Women were so confusing.

"Morning," Levi mumbled as he stumbled to a chair and sat. He rubbed his temples with his thumbs, then fixed his gaze on sweet, beautiful Elsie. She'd hung her coat and bonnet up and was carrying two plates over to the table for Abigail.

Levi's palms sweated and he swiped them against his pants. His mouth dried. Oh, what she did to him! He fought to get his reactions under control. "What brings you by so early?" he asked, then grimaced. That sounded rude.

"My horse is lame and I needed to borrow Elsie's to get to work," Noah said. "I'll pick her up after five on the way home. *Daed* is going to try to get my horse to the farrier today."

"So you can't stay?" Abigail sounded disappointed.

"Sorry. I already ate breakfast, too, but this smells delicious. If you don't mind, I'll take it for my lunch."

"But it'll be cold," Abigail objected.

Noah winked—winked!—at Levi's sister. "As the last verse of a child's nursery rhyme goes, 'I like it hot; I like it cold.'"

Abigail's cheeks flamed redder. But she nodded and went to get an empty plastic container that they used to store leftovers.

Levi frowned and glanced down at his fisted hands. He never took Noah Miller as a flirt, and he didn't appreciate him leading his sister on. Not one bit. But he also didn't want to crush Abigail's hopes and dreams.

His throat clogged. Maybe he was doing the same with Elsie, kissing her the way he did, hiring her, and saying some of the things he had. She must be feeling false hope, too.

Noah clapped Levi on the shoulder. "I'll be seeing you. Take care of our sisters. Yours and mine."

Levi looked up.

Noah held the plastic dish in one hand. His grin was easy, friendly—as if he believed Levi's intentions toward

Elsie were pure and marriage minded. Then he hurried out the door.

Leaving Levi alone with two starry-eyed females and a man destined to destroy their dreams.

* * *

Elsie knew better than to entertain any false hopes. Especially when Levi refused to even look at her, and the few words he'd spoken—"Let's pray" and "Amen"— were gruffly mumbled. But that would change, especially when he came home from work tonight to find his office in better condition and the house smelling of Christmas cookies, fudge, and other goodies.

And if Abigail was agreeable, Elsie would help her plan a youth frolic with a taffy pull. Judging by her reaction to Noah's friendly visit, it would do her good to be around young people. Levi, too. He never attended frolics, and he didn't take Abigail to the meetinghouse on church Sundays for some reason. Maybe it was too difficult or she refused to go. Elsie would try to find out the reason and attempt to fix it. They were turning into recluses.

She glanced at him as she sipped a cup of coffee. She'd eaten breakfast already, too, so she left her untouched plate on the counter with a quiet explanation for Abigail.

Levi kept his head averted, his gaze down, and ate silently and quickly. He closed his eyes again for a final prayer, then stood. He focused on Abigail. "I'll be working in the shop today. I'll be in for lunch."

Elsie swallowed, tempted to direct his gaze toward her like she had the night before. She wanted some sort of acknowledgment from him, but it seemed as if she was destined for a whole lot of nothing. At least they'd see each other occasionally.

Maybe.

Make that definitely. If he was working in his shop, she could find an excuse to go out there. Or maybe not. That'd be too much like chasing him, and one thing she learned from the youth leaders was that men liked to be the pursuers, not the prey.

With that in mind, she needed to stick to her original plan and kill—er, make that win—him with kindness.

Levi nodded her way but kept his gaze averted, grabbed his outerwear, shoved the items on, and went out the door. A moment later, he stuck his head back in. "It's snowing, Abigail." Then he shut the door and strode past the window on his way out to the barn.

Abigail rolled over to the window.

Elsie followed. "When was that winter storm warning for?" She peered out the window at the gently floating flakes. Tiny ones. This wasn't accumulating snow.

"I don't know, but isn't it pretty? I love snow. *Daed* always used to make a row of snow people. One for each member of the family." Abigail's voice broke and she sniffled.

Elsie remembered the row of snowmen. "But last year there was...one." Oh. Why hadn't Levi built two? Or more, in memory of his family?

Abigail swiped at her eyes. "He was bawling by the time he finished one."

Elsie sucked in a breath. That explained so much.

"The tears froze on his face," Abigail said. "I'm not even going to ask this year."

Elsie swallowed the sudden lump clogging her throat and bent to wrap her arms around Abigail's shoulders. The teenager reached up and clung to her. Elsie hugged her, but she had no words. Her eyes burned.

And shame filled her. Instead of plotting how she could win Levi's heart back, she would focus on how she could help the two remaining Wyses heal.

The trouble was she didn't have the foggiest idea where or how to begin.

CHAPTER 10

Levi stood in the doorway of his cold, dark workshop and slumped. He didn't know where to even start, which was beyond pathetic, because ordinarily he'd have no problem moving on to the next step, the next thing.

It seemed that having an impossible deadline stalled his creativity.

Either that or it was the darkness that permeated his soul. His life. His vision.

Would he be excommunicated if he went to the bishop and confessed that he killed his family? Some Amish believed murder was unpardonable and would destine him to spend eternity in hell. And even though it was accidental and unintentional, the fact remained that his failure to return to the house and turn off the gas had caused the explosion.

He didn't deserve forgiveness, but he wanted to be free from the guilt, the pain, the weight. He wanted to breathe in a great big breath of grace.

Gott's grace. And mercy. Forgiveness.

Too bad it wasn't intended for him.

He sighed heavily and flicked the light on.

At least he'd shed a little light on the subject.

But the room was cold, so very cold, and the heaters took forever to even begin to make a difference. It'd help a lot if he could paint in the house. Abigail didn't like the odor of paint fumes, but maybe she'd make an exception during this bitter cold snap. He'd ask her at lunch. It'd help considerably if he could paint after dark when he was inside anyway. Not to mention they'd dry ever so much better.

Abigail might even enjoy painting animals. It'd be something quiet and enjoyable to do, unlike the endless job of darning his holey socks. He couldn't imagine how that was fun.

And it would save him time while also helping get the order ready that much faster...

He shut the door to his workshop, flicked the pitiful space heaters on, and grabbed a block of wood. The obvious first step would be to finish the train. He needed three more cars for this one, then seven cars, an engine, and a caboose for the other train. The animals could come after the trains were finished. He glanced at the partially completed train. If he focused, he should be able to make all three cars in very rough form today. The sanding and carving and assembly would take longer. But once the pieces were cut, he could then sit on a stool to focus on the detail work.

Focus.

Levi gave a soft snort. How was he supposed to focus, knowing that Elsie was in his house, so close but oh so far away? That she'd been in this very room? That she had left half of her candy cane here on an unfinished boxcar? And it was still there, reminding him of Elsie. And her kisses. How was he supposed to work, knowing she willingly was in his arms last night, exchanging kiss for kiss?

His body heated.

This was not going to work. Not at all.

Something creaked, and Levi clutched the rectangular wood block tighter and swung around, half expecting to see Elsie standing there in the open doorway, candy cane in hand, ready to have that talk she said they needed to have. The conversation he beyond dreaded.

She wasn't there. Good, because he didn't have the energy for her right now. Nothing would be resolved, because there was no atonement for his sins. He could confess everything to her, but what good would it do? She still wouldn't understand and would want to solve his many problems, and he was mentally too exhausted to even attempt to find the words he needed.

With a sigh of relief he turned to get back to work.

Another creak. Closer.

Had he just not seen her? He looked again.

The door was closed, just the way he'd left it. No Elsie was in the room with him. No one was.

He was alone.

Except for another creak of a floorboard.

Creepy.

Levi clutched the wooden block, strode over to the door, and swung it wide open.

"Don't hit me!" An elderly Amishman, face obscured by a black scarf and wielding a cane, shrieked in terror and threw a small metal toolbox he'd held in his other hand at Levi. It fell with a clatter and opened, spewing tools all over the barn floor. He swung the cane at Levi's lower leg. It connected with a not-very-painful thump.

What? He wouldn't hit anybody. Levi held out the block of wood.

The man—Levi thought he recognized the fear-filled eyes and the gray beard hanging below the scarf— bellowed and swung the cane again. Harder.

This time the cane hit with a not-so-satisfying—and very painful—crack. It probably left a bruise.

The man let the now-broken cane drop as he whipped his scarf off and held it out like a shield or as if he were a matador in a bullfight. And Levi recognized him.

"George?"

"Now look what you've done!" the semiretired buggy repairman shouted. He only knew one volume. Loud.

"I can make you a new cane," Levi said. It'd be a whole lot easier than making a train.

"What's that? A new game?" George cupped his ear.

"Cane!" Levi nudged the broken one with the foot connected to his injured leg. It hurt to move.

George frowned. "Came? Why, because when I was in town I heard you needed a train. There's only one reason to need a train and that's because your buggy is broken. And I fix buggies!" George yelled.

That explained the toolbox.

Levi rubbed the base of his neck. His head ached worse. And he didn't know how to explain to George that his buggy wasn't broken. It just seemed easier to accept than to attempt a shouted and sure-to-be-misunderstood explanation.

He held up his finger in a silent "wait a minute" and hobbled into his workshop to grab a walking stick he was planning to sell come springtime. He handed it to George, then knelt to gather the scattered tools. George pointed to each with the walking stick and shouted directions on precisely where to place it in the toolbox.

Hopefully, George wouldn't want much money for "fixing" a not-broken buggy. And it would give George the attention he craved—according to Levi's *daed*—when George broadcasted his rather-doubtful and paid-for good deed around the community. Of course, he wouldn't mention the doubtful or paid-for parts. Just the good deed.

On the positive side, this unplanned—and unwanted—visit served to take Levi's mind off of the also unplanned and unwanted deaths of his family members, as well as Elsie's presence, which somehow triggered all the other memories and thoughts running through his mind. Not to mention the desire...

And with lightning-flash speed, they all returned. He groaned.

Thankfully, George didn't hear.

Levi looked up as he picked up the last tool. Movement in the open barn doors caught his attention. A figure darted out of sight. He closed the toolbox, handed it to George, and went to investigate.

And there was Elsie, speed walking back to the house, skirt swaying.

Levi let her go, but, heart pounding, he watched every step.

He'd talk to her about spying later.

Except, that *was* in the job description of an elf.

* * *

The best-laid plans of mice and men, Elsie thought as she hurried through the cold to the house. *Mamm* always quoted that line, though Elsie had no clue where she'd gotten it from. Did mice actually make plans?

No matter. The point was that all her plans to help Abigail first had been for naught. Abigail had wanted to be left alone while she did dishes and laundry and pointed Elsie to the loft office.

It was a good vantage point for watching the barn, so she was able to see an elderly Amish man skulking around the barn. And *jah*, she probably shouldn't have followed him, but she arrived in time to witness the fatal blow to the cane. She'd smothered a gasp, but seriously, why was George beating Levi, and why did Levi take it without a word? Although, to be fair, turning the other cheek was grilled into them, and Levi usually was just plain nice.

Unless he was avoiding her.

Or accusing her of lashing out irrationally.

She went inside the warm house and checked the fire. Abigail was singing in a back room. Elsie poured herself a mug of hot peppermint tea, then hurried to the loft. She might not be able to save Levi from the cane-whacking George, but hopefully she could save him from this death by paper pile.

She sighed as she returned her attention to the loft office disaster. Another of *Mamm*'s sayings came to mind. *Things always get worse before they get better.* That was certainly true of this office. She'd started sorting the papers in piles on the floor by business or customer name. What a mess! There were so many different piles she couldn't move without stepping on something.

Impressing him with her organizational powers wouldn't be happening today.

She opened the file cabinet and cheered. It was conveniently empty, except for an unopened box of multicolored hanging file folders, but it wouldn't be for long. She opened the box, scooped up a colorful blue folder, labeled it with the name on one of the piles, and hung it on the thin metal bars. She'd organize by date later. This part had to come first.

She'd barely made a dent in the mess when a door shut downstairs. She peeked outside. George's buggy was still there. Maybe Abigail needed something. Elsie headed for the ladder stairs but stopped when Levi appeared in the opening.

His eyes met hers for a too-brief moment then swept across the messier mess of his office. His brow furrowed, a muscle worked in his jaw, but to his credit he let a minute tick by before he opened his mouth.

"Have you, um, seen my checkbook?" His gaze seemed doubtful as it shifted back to Elsie. "George fixed my buggy."

Elsie glanced around and spied the checkbook on the desk. "I didn't know it was broken," she said, then grimaced. Of course she didn't know it was broken. Levi had no reason to think she needed to know everything.

Something flickered in Levi's eyes. "I didn't, either," he said. "But he says it's fixed now. At least I hope he didn't break it." He shrugged.

That was a concern. Elsie had heard rumors that George's mind was slipping. His wife had said something about early stages of dementia. Elsie swung around, grabbed the checkbook and a pen, and handed both to Levi.

He took them but lingered. "Why aren't you helping Abigail? She needs help. That's mainly what I hired you for."

"She said she wanted to be alone and told me to start up here." Elsie lowered her voice. "I think she wanted to daydream about Noah."

Levi frowned. "I was afraid of that." He sighed heavily.

Elsie bristled but took a couple of deep, calming breaths. "Noah is a good man, Levi."

Levi hesitated another moment. "*Jah*. I'm sure he is, but—"

"Let her dream. She's a normal teenage girl."

There was another long silence; then he nodded. "You're right. Of course. I'll let her dream. I'll…I'll just go"—he looked down at the checkbook—"pay George."

"You do that," Elsie said.

He looked up again, his gaze skimming over her, then lingering for a heart-pounding moment on her lips.

She resisted the urge to lick them.

There was a troubled light in his eyes when he raised them to meet hers. "Did you smuggle peppermint in?"

She attempted to look innocent. "Who, me?"

His lips flickered ever so briefly. "*Jah*, you."

"Couldn't be. You told me no candy." She tried to keep a grin at bay at the memory of another cotton ball dab with peppermint essential oil that morning.

"Then who? I smell peppermint."

"Maybe because you *want* to," she teased.

His gaze lowered to her lips again. Then he shook his head. "No. Couldn't be."

Was she that repulsive? The smile that'd been flirting died as he backed down the ladder.

* * *

It couldn't be, but it was true. Levi wanted to kiss her again with every fiber of his body.

Instead, he carried the checkbook and pen through the house and tried not to breathe. It was impossible, but it seemed the scent of peppermint permeated the air, filling the entire house. Did he subconsciously want to smell peppermint so badly he imagined it?

He went into the barn, found George, and wrote a check, trying to ignore the various buggy parts strewn all over the floor. It was just one more thing Levi needed to do. Fix the buggy George just "fixed." George probably needed the money anyway. His house and his health were both falling into disrepair.

George pocketed the check with a big smile. "Now there's no reason for you to take the train," he shouted.

If only. Levi managed a weak smile—or something he hoped resembled a smile. It'd been so long the movement felt strange to his facial muscles. "It's puzzling how you..." He was going to say something about George's bad ears and yet his surprising ability to hear Mark's comment since Mark never raised his voice, but that'd probably be rude.

"Suffering, you say?" George yelled as he patted Levi's forearm. "Suffering is a part of life. I've never met a strong person who hasn't suffered."

Levi attempted another polite smile but froze. Wait. That was actually a nugget of wisdom worth pondering. He'd definitely become stronger by being forced to step up to the plate and care for himself and Abigail. Though probably George referred to something else entirely. He never could tell with George.

George patted Levi's arm again. "Call me if you have any more trouble with your buggy. I fix buggies, you know. Beats having to take a bus or a train."

Levi looked at the scattered miscellaneous parts on the dusty floor. Somehow he managed to keep his mouth shut and acknowledge George with a nod. But really Levi wanted to cry. Why hadn't he thought of writing a note to explain things to George? Or taking him into the workshop to show him the train? Why did he think of these things too late?

George grabbed the walking stick Levi had given him, picked up the toolbox, and headed outside. Levi gathered the spare parts and his own toolbox, checked to make sure George was gone, then shimmied under the buggy to finish fixing it. Despite his stalled creativity, at least he had a reason to stay busy out here.

Sometime later, he put the toolbox away and dusted off his backside, satisfied that the buggy was fixed to the best of his ability. He was glad he took the time because at least one of the wheels would've come off on the road.

He needed a hot mug of coffee to motivate himself to get back to work on the train, but he'd lost the whole morning, due to the semiretired buggy repairman. He'd get the coffee to go. And then he wouldn't have to see Elsie.

Levi scurried toward the house and opened the door to two lined cookie sheets filled with homemade peppermint patties. Two smiling females. A house filled with the scent of the mint.

And the overwhelming desire to kiss a certain someone senseless.

CHAPTER 11

Elsie had seriously needed a break from all the paper-work. Her eyes were burning. Too bad she'd forgotten her reading glasses. Or rather, not forgotten, but had been too proud to bring them and let Levi see a sign of weakness. Maybe not weakness, but imperfection.

Silly of her, really. She was far from perfect.

She'd wanted to look pretty for him, too.

Especially since he'd never seen her with glasses, and what if it repelled him?

At least she'd know. Tomorrow, if she still had a job, she'd bring her glasses.

Besides, if she focused on Levi's healing and her future in Chicago, it didn't matter if glasses repelled him.

It'd been a blessing when an hour ago Abigail called for her and suggested they do something fun. And Abigail had been the one to suggest peppermint patties. She claimed they were Levi's favorite...or used to be back when—whenever "back when" was—and she wanted to soften him up for a conversation they needed to have. She wouldn't say about what. It was none of Elsie's business anyway.

Levi strode past the porch window. Elsie's heart pounded.

The door opened. He stepped inside.

And froze, his gaze fixed on the table.

The moment of truth had arrived.

Elsie figured she'd be the one blamed for the peppermint patties—and maybe she should be. She'd bought the bottle of flavoring. Not imitation, either. The real stuff.

Jah, she wanted him to think about kissing her.

She'd told him to let Abigail dream, but maybe she shouldn't have. Abigail could end up getting hurt.

Elsie *would* be hurt if she dared to dream. No doubt about that. And not because of Abigail's dreams, but because of her own. Levi had made it more than clear that while he may want to kiss her, he wasn't interested in renewing their relationship.

She wasn't interested in becoming his plaything. Well, maybe she was, but only within the confines of marriage.

And therein was the problem. Marriage wasn't in their future.

No. Her job was to help him heal so he could find happiness with some other woman.

That hurt.

Her future was life without her family and friends in Chicago. That hurt, too. But at least she'd have Sam and Sammy and she'd make friends. Eventually.

She wished she could run back to the eye-burning

paperwork, but she needed to get the candy on the waxed paper-lined baking sheets and into the refrigerator to chill.

"Peppermint patties?" Levi asked, his voice strangled.

"Abigail said that they're your favorite." Elsie nibbled her bottom lip. Maybe she could invent a reason to escape the kitchen...

"They used to be." He lingered in the doorway.

Abigail looked up from a recipe card she was reading. She frowned. "Used to be? Not anymore?"

"I haven't had them since the...the last Christmas we had with the family. Elsie brought them over for everyone, along with a gift just for me." His voice broke.

Oh. Elsie slid another peppermint patty onto the baking sheet. She hadn't meant to stir up bad memories. Or to hurt him. But it was Abigail's idea to make them. Elsie had provided the ingredients, though. Should she go hide in the bathroom for a while? Just to get away from the tension?

"We need to talk." Abigail placed the recipe card on the table and fixed her gaze on Levi.

He paled. His gaze skittered from the candy to his sister to Elsie then back to Abigail. "Now? With her here?" He glanced back at Elsie. "I didn't mean to be rude. Just that it's private. I think."

Abigail nodded.

Elsie stepped away from the table. She wasn't wanted? At least not for this conversation, whatever it was about. "I'll be in the loft."

"I'll call you when we finish," Abigail promised.

Levi came closer to the table and handed Elsie the checkbook. He seemed to try to be careful not to touch her, but despite his efforts their fingers brushed. Sparks flared. "Is there any coffee made?"

"Peppermint tea," Elsie said with a slight grin. Then she fled from the room, her face burning. She'd made it for herself and not him, but still...

How unintentionally obvious could she get?

* * *

Levi watched her go before he glanced back at his sister. "Tea?" He wouldn't use the word *peppermint* again. Was Elsie doing the peppermint thing on purpose to keep him thinking of her and wanting to kiss her? "Do you mind if I make coffee?"

"I'll get you some. There's still some left from this morning, since Elsie isn't a coffee drinker. You go wash up. I'm going to check on the pretzel dough I have raising."

"Pretzels, too?" Levi's mouth watered. He loved Abigail's pretzels. He nodded and backtracked long enough to take off his shoes, coat, and hat; then he headed for the bathroom to scrub up.

When he returned, Abigail had a steaming mug of coffee as well as two peanut butter cookies waiting for him. Where had they come from? Had Elsie brought them? He sat at the chair nearest to them.

Abigail parked so she faced him and set her brakes.

Levi reached for the coffee mug, then hesitated and reached for her hand instead. "I'm sorry for abandoning you last night. I should've been available in case you needed me."

Abigail wrinkled her nose. "You were here. If I'd

needed you, all I would've needed to do was call you and you would've come, right?"

"In a heartbeat. But...I thought that was why you were frustrated with me. Is it because I..." He pulled in a deep breath. "I kissed Elsie?"

Abigail sighed. "I never expected you to kiss and tell. No."

Levi gently squeezed her hand, then released it. "You're confusing me, Abigail. What did I do? How can I fix it?"

Abigail sucked in a noisy breath. "There might be this guy that might ask me out, and if he does, I want to go." The words tumbled over each other in a rush.

Levi blinked twice and gaped at her. "There *might* be?" And Elsie had said to let her dream. Did she know?

"There might be." Abigail's cheeks reddened.

"And his name might be Noah Miller?" Oh, this hurt.

The red deepened. "It might be."

Levi forced himself to breathe. "Why do you think he might ask you out?" Although the man had flirted with Abigail when he was here.

Abigail looked away.

Oh. It was wishful thinking. Levi tried to think of appropriate words of comfort, but it was hard, especially when he wanted to shout in relief.

Tears glistened in his sister's eyes when she looked at him again. "Because ever since the accident, he's been coming by occasionally to talk to me. Because he said he'd like to take me out. If you agreed to let him."

Levi blinked. Never in a thousand years had he expected that. Noah had been calling on Abigail for the past year and a half and Levi was just now hearing about it?

Elsie had said to let Abigail dream—did that mean she'd known? She must've. Why hadn't she warned him? It would have been nice not to be so blindsided.

And this was why Abigail had been fixing his favorite foods? To soften him up so she could go out with a man? And not just any man, but Elsie's brother?

Oh, this was bad. Very, very bad.

For a half second, he was tempted to get up, find Elsie—who was probably spying—and have a chat with her. One that might involve him lashing out irrationally at her like she had with him right before they broke up, but he forced himself to sit still. It was best to think before he said anything. And sometimes it was best just to keep thinking and say nothing at all.

"Please? If he asks?" Tears beaded on Abigail's lashes.

Levi gulped. Oh, Noah would ask. He'd already asked Abigail to okay it with Levi. Which meant either Noah was a coward and afraid to ask Levi—which didn't fit— or Abigail was afraid of his reaction.

That saddened him. He'd do anything for her. Well...almost anything.

Levi forced himself to breathe. Deep, cleansing breaths. Then, to give himself time to calm down a little more, he reached for his coffee and took a long drink. He returned the mug to the table.

The tears on her lashes spilled over. Just a couple, but it broke his heart more. He shut his eyes for a moment, then opened them. "*Jah*. If he asks, and if you want, he can take you out."

And Levi would try not to terrorize Noah before the date with the "*daed* talk." He'd been scared spitless when Elsie's *daed* had it with him.

Abigail squealed and somehow—he wasn't quite sure how—launched herself out of the wheelchair, took two or three stumbling steps forward, and threw herself into his arms. Then she clung to him, laughing and crying. At the same time.

His throat burned. "*Ich liebe dich*, Abigail."

"And I, you." She wobbled and clung tighter. "Help me back to my chair."

Levi adjusted his grip and eased to his feet; then he held on as he slowly backed her up enough to sit. He crouched in front of her. "Abigail, you walked." He felt a twinge of hope that someday she could live her life the way she had...before.

She cried harder. "Just a couple steps."

"You have to start somewhere." And that was true for himself as well, with those circus train orders. He had to do something, other than stress over them. "Even two steps is progress."

She reached for a paper napkin and blew her nose as his stomach rumbled. She giggled. "Get Elsie and we can get the noon meal ready."

He glanced at the table covered with candies, cookies, and baking supplies but nodded and went into the other room, fully expecting Elsie to be darting for the loft ladder after eavesdropping on their conversation. She wasn't. Nor did he see her in the short hallway when he peeked. He climbed up into the loft, and there was Elsie, sitting cross-legged on the floor, stacks of papers spread out around her and another pile in her lap. She'd been here awhile. Working. Not eavesdropping.

But then, why would she need to eavesdrop? She'd known her brother planned to ask his sister out. He stepped closer to her and sighed. "Why didn't you warn me?" He tried to keep his voice calm. Quiet.

Elsie glanced up with a frown. "About what?"

"Your brother and my sister."

Her frown deepened. "That she likes him? I didn't know until this morning, the same time you found out. Is that a problem?"

"It might be. Did you know he's been calling on her? That he's been talking about asking her out?"

Elsie blinked. "No, I didn't. I thought he was seeing someone, but I never dreamed..." She put the stack of papers down and stood. "Is it a problem because of us?"

He used to be able to read every emotion on her face. He wasn't sure he could anymore, but he was as certain as he could be she was telling the truth. She hadn't known. Relief filled him. "No. *Jah*. I don't know. Maybe. If only there was some way for me to keep an eye on them when he takes her out," he said.

"I don't understand why you think you need to, but there is. We—"

"No! I won't go on a double date with you and them." He'd want to be alone with Elsie, making out under the stars at Hidden Springs. His body warmed. Inappropriate thoughts, those.

"Of course not." She gave a little laugh, one that sounded bitter. "We both know how you feel about me."

"You know?" His breath strangled. But then of course—he'd flat out told her.

"You've made it plain. You may want to kiss me, but you can't stand to be around me." Her smile was sad looking. Resigned.

How could she be so wrong? But it was a hedge of protection for both of their hearts.

"But it's okay because I..." She hesitated. "I, um, never mind." She looked away as if she felt guilty.

She what? Didn't love him anymore? He knew that. But why would she feel guilty for that?

Elsie pulled in a breath. "No. Not a double date. I was thinking a taffy pull. Here, at your house. I'll organize the whole thing. That way you'll be here."

"In the barn. Working." Since he had a deadline. And even if he didn't, he couldn't risk letting his feelings be known to everyone who might attend. Couldn't risk the intrusion and matchmaking and endless questions...

"I kind of thought in the house. Chaperoning." Her hand landed on her hip and she jutted it out.

Impossible. His focus would be completely on Elsie. Like it was now. But against his better judgment, he nodded. "Ask Abigail if she wants one." She would. That was painfully obvious. He needed to change the subject before he lost control of his severely frayed good sense and kissed Elsie. Again. A dish clattered downstairs. And that reminded him..."I, uh, was sent to ask you to help her get the noon meal ready." Abigail clearly needed help, which was why she shouldn't date until she had improved more.

"It was great talking to you, Levi." Elsie's smile looked real.

"*Jah*. It was." Except, now he had other methods of communication on his mind. He forced himself to slightly turn away before he touched her soft cheek. Kissed her sweet lips. *Lord, help.* He caught his breath. "I'll be in the barn. Call me."

"No. You call me." And she winked.

Maybe he imagined the flirty tone. Or maybe not.

When he added in the wink...definitely not.

But he fled before he answered her *call* and got them both into trouble.

* * *

Elsie chastised herself for teasing him as she followed him downstairs and into the kitchen. She'd have to ask Noah to shoot down some mistletoe to hang in Abigail's kitchen. But that might encourage Noah to take advantage of it, and Levi would be sure to have a meltdown if he witnessed that.

Noah and Abigail.

It was so sweet!

One of the Millers should have a happily ever after with the Wyses, and if it couldn't be her, then it should be Noah.

It'd be better if it were both of them. But she needed to focus on helping them heal. Not on flirting. It was just that flirting came naturally when she interacted with Levi.

She still loved Levi Wyse.

She always would. Always and forever. A woman never got over her first love.

CHAPTER 12

Levi didn't make much progress. In fact, it seemed he'd barely finished cutting the wood into the beginning shape of a train's boxcar when the dinner bell clanged.

For a moment, disappointment filled him. He'd hoped Elsie would make the trip out to the barn to tease his senses with peppermint when she called him in. But it was better this way. He needed to keep his distance from her if he wanted to keep his infatuation with her somewhat managed. Not to mention his traitorous heart that never stopped loving her. It probably never would.

He quickly put his tools away even though he planned to return, turned off the heater that had barely affected the bitterly cold temperatures, flicked off the lights, and strode to the house.

The kitchen was empty when he arrived, but the table was cleaned off and set, and a delicious scent filled the air—and it wasn't peppermint. He grabbed pot holders and opened the oven. Meatloaf and scalloped potatoes. Mixed vegetables simmered on the stove.

And Abigail's wonderful soft pretzels, covered with butter and sea salt, waited on the counter.

His stomach rumbled.

"I'll get the food ready to be served, if you want to wash up," Elsie said as the scent of peppermint enveloped him. It sounded—and smelled—as if she was standing right behind him.

He slowly turned.

She was definitely close enough that he could reach out and touch her. If he wanted. And he wanted to. Very, very badly.

"Where's Abigail?" His voice shook.

Elsie gestured toward the pantry. "Packing up some peppermint patties and peanut butter cookies for me to take home. I told her we didn't need them, but she insisted. The way to a man's heart is through his stomach, and all that."

Levi frowned. "I've heard that quote before, but I'm not sure how true it is. That's rather..." He hesitated, searching for the correct word. He couldn't find it. He shrugged. "Sexist? Judgmental? Biased? I think there's a lot more involved than food."

"Like what? Beauty? Sex appeal?" She took the pot holders from him and stepped around him to the still-open oven. "Peppermint?" Her tone turned flirty.

He turned to watch her. "Um, friendship. Common interests. Attraction that isn't necessarily based on looks but maybe personality."

"And me?" She lifted the meatloaf out. "Why were you attracted to me initially? Not now." The scalloped potatoes joined the meatloaf on the counter. She shut the oven door.

"All of the above and more. You completed me. I felt like part of me was missing when we were apart." He still did.

She turned to face him and silently studied him.

He shifted and averted his gaze. He couldn't let her see—

She took two steps forward and wrapped her arms around him. Her softness pressed against him as she hugged him. He gasped for air and stiffened to keep from gathering her closer and kissing her the way he had last night. She stretched up and bussed his cheek, then released him and stepped away. "That's sweet, Levi. I honestly hope you find that again."

His appetite faded. "There is no hope of that. None." He backed away. "I'm not hungry anymore. I'll be in the barn."

"Sorry I repulse you now." Her voice hitched. Broke.

His eyes shot to her. Why would she say that? Didn't she know…she had to know—

"Levi," Abigail said quietly.

He spun around.

"You're staying in to eat. We need to talk."

"Again? More?" What now? Dread settled in his stomach, heavy, like a rock. Would this be the conversation about his many failures, or had Noah snuck back and proposed while no one was looking? Though, that thought seemed like pure foolishness.

"Again. More," Abigail parroted with a gentle smile. It took the sting out of her teasing. "Go, sit. Elsie and I will bring the food over."

He nodded and, to help out, grabbed the green glass bowl of applesauce sitting on the counter and carried that to the table. Then he took his seat, bowed his head, and prayed for guidance, for wisdom, for clarity of thought, and for the right words for this new issue.

Both women were at the table when he opened his eyes and looked up.

"Praying without us?" Abigail asked. She must know how flustered he was.

He managed a nod. Elsie, the impossible deadline, and George had all contributed to throwing his day off track. He needed all the prayer time he could get. He didn't dare glance at his green-clad, strawberry-blond, peppermint-scented elf. "Shall we pray?" He bowed his head again and waited long enough for a speedy recitation of the Lord's Prayer. "Amen."

Abigail raised her head and lifted a slice of meatloaf to her plate. Elsie didn't open her eyes for a few more moments. Maybe she needed more prayer time, too. When she did, she quietly stood, walked over to the stove, poured him a cup of coffee, and carried it to the table. Her fingers brushed against his shoulder as she pulled away. His skin burned through the thin fabric of his shirt. He tried not to show any reaction to her accidental touch. "*Danki*," he said, then reached for the bowl of mixed vegetables even though his appetite still hadn't returned. He spooned some on his plate, passed the bowl to Elsie, and turned his attention to Abigail. "What did you want to talk about?"

Abigail clasped her hands like a little girl. "Elsie mentioned something about maybe having a taffy pull, if it's agreeable with you."

It wasn't okay with him, not in the least. But for Abigail… "She mentioned it. I guess you're interested. When do you want it?" The twelfth of never would be a good time.

Abigail beamed and somehow bounced in her wheelchair. "As soon as possible. Before Christmas, obviously. When is that ice storm forecasted to arrive?"

Levi shrugged. "Whenever it wants to arrive or not at all. When I was in town yesterday, I heard it had stalled out in the Dakotas and the weathermen weren't sure how it would track. It will be delayed. However, the *Farmer's Almanac* is predicting a colder-than-normal year with more wintery accumulation than usual. And that is all I know."

"Would this Friday be too soon? Two days from now?" Abigail directed that question to Elsie.

Levi spooned out a serving of scalloped potatoes and passed them. His stomach growled. Maybe he'd be able to eat after all.

"It's short notice, but I'll spread the word. I think most will cancel plans and come here instead because people haven't seen you in forever." Elsie passed the potatoes to Abigail.

"They know where to find me. I just figured they don't care. Not really."

And there went Levi's appetite again. How many people had Levi discouraged from visiting because he hadn't wanted them gawking at her or pitying her? And she thought they hadn't cared? Wow. He was ten times a jerk. Never mind that his motives had been pure and he'd only wanted to protect her.

Elsie frowned. "No one has stopped by? In almost two years?"

"Just you and Noah and the *Englisch* social worker. And you only recently, that day I prayed for help and you came."

That was Monday, Levi recalled. And here it was only Wednesday. So much had happened since then.

Elsie shook her head, silent for once.

"People might've come when I was in a coma," Abigail continued. "Noah said he did and he brought your sister Mandy with him once."

Jah, that was when Levi put a stop to visitors. The nurses said that the Amish went in there and loudly mourned or made discouraging remarks about how it was too bad and so sad, and even though Abigail was in a coma, it depressed her. They insisted that coma patients could hear. He'd have to somehow find the words to explain that. And now would be the perfect time since they were on the topic.

He pulled in a deep breath for courage, one that might have been a little loud because both Abigail and Elsie looked at him. He fisted one of his hands on his lap. "It's my fault," he said, then shoved a forkful of food into his mouth. Hopefully, that explanation would be good enough.

"What is your fault?" Abigail asked. Both women looked confused.

He should've known better. Nothing was ever so easy.

Levi chewed and swallowed, then put his fork down. "No visitors," he said. He might as well say why because they'd ask, and so he launched into a rather pitiful recitation of what the nurses had said about how Abigail's visitors were behaving. "And that's why I discouraged visitors once you came home. I was trying to protect you." He was working insane hours to pay their bills and doing all he could to protect her emotionally as well. But obviously failing. Like he might fail with the circus train order, too. Good thing the biggest bills were paid since his income was about to take a big hit.

"You're so sweet," Elsie said when he finished, and reached out a hand to hold his, the way she used to when he courted her. A sign of support, she'd always said.

He grasped it and clung although he'd probably regret it later. Warmth spread up his arm, somehow calming him.

Abigail started crying. Again. Elsie must affect his sister's tear ducts somehow. All that peppermint, maybe. Abigail must be allergic or something. He'd have another talk with Elsie about the smell. Possibly he should suggest a shower right before she came to work, although that might not go over so well. She probably sucked on the candy so much she was permanently scented.

Which meant his sister might be allergic to him if he held Elsie's hand.

He quickly let go and took another bite of his now-cold food.

Not to mention he'd probably smell peppermint in his sleep.

And then kissing her would not only fill his thoughts, but also his dreams.

* * *

Working for the Wyses was educational. Elsie gathered up the dirty dishes after Levi left the house and carried them over to the sink, her thoughts spinning. Of course

Levi would've mourned the loss of his family, but she'd never dreamed he'd cry over snowmen. It spoke volumes about how steeped in tradition he was. It was a good thing but so sad that he'd lost his whole family—except for Abigail—in one horrible moment.

And protecting Abigail the way he had by forbidding visitors—although the loud wailing seemed out of character for most Amish. They were usually more stoic when it came to death. "It was his or her time," and that was the end of it. Unless they were crying over Abigail's life hanging in the balance. For a while in there, the doctors had been rather grim about her chances of survival. Of course, after Levi forbid any visitors, Elsie had stopped getting any updates other than Levi's rather cryptic "No change" on the rare occasion he came to take her out on a date. He'd been withdrawing even then. Until the day Abigail woke up. Levi had come over so excited to share the news, and that was when he'd invited her to his third cousin's wedding—the wedding that had sounded the death knell for their relationship.

Elsie sighed as she ran hot water into the sink. Had something happened to Abigail that weekend—something bad enough to make him forget about her and everything and rush home to his sister?

She peeked over her shoulder. Abigail hummed as she wrote something on an index card. She'd said she was going to write a shopping list for Elsie while she did dishes. Elsie guessed she'd be doing the shopping in the morning and then helping Abigail deep clean the house to get ready for the taffy pull. Although, Levi would need to approve the list and give her the money.

They had a lot of work to do in a very short time, but

it was a miracle, pure and simple, that Levi agreed to let her suggest it. And with his silence, he'd agreed for it to happen in just two days' time.

She added a squirt of dish detergent to the hot water, stirred it in, and turned the faucet off. She'd have to see if Noah would take her to a few places to find a couple of chaperones, in addition to getting the word out about the frolic.

She'd mentioned chaperoning to Levi, but the truth was both he and she were single, and married couples acted as chaperones, not singles of courting age. Levi must've forgotten or else he would've flat out refused.

A flutter of excitement tickled her belly. Aware of it or not, Levi Wyse was about to be her date to the taffy pull. And with that in mind, Noah *had* to shoot down some mistletoe before Friday evening. Elsie's future happiness was at stake.

Instantly guilt filled her. Helping Levi and Abigail heal was more important than conniving and manipulating to get him back.

Though wouldn't being forced to be part of a two-some at a frolic be part of the healing process? And who better to be with than her. She was obviously the one he'd be most comfortable with, even if he didn't like her anymore. It'd be better than having him hide in the barn the whole time.

Elsie finished washing the last dish, drained the water, and grabbed a towel to dry the dishes. As she wiped the first plate, she turned to Abigail. "What would you like me to do next?" It kind of hurt to ask. But Abigail was her employer and Elsie couldn't just assume.

Abigail pursed her lips. "Sweep and scrub the kitchen

floor. That's a job I can't do very well from a wheelchair, and I think the kitchen should be super clean for
candy making. Besides, everyone will be judging me—
and you—on our housecleaning skills, and I don't want
us to be found lacking."

Elsie nodded, but she wasn't sure the focus would be
on judging housekeeping. She went to visit with friends
and have fun and didn't care whether the floor was clean
enough to use for a plate. Of course, being an Amish
home, the assumption that it was would be there.

"The cleaning supplies are in the mudroom." Abigail
pointed to the laundry room.

Elsie headed that way. There was another outside
entrance and a direct entrance to the bathroom so a
muddy farmer could strip in the laundry room and head
straight for the bathroom and a shower without anyone
seeing him or her. Convenient. She peeked out the small
window on the back door and stifled a scream when
her gaze locked on Levi's serious gray eyes. She hadn't
expected him to be standing there.

Levi jerked open the door and stepped inside.

Elsie stumbled back a couple of steps.

"What are you doing?" he whispered.

Why was he whispering? "Looking for cleaning supplies," she said just as quietly, opting to tell the truth.

Confusion crossed Levi's face. "Outside? Through the
window?"

Elsie frowned. "Oh. No. Just wondered where this
door led. That's all. You didn't show me this room."

"I didn't think of it, but a mudroom is a mudroom."
He shrugged. "Cleaning supplies are in that cupboard."
He pointed but then edged closer. "It probably won't do

any good to tell you this, but I think Abigail is allergic to peppermint."

"Why do you think that? And why wouldn't it do any good to tell me?" Elsie tilted her head.

"I was going to suggest showering before you come, but then I figured that wouldn't do any good because you probably eat so much peppermint you're permanently scented. I think she's allergic because I've never seen her cry so much. It must be making her eyes water."

"Oh. She's just happy." Elsie reached out and patted his arm. The man must be an idiot to not realize her scent was due to more than simply eating peppermint. But maybe he was attempting to protect himself by using his sister's needs.

"Happy? Why would she cry if she was happy? That makes no sense." Levi moved a little closer. He smelled of sawdust. Of coffee. And of chocolate-covered peppermint patties. He gazed down into her eyes.

"Because you agreed to a taffy pull. Because you love her so much you tried to protect her when she was in a coma. Because you gave permission for her to start living like a normal teenager."

"I never told her she couldn't." Levi frowned and moved closer still. Close enough she could rise up on tiptoes and kiss him. Close enough that if he were any other guy, he'd be violating her personal space. He'd lowered his voice even more so that it felt even more intimate and made her shiver. "But how is she going to get to all the teenage activities? I'm a working man and not available to lift her in and out of buggies regularly." His gaze dipped to her lips. Rose. Then lowered again, lingering.

"We'll figure it out." Elsie's breath hitched. She should move away, but the hungry desire in his eyes caught her and held her captive. "The reason you abandoned me at the wedding eighteen months ago—was it…had…um…Did it have something to do with Abigail?"

His hands rose and cupped each side of her face. His fingers slid over the curve of her cheeks. His eyes darkened. "Mm-hmm. She fell and had a major setback. The doctors didn't think she'd survive."

Elsie's heart pounded out of control. The rough timbre of his voice combined with the look in his eyes reeled her in. She moved a centimeter closer and raised her head to his, a silent invitation for his kiss. "Why didn't you tell me?"

He groaned and lowered his head enough so his breath whispered across her lips. "You broke up with me before I could."

So their breakup was truly her fault. Regret filled her. If only she could communicate her love still remained…

There was something mixed with the desire in his eyes. Heat. Something.

He groaned again. His thumb traced over her lips, igniting a fire deep inside. "Elle—"

She shivered and surged against him, her arms going around his neck as he backed her against the washing machine and pressed against her.

The next instant his lips were on hers. Teasing. Caressing. But holding back and not committing. Driving her mad.

Two could play that game. She whimpered, weaving her fingers into his hair and wiggling against him.

He made a growling sound deep in his throat. The next second she was seated on the washing machine, being held closer than he'd ever held her before, and his lips working some kind of magic that erased every thought from her mind except Levi and what he was doing to her.

* * *

He was out of control.

Somewhere in the hidden recesses of Levi's mind he recognized that fact, but he didn't want to acknowledge it. He mentally slapped the blaring alarms silent, his fevered kisses moving from her lips to her ears, down her neck, his hands cupping her hips and urging her off the machine, completely into his arms, her legs wrapping around him, and...and...

What. Was. He. Doing?

Oh, good Lord, have mercy.

He redeposited Elsie on the washing machine and wrenched himself away, his eyes burning. "I'm sorry. I'm so sorry."

Her sweet lips parted, swollen and probably bruised. She reached out as if to tug him back into her embrace, but he stumbled backward, then veered toward the door. What had he returned to the house for anyway? He couldn't remember. All he knew was...

Oh, good Lord...

"This changes nothing. Nothing." He grasped the doorknob and with a twist wrenched the door open. "I still can't marry."

"Can't," she repeated. Her eyes glistened as if she were about to cry.

He wanted to cry with her.

"Why *can't*?" Her voice broke.

He gave a mute headshake and...

And...

In what could only be lousy—or perfect—timing, Abigail wheeled into view. Partially. He saw her feet as she propelled her chair.

He motioned in that direction, and as Elsie slid off the washing machine, he slipped out the door. A tear or two escaped and ran down his cheeks.

Lord, help.

How could he continue to have Elsie work for them? But how could he not?

CHAPTER 13

On Thursday, Elsie deep cleaned the entire house per Abigail's directions, though she really didn't think some of it was necessary. Who would check for dust above door frames? Even when church services were held in homes every other Sunday, Elsie had never seen anyone reaching up high to check for dust. And ever since the terrible tornadoes that almost destroyed Hidden Springs, the bishop and preachers decided to build a common meetinghouse for services instead of having them in homes. Apparently several other districts were doing the same thing. And who dusted door frames in a church?

The house smelled of lemon-scented bleach when the door opened and Noah strode inside carrying the empty leftover dish. He'd been kept late at work Wednesday evening and Elsie's brother Sam had picked up Elsie, full of talk about Chicago and how he'd rented a two-bedroom apartment for them starting January first. They could move in sooner; the landlord was painting now. Elsie guessed she'd share a room with two-year-old Sammy. The clock was ticking. She didn't have much time left with the rest of her family and friends.

"The baked oatmeal was just as good as I imagined. You'll make a good wife someday." Noah winked at Abigail, who was sitting at the table slicing carrots and celery sticks to eat raw for part of supper.

She put down the knife and blushed. "*Danki*. I'm glad you enjoyed it."

Noah set the dish on the table and sniffed. "Smells like you've been cleaning."

"Elsie has. I wrote out a shopping list for her yesterday." Abigail nodded at Elsie on the other side of the table.

"I'll be ready to go as soon as I finish preparing meatloaf sandwiches." Elsie smeared mustard on the already sliced bread.

Noah shrugged. "Take your time. I'm not in any hurry to leave." He pulled out a chair and sat next to Abigail.

Elsie tried to not be obvious about studying them. She should have known about this long before now. She certainly had plenty of questions for Noah during their ride home. Starting with why he never brought her along when he visited Abigail.

"Can you and Elsie stay for supper?" Abigail asked.

Noah raised his eyebrows as he glanced at Elsie before answering. She gave a slight shake of her head. She'd love to and their parents wouldn't mind, but Levi probably had enough of her. He'd been gone when she arrived this morning and still hadn't made an appearance. Besides, he was sure to be uncomfortable after kissing her the way he had yesterday. It kind of embarrassed her, too. He'd never been so passionate when they were dating. It was almost as if he couldn't get enough. Maybe he sensed, as she did, that time was running out and all restraint was gone.

As if he was refilling his...thoughts, memories, something...before they parted again. Permanently this time. Because she'd be heading to Chicago with Sam and Sammy.

Oh, that hurt. Especially because she'd likely be shunned.

"Sorry, we can't stay." Noah sounded regretful. "Maybe another time."

Elsie didn't want to come between Noah and Abigail, either. But...

Abigail sucked in a breath. "Levi said we can have a taffy pull tomorrow," she blurted; then her cheeks flared red.

Elsie cringed. The poor dear. Abigail's crush on Noah was almost painful to watch. But maybe they felt the same about her obvious feelings for Levi.

Of course, her feelings were painful to experience, too. How should she react to a man who seemed to want her physically but not in any of the other ways that mattered in a forever romance—er, relationship? One that included marriage and a happy ever after.

There was no forever in their extended relationship forecast. And if she were smart, she wouldn't let him steal any more kisses—not that he stole them. She gave them away willingly. They should be saved for her future husband.

Not that anyone was lining up to court her. She had

dates. Dates! Sometimes two...never three. Seemed as if her lack of longevity at jobs extended to relationships, too.

What was wrong with her?

Maybe that'd change in the *Englisch* world, too.

She mentally shook her head and focused on her brother, who gazed at Abigail as if she were the only woman in the world.

"Friday is short notice," Noah said, "but we'll make it work. My big concern is the weather forecast. When we were talking at work, I heard we're supposed to get a bad ice storm with enough accumulation to down power lines followed by a blizzard with several feet of snow on top of the ice. The grocery stores are sold out of the necessities."

Brow furrowed, Abigail went to retrieve her shopping list and skimmed it. Then she shrugged. "Get what you can." She shoved it nearer to Elsie.

Elsie glanced at it. "Most of it is for candy making anyway and snacks for the frolic. You should be fine except for milk. And we have enough to spare at our house. I'll bring a gallon in the morning."

"Oh, I haven't had real milk fresh from the cow in forever. The whole milk from the grocery store just doesn't taste the same. *Danki*. When is that storm forecasted for?" Abigail turned to Noah. "Levi said he heard it was stalled over the Dakotas."

"It was." Noah shrugged. "And they still aren't sure which way it will go. If it tracks our way, it'll arrive late Friday night or early Saturday morning. So the taffy-making frolic shouldn't be affected. Everyone should be home by the time it starts. I think." He eyed Elsie's stack of meatloaf sandwiches. "I'm going to head out to the barn and say hi to Levi; then I'll be ready to go." He winked at Abigail again.

She looked down, her cheeks flaring red again. So sweet.

"I'll meet you at the buggy," Elsie said, then looked at Abigail as Noah stood and left the house. "I think I made plenty." She motioned toward the stack of sandwiches that used up all the leftover meatloaf. "But whatever is left you can set out at the frolic."

"*Danki* for all your help." Abigail picked up the knife again. "I'm so happy you and Levi are back together. You complete him. I can't wait until we're sisters."

Elsie paused in putting the lid on the mustard jar. She stared down at it. "We're not back together. Probably never will be." There was no probably about it. "I didn't mean to give you that impression. He's my boss and that's all." She couldn't even claim to be his friend. He'd be shunning her with all the rest.

Abigail frowned. "But Levi said he kissed you. He'd never do that if he wasn't in love with you."

If only that were true. And it rather hurt that Levi kissed and told, as if she were some kind of conquest. Elsie forced a shrug that she hoped looked nonchalant. "Levi can't stand me and the only reason he hired me was because of you. He said so."

Abigail scoffed. "Then why'd he kiss you?"

Peppermint. He'd told her so. But Elsie lifted her shoulders again. "We're history. The most we'll ever be in the future is friends." And that was stretching it.

"Think what you will. He's my brother and I know for a fact that he's still in love with you."

Whatever. But did Abigail know why Levi said he "can't" marry? Maybe she could ask Abigail. But not today when her emotional roller coaster had already taken her for a ride.

Elsie put the sandwich supplies away, cleaned up her mess, and headed for the door. And her coat. "I'll see you tomorrow."

* * *

A floorboard creaked.

Levi put the block of wood down on the workbench.

George, again? At least Levi had made significant progress between yesterday's and today's visits. The trains' cars were all cut out in rough form and ready for the hand shaping with his whittling tools. And maybe if he showed George the toy train cars, he wouldn't take apart the buggy.

He turned toward the door as it opened, spread his hands out so George could see he was unarmed—and hopefully wouldn't attack him with the walking stick—and looked at...Noah.

Noah, who wore a serious, intentional expression that warned Levi this would be a conversation he didn't want to have. But at least it wasn't a total surprise, so maybe he wouldn't come across as a jerk.

Levi tried to muffle a sigh, brushed the thick layer of sawdust off a stool, and held his hand toward it. "Hey, Noah. Have a seat." And then he cringed because that sounded rather abrupt. "Good of you to stop by." Better late than never, right?

Noah smiled, his ability to appear at ease whether he

was or not—like Elsie's—somewhat annoying Levi. The original facial expression had implied that Noah had to be as nervous about the upcoming conversation as Levi was. Noah straddled the stool and gave an exaggerated shiver as he glanced around. "A bit chilly out here, ain't so?"

Levi hadn't noticed, but since Noah brought it up… "Now that I'm not working it is." Levi crossed his arms and leaned his back end on the edge of the workbench. Time to cut the small talk. He wasn't good at it anyway and preferred to get to the main point. "What do you need?"

Noah's smile faded. "You aren't going to make it easy on me, are you?"

"Should I? It's about one of our sisters and—"

"Both." Noah jutted out his jaw. "I was going to ask permission to court Abigail, but maybe I should ask about your intentions regarding Elsie first."

Time to do damage control. Levi tried to muster a pleasant expression and find a calm yet firm tone of voice that would indicate he was the alpha dog here. Not Noah. This was his home. His family. "Permission granted. I know I don't need to tell you that she's fragile and still healing. Her recovery is slow and ongoing and—"

Noah held up a hand, his expression open and friendly again. "I know. I've been seeing her as a friend for over a year. Close to two years. She's my best friend. I didn't expect to fall in love."

"Taking her out has its own set of challenges." Levi had to warn the man. Noah had no idea what he was getting himself into. Lifting her in and out of the buggy, making sure where they went was wheelchair accessible, protecting her from unkind comments and gawkers…

"Abigail told me. But our first date is going to be at your house at your taffy pull." Noah spread his hands out. "You'll be there, watching."

Watching? Hardly. Levi tried not to scoff. "It's not my taffy pull. It's Abigail and Elsie's. I won't even be there."

Noah's smile flickered. "I think Elsie is kind of expecting to be your partner at the frolic."

"I don't know why she'd expect that." Except, he did. And worse, Noah witnessed that first passionate kiss since Levi and Elsie reconnected. Because he was strong-armed into hiring her as his elf. He unfolded his arms and waved a hand at his messy shop. "I'm on deadline." An impossible one. "I told her I'd chaperone the barn area while I work." At least he was pretty sure he had.

"You and Elsie can't be chaperones. You're singles of courting age."

"But we wouldn't be together in the same building." And he wasn't courting. Elsie might be in a relationship, though. And it made Levi lower than a snake to kiss another man's girl. But then again, Elsie hadn't exactly tried to stop him. Nor had she complained. Of course, that still didn't make it right.

Noah's face screwed up as if he'd tasted something sour. "You're not? But you...she...huh."

The man was holding back, clearly respecting Levi's implied alphaness by not challenging him. But still, his facial expression and body stance spoke volumes.

Time to change the subject. Or at least direct it away from him and Elsie. Levi crossed his arms again. "Your sister brought up the taffy pull, though I can't remember why." He'd kissed her since then. "She asked my permission to mention it to Abigail. I gave it, but I'm not real good at socializing, as I'm sure you know. Elsie suggested we chaperone."

"She knows better," Noah muttered.

Jah, and come to think of it, Levi knew better, too. Which meant Elsie had deliberately set out to mislead him—the conniving, manipulating, tempting...

"Elsie can be persuasive."

Persuasive was a whole lot nicer a word than the ones Levi struggled to think of. Probably truer, too. Elsie, like Noah, was just plain nice.

"Abigail was all over it when Elsie brought it up." Levi looked down at his tennis shoe–clad feet and scuffed a toe in the thick layer of sawdust. "I didn't realize how lonely she was."

"She's alone all day. You're around other people at work all the time."

Noah was a whole lot more forgiving than Levi, too. He could learn a lot from the Millers.

"You should make an occasional appearance at the taffy pull, just to show your support to Abigail and Elsie." Noah shifted on the stool, causing it to creak.

He was probably right. Levi sighed and glanced up, ready to agree, but he caught a glimpse of the unfinished trains. The block of wood he'd just cut out taunted him. How could he possibly consider going to the frolic? There was no way this order would get completed if he wasn't the adult, keeping his fingers on the sandpaper.

Noah stood. "I'll let you get back to work. I need to get Elsie home and Abigail almost has supper prepared." He gave Levi a pointed look.

A broad hint that Levi should temporarily close up

shop and come say goodbye and stay in long enough for dinner. But saying goodbye would stretch the limits of his control. Especially after kissing Elsie the way he had. It was far wiser to keep his distance physically and mentally and think about the reason why he couldn't marry instead of letting his strong feelings for her overrule his good sense.

"I'll be along in a bit," he said and deliberately picked up the roughly cut-out boxcar.

Noah huffed but left without another word...and after a moment, Levi followed, but just far enough to lurk in the shadows inside the open barn door.

And from the safety of the darkness, he watched the sway of Elsie's hips as she walked around the buggy and climbed in, the blood in his veins heating as he relived the too-short moments he held those curves in his hands.

Keeping his distance was his only hope of surviving this.

As he watched Noah drive the buggy toward the road, Levi's cell phone rang in the workshop. Levi hurried back into the room. It was an unfamiliar number. Probably more work, but Levi didn't need to look at his nonexistent planner to know he wasn't available until after Christmas. Of course, that was factoring in the toy orders.

"Wyse and Sons Construction." He really should change the name of *Daed*'s business considering there were no sons—other than Levi—anymore. Never would be. "Levi speaking."

"Levi. This is Elsie Miller's friend Jane Turner. I need some information about toy prices. Elsie didn't know what you charged."

Levi frowned. "I can answer your questions, but you need to know I'm booked solid until after Christmas."

"That's fine. So am I. We'll go with an Easter delivery date for the toys. I can't set up your website yet, so I'm listing them for sale on a popular crafter's site. I—"

"What?" He might have shouted the word.

The woman hesitated, then started repeating herself. At least she added more information. "Elsie contacted me about building a website for Santa's Workshop and she sent pictures of your creations. I think they'll sell well, and—"

Elsie contacted... building a website... the words fell into repeat as Jane continued talking. He might have answered Jane's questions though he didn't remember doing so. His brain was numb. His temper was not.

Who gave Elsie Miller permission to have a website built for his *hobby*?

And when did she take pictures?

Was the bishop aware or would Levi be the one in trouble?

He needed permission from Bishop Nathan before proceeding. He opened his mouth, interrupted Jane, and told her so.

She acknowledged it with a scoffing sound.

But as far as he was concerned, that was handled.

"Thanks for calling. I'll get back to you when I have permission," he said. But he had no intention of following through either with Jane or the bishop.

Furthermore, he needed to have another talk with his elf.

* * *

Elsie had to let Noah use her horse and buggy again the next day since his horse was still lame. He drove out to Zooks' Salvage Grocery first, since she needed to fill Abigail's grocery list. It still turned Elsie's stomach to go there since she'd been unfairly fired—in her opinion—after only a few hours of work. No wonder Zooks' were desperate for help if they fired everyone for no good reason. But unless she wanted to have Noah drive her to nearby Arthur to grocery shop, Zooks' was the only option in Hidden Springs. And the trip to Arthur would take both of them out of their way, making Noah late for work at the cabinet shop.

The sky was heavy with dark-gray clouds that appeared so packed with moisture that they hung close to the ground. Not foggy, since it'd been so frigid that both the air and the ground were cold. Still, the dark, heavy clouds added an eerie feeling that spooked Elsie's overactive imagination. She really shouldn't have stayed up into the wee hours of the morning reading that romantic suspense under the covers by flashlight so she wouldn't disturb her sisters.

"It smells like snow," Noah said for what seemed like the umpteenth time since they left home that morning. His voice was filled with dread.

Elsie didn't see it as a huge problem. She'd just stay home this weekend and into next week if it got that bad. And maybe that "absence makes the heart grow fonder" quote would be true this time around. For both Levi and her family and friends. A girl could dream, anyway. She hated to leave them, but it was for the greater good: a future and a hope.

Would the blizzard postpone her and Sam's leaving? If it did, it wouldn't be by much.

Noah had a bigger problem with the snow because the Amish-owned company he worked for relied on *Englisch*-owned construction companies or worked for the *Englisch*, and when roads got really bad, travel was discouraged unless it was an emergency.

Horses were fine on ice or a slick concrete parking lot. Their shoes were covered with grill tec that enabled them to grip ice. It was ever so much safer in a buggy with ice than a car, as drivers could lose control faster than a buggy driver.

She grabbed her purse, double-checked to see if she still had Abigail's list, then climbed out of the buggy and trudged into Zooks' as Noah secured the horse.

"Free ice cream!" Thomas Zook bellowed as the sleigh bells rang on their hook over the door. They were new since Monday. "Buy two full price, get one free. Discounted flavor my choice."

"Dill pickle, per chance?" Noah quipped behind her, a hint of laughter in his voice.

Thomas Zook appeared around the endcap, scowling. His eyes narrowed as they rested on Elsie. "You," he growled.

"Me!" Noah boomed.

She waved the shopping list. "I've come in peace." But her face burned.

Thomas Zook muttered something under his breath and turned away. "Let me know when you're ready to check out." At least that was said in a much nicer tone.

"I do need ice cream. But Abigail specified vanilla. It's for the punch. And I would be embarrassed to give her dill pickle ice cream." Elsie grabbed a basket and headed for the back of the building, where the perishable items were kept. On the way she grabbed the other items on Abigail's list. Finally, she stopped at the ice cream display and sorted through it. Not a vanilla in the bunch. The closest they had was eggnog.

Noah leaned over. "It's a fruit punch, right? They have pumpkin flavor." He straightened, clutching a box picturing a light-orange-colored ice cream.

"I don't think so." Elsie made a face at Noah.

He placed the box back into the case and frowned. "Eggnog might work. I guess. Maybe. Or I could make a side trip into Arthur to another grocery store before I come for the taffy pull tonight, but then I'd be late."

Elsie shrugged. "We'll try eggnog. If she doesn't want to, I'm sure some of the guys will eat it anyway."

"I would." Noah grabbed two boxes. "We gotta take advantage of that buy-two-get-one-free offer."

Elsie glared at him.

He chuckled but kept both boxes as he walked toward the exit.

She rolled her eyes and headed for the front and the lone checkout where Thomas Zook waited.

Noah held the two ice cream cartons high.

Thomas Zook grinned. "I am so excited to gift you with a free cartoon of dill pickle ice cream." He turned, grabbed a box from a small freezer on an open shelf, and set it on the counter. "Enjoy!"

"And I am so excited to receive it." Noah waited until all the groceries were rung up and paid for; then he found the package of dill pickle ice cream in one of the plastic bags and, with a wink at Elsie, placed it in the benevolence box that went to the needy in the community.

Then, while Thomas Zook spluttered, Noah grabbed

the plastic bags full of the purchases and carried them out the door.

Elsie hurried after him. She wanted to be long gone before Thomas Zook found his voice. "You are *so* bad," she said to Noah as she scurried into the buggy.

"*Jah*, and *Daed* will hear about it, I'm sure. But it will be worth the end result."

"I hope. He might make us apologize."

"Maybe to the needy." Noah laughed. "Possibly a cursory one to Zook for tricking him." He climbed in and backed the horse away from the hitching post. "I don't think it's kneel-and-confess-before-the-church-worthy."

Elsie hoped not. That'd be so embarrassing. Especially in front of Levi. But at least she wouldn't have to do it alone. Or at all since Noah was the one to do the buying and "gifting."

As they pulled onto the road, a horse and buggy approached on the opposite side of the street, and even though the driver wore the standard black coat and hat, she could recognize Levi anywhere.

Apparently, he felt the same way because his gaze locked on hers.

Noah raised a hand in greeting, but Levi kept his focus on her until they passed each other.

She adjusted the rearview mirror to keep his buggy in sight.

And smiled when a hand came out of the other buggy, adjusting his.

CHAPTER 14

Friday evening when Levi returned home from work finishing the bad plumbing job, the yard and pasture were full of buggies.

What? Why? What had Elsie done now? This on top of the website issue seemed too much.

Levi took his hat off to eliminate the shadows it created and rubbed his tired eyes, then looked again. There were definitely dozens of buggies there. Had she invited all the *youngies* over? Wait. She had. A taffy pull so Abigail could spend time with Noah.

Levi exhaled heavily. It was amazing how quickly Elsie and Noah got the word out about the taffy pull. Abigail was probably over-the-moon excited. And all these people were there before the supper hour, which meant two things: They brought food for snacks or supper, and more people would likely be coming when they got off work or finished chores.

It also meant he'd be hidden in the barn. Working. Freezing because his space heaters didn't put off much heat. Hiding from all these people and the desperate-to-be-married females of the group who thought he was fair game. And starving just thinking about all the food.

On cue, his stomach rumbled.

He steeled himself and drove the buggy toward the open barn doors. Open! He was certain they were shut when he'd left in the morning, which meant someone or more than one someone was lurking in the barn—in Levi's personal space. He'd shoo them out in short order. He parked the buggy and was unhitching Trouble when George tapped his way into the area from somewhere. Hopefully, he hadn't been in Levi's workshop messing with tools and the toys.

"Horses and buggies outside," George bellowed.

"I live here," Levi shouted back. It strained his vocal cords. He wasn't used to raising his voice.

George halted, frowned, and scrutinized Levi, then apparently decided he was telling the truth. "Okay. Take care of the horse then get to the house. No one is supposed to be out here. Including you. Abigail's orders." Everything was said at top volume.

Levi frowned. There was notepaper in his shop, but it would take too much yelling to try to make George understand that Levi needed paper to explain why he needed to be in the barn. Maybe. He pointed toward his workshop. "Deadline," he shouted, unintentionally, then cringed.

George's face screwed up. "Dead? Who's dead?"

"Paper," Levi yelled.

"The paper's dead?" George loudly asked. He looked at Levi as if he wondered whether Levi was mentally off.

Why was George there guarding the barn anyway? Did someone seriously ask him to chaperone? Although if the elderly man did catch someone making out in the barn, all the shouting would ruin the mood. And if it didn't, one good whack from that very sturdy walking stick would do the trick.

Something to keep in mind on the off chance he was alone with peppermint-scented Elsie.

Although, maybe she had a date. A very attentive date.

Oh, that thought hurt. But it was a very real possibility.

Levi slowly finished unhitching and taking care of Trouble while George the chaperone stood guard; then he trudged toward the house. He'd write out the note, have Abigail sign it, and take his permission slip back out to his own barn to work in his own shop. There had to be some humor in that, but Levi couldn't find it.

The house was alive with the sounds of laughing and talking, things that had been missing for close to two years. The acute pain hit him with a force that almost brought him to his knees. He stumbled to a stop at the bottom of the steps to the front porch, staring at the brightly lit and very alive-sounding building. How could he go in there? His eyes burned and his throat threatened to close up. Going out to the barn without a permission slip wasn't an option, yet he couldn't enter his own home.

He stood there in the freezing cold, staring at the building, then finally went around the side to the mudroom entrance. At least he could clean up in the bathroom and go through the other door to his bedroom, where he could change clothes if he wanted to. But he was just sawdusty, and since he didn't plan to stay in the house, that didn't matter. Abigail would just have to understand. He was doing this taffy pull for her, not for him. Everything he did was for her.

He didn't need or desire socialization, nor did he deserve to have fun.

He quietly slipped into the mudroom, shut the outside door with a quiet click, then scurried across the expanse to the bathroom, which was thankfully empty. He scrubbed his arms and hands and face, then darted out the other door to his bedroom.

That room had already been invaded by a bunch of nameless, faceless strangers who'd left his bed piled full of black coats, bonnets, and hats.

For a few minutes, he silently chafed at the violation of his personal space, but then he forced himself to put it aside. It made sense, after all. They had to put that stuff somewhere. At least no one was lurking in the corners.

He looked on his dresser for a slip of paper and found a receipt, blank on one side. He grabbed a pen and wrote himself permission to be in his own barn, then carried that and the pen out of his room and into the crowded main living areas for Abigail's signature. This was beyond ludicrous.

"Hi, Levi!" a bunch of people called out.

His stomach churned, his face heated, and his hands started to sweat as what seemed like all the attention swung to him. This was why he never bothered with youth events. Well, this, and other reasons.

He mumbled some sort of greeting, not exactly sure what he said, while searching for Abigail in the crowd. He couldn't see her or her wheelchair. Maybe he could find Elsie. But she was petite, like a real elf, her head not even reaching his shoulder. Almost everyone towered over her. Girls approached, surrounding him, all talking, giggly, and flirty, batting their eyelashes. He was going to suffocate. He stopped in the center of the girls, afraid to move. He might accidentally touch one. He fought for air and stiffened as the girls edged closer. He had to escape. *Lord, help.*

He wished for a moment that super loud, stick-wielding George were inside the house so Levi could sneak out the back door.

The crowd parted as Elsie, the little dynamo, somehow found an opening and appeared at his side. "There you are. Abigail was looking for you. She saved you a seat next to Noah." The crowd parted as she led the way out without touching him.

He didn't need or want a seat next to Noah. "I have a note," he said.

Elsie paused under a sprig of mistletoe. He glanced at it, then her, hating that he noticed. His gaze dipped to her lips. What was the point of hanging mistletoe inside, in plain sight, when touching was discouraged? Kissing was forbidden. Elsie appeared guileless, unaware of the parasite plant sprig above her head.

"Let's see the note." She held out her hand.

"No. I don't trust you not to rip it up."

She appeared hurt. "Really? You think I'm an immature child?"

No. Not even close. But still... "You can look but not touch." That came out wrong. Her cheeks reddened. His heated. Burned. He shoved the note toward her. "Just read." That might've been growled.

She made a show of clasping her hands behind her back, then scanned the words. "You wrote that."

No kidding. He didn't say it but thought it very loudly.

Elsie gave him a sympathetic look. "Abigail says you must stay in for some of it."

He blinked. "But I'm on deadline." He'd shared that with Abigail, right? But maybe not with Elsie, because she looked confused. "I have a large toy order that needs to be done by Christmas." Toy order. That reminded him . . . "By the way—"

"You're turning into a hermit. All work and no play," she began, then blushed. "Well, you're hardly a dull boy." She looked away. "Abigail is at the table. The taffy is almost ready to pull. Give her the note and see what she says. But if she wants you to stay in, you will change your clothes, clean up, and stay for a little while. And you can pick whatever girl you want as a partner." She motioned toward the cluster of still-giggling females.

He didn't even glance at them. "I choose you."

*   *   *

Elsie couldn't look away from Levi's piercing gray eyes. If only he were serious. But the only reason he'd pick her was because she was safe. No expectations. No commitment.

His gaze searched hers. "Unless you've made arrangements with someone else."

She gulped. "There's no one else." No one but him. Ever.

His eyes darkened for a moment before he pressed his lips together, nodded, then tightened his fingers around the note and turned toward the table. "I'll try to sweet-talk Abigail into signing." He walked off.

There was no reason to stand there wishing and dreaming and hoping and scheming. Unless Abigail had considerable power over Levi, he would do what he wanted. And he didn't want to be at the taffy pull. Elsie sighed and turned away, going to greet a girl, Leah Zook, who'd just come in. Thomas Zook's daughter.

Judging by the way Leah's eyes widened and she clutched her chest and gasped, "Levi Wyse. Oh my word, he's actually here," she was probably another one of Levi's admirers. "He's so hot! Like, literally, he's hot stuff."

"*Jah*, he's here," Elsie agreed, "tempor—"

"And he's coming this way!" Leah squealed, grabbing Elsie's arm. "He's my destiny, you know. Both our names start with *le* and are four-letter words. Not only that but our last names are also four-letter words and at the end of the alphabet."

Huh? That made Levi her destiny? Elsie blinked at Leah, then started to turn, but a hand landed on her shoulder and he leaned down, his warm breath tickling her ear as he whispered, "I'm staying for a short while. I need to clean up, but you're my date."

Abigail had more control over him than Elsie thought.

He released her shoulder and left; then Elsie met Leah's glare. "I guess no one told him."

"Seriously, once you break up, you need to have enough common courtesy to stay broken up," Leah hissed, then shoved past.

It seemed pointless to mention that they were still broken up. He was just using Elsie for protection detail.

Especially since Leah chased after him. "Levi? Yoohoo, Levi! Where do I put my coat?"

He turned, stared at Leah, and then gave Elsie a panicked look.

She smirked and added a couple of eyelash flutters. *Jah*. Good luck with her, *hot stuff*.

* * *

Levi pointed Leah in the direction of his room. He didn't say anything, but she'd figure out how to put her outerwear on the bed. He also didn't mention it was his room, but she'd likely figure that out, too. He lingered in the living room, not wanting to be anywhere alone with her. Not even in the hallway. Why couldn't Elsie have shown her to the bedroom? He slumped. It was another indication that she wasn't interested in him. It shouldn't matter, but it did.

After what seemed like forever, Leah finally exited his bedroom, gave him a flirty look as she passed, and whispered, "I'll save you a seat."

Of course, she might not have heard him claim Elsie as his date. He shook his head. "*Danki*, but I'm with Elsie." He was with Elsie, but it wasn't a date. She was safe.

Safe. *Jah*. About as safe as lit dynamite.

What was that saying about how if you play with fire, you'll eventually get burned?

Truth.

He grabbed a clean pair of clothes, went into the bathroom, and locked both doors, then took a quick shower. He tried to keep his irritation at being forced to attend the frolic for a while masked. It was sweet of Abigail to want to include him, but he couldn't stay long. And she promised to sign his excuse when he had enough.

He had enough already, but he knew better than to ask. Not without giving the frolic a fair shake.

Everyone was seated when he returned to the main living area. He slid into the empty seat at the end of the table, next to Noah and across from Elsie. His safety zone, with his sister and his girl who wasn't his girl. He didn't look for Leah, but hopefully she found a partner.

One of the chaperones, Elsie's married friend Gracie, placed some candy between him and Elsie. "Be sure to oil your hands. And be careful. The candy feels cool enough to touch, but it might still be hot underneath."

As Elsie oiled her hands, Levi lifted the green, possibly spearmint-flavored taffy from the pan with an oiled spatula and formed it into a cylindrical shape like he'd done in years past. She reached across the table and took one end, pulling it toward her. It sagged in the middle. He was surprised he and Elsie weren't given peppermint-flavored taffy.

Others laughed and talked around them. She grinned at him as they began working together, pulling and twisting, mixing in the syrup, until the taffy finally began to hold its shape. He didn't smile at her, but he never smiled anymore. Hadn't since... since the accident. He tried to force his lips in that upward direction, but it felt strange. Probably looked strange, too, since her grin faded, and she peered at him, studying his expression. What did she think? Abigail worried he'd be prematurely wrinkled since he carried so much emotional and mental weight. Did Elsie agree? Or did she still think he was handsome? He knew Abigail was concerned about him—thus the forced attendance at the frolic—and she probably shared her fears with Elsie.

It probably was wrong to use her this way, keeping her from whoever her current admirer was, but honestly this terrified him. He tried to think of something to say— something nonconfrontational, which meant the website issue was out—but his brain cells were stalled, due to fear, maybe, or possibly due to being so close to Elsie, pretending they were a couple.

He squirmed in his seat, eyeing the note he'd written, that Abigail now kept beside her, receipt side up so no one would know what a coward he was. Had she signed it yet? Could he grab it and go, lose the contents of his fear-induced roiling stomach, then hide in the barn with George? He could put George to work sanding train cars. Except he couldn't imagine trying to explain what he needed to have done…unless there was lots of paper out there for notes.

He was pretty sure there wasn't.

Noah elbowed Levi in the ribs. "Great turnout, *jah*? I even found chaperones."

Levi nodded, swallowed the knot in his throat. His gaze went to Elsie's friend Gracie, cooking another batch of taffy on the stove, and her new husband, Zeke. They'd met a year ago during some awful tornadoes and married this past spring. Zeke was on the other side of the room, showing someone what to do. One of the special-needs teens. It appeared to be Gracie's sister, Patience.

"I saw George in the barn," Levi said, scanning the room. "I don't see his wife, though."

"Mildred had to stay home to feed their cats and start a new pot of bean soup." Noah's voice held humor.

Levi's lips twitched. George had his idiosyncrasies, including dozens of felines and an insane fondness of bean soup.

"George might be more than a little concerned about the cats going without food if the storm comes in that they're predicting," Noah continued.

Levi shrugged. There had been some freezing drizzle earlier but no accumulation yet. However, rumor still continued to speculate...

Gracie appeared between Elsie and Abigail, her face holding a greenish tint as she clutched her stomach. She whispered something to the air between them; then, while a horrified expression crossed Elsie's face, Gracie spun and headed for Zeke, gagged, and ran outside. Without her coat.

Abigail's eyes filled with tears.

Noah dropped his end of the blue taffy they held and reached for Abigail's hands. "What's wrong, Abby?"

Zeke followed Gracie outside.

Levi looked at Elsie. She stared down at her hands. A tear rolled down her cheek, followed closely by a second. Levi gulped, then followed Noah's lead and reached for Elsie's hands. Except, she jerked them away, bolted to her feet, and dashed for the mudroom. Another minute passed before Levi pushed past his hesitation and followed her. What was wrong with Gracie and why would Elsie and Abigail cry about it?

He found Elsie sitting on her backside, wedged between the washer and the bookcase used as a cupboard for laundry supplies. Her knees were hugged up to her chest, her hem tugged enough to cover her ankles, her body hunched enough so her head rested on her knees. Face down.

She looked up.

He wanted to fix whatever was wrong so Elsie—and Abigail—would stop crying and smile again.

He crouched in front of her. Reached out his hand. It trembled as it brushed against the dampness of her cheek. He wiped the tears away with his thumb. Her lips quivered and more tears took the others' places. He slid his hand down, brushing the corner of her lip, over her jaw, and around. His hand shook more as he fingered the loose strands of hair on the base of her neck. "Elle, honey—"

The endearment slipped out unintentionally, shocking him as much as she did when she raised her head the rest of the way, lurched forward, and buried her damp face against his neck. Her breath feathered against his skin, her arms wrapped around him, and she cried, the tears soaking his shirt.

He awkwardly patted her back, then rubbed it, trying to comfort her as he struggled to think who the third couple chaperoning might be. Would whoever they were be lenient? Failing to come up with who the chaperones were, he tried to think up a good reason for him and Elsie to be violating the unwritten public-display-of-affection rules when they were caught, but without knowing why she cried, he wrestled with that, too.

Finally, she sniffled and pulled away, enough to dry her eyes with her apron. He scooted back far enough that if a chaperone appeared, they'd be "okay," but remained on the floor. "What was that about?"

"Ice cream," she whimpered.

Of all things! "Ice cream?" He almost hated to ask. "You're crying about ice cream?"

She nodded. "Abigail wanted ice cream for her fruit punch and she asked for vanilla, but the closest they had was eggnog, and Noah thought it would work so we got it, but Gracie is, well, you know, and the smell and taste made her sick and now Abigail's punch won't have ice cream and it's all my fault because he fired me! Besides, I should've brought the dill pickle kind," she wailed.

Levi blinked. And that was supposed to make sense? "I don't think dill pickles would go very well with fruit punch," he said slowly. "And if Gracie is sick, why is she here?"

"She's...she's...you know." Elsie struggled for breath.

No, he didn't know, but as long as she wasn't contagious, it didn't matter. Wait. "Is she contagious?"

"Seriously?" Elsie barked a "ha" while still fighting for air. "I...hope...not." Each word was punctuated with a gasp. "Maybe. If I drink the water."

Okay, then. "Don't drink the water." Was she hyperventilating? Maybe. He swallowed. "Breathe, Elle. Just breathe. There are worse things to go wrong than ice cream." Far worse. He should know.

A shadow appeared in his peripheral vision and he glanced that way. Jon Lantz peeked in. Ah, the other chaperones. Jon and his new bride. Their wedding was postponed due to his injuries after falling from a barn rafter, and they married around the same time as Gracie and Zeke.

Jon lifted a hand in greeting and moved on. Good.

Elsie still struggled to breathe.

Levi scooted closer and opened his arms wide, wrapping them around her, pressing her against his chest. "Breathe, sweetheart. Slow and easy, now. Shh." And he started humming the only song he could think of while holding her in his arms. The doxology. *Praise God from whom all blessings flow...*

Praise *Gott* for a wise sister who insisted on his presence at the taffy pull so he could be here for the ice cream disaster, even if he didn't understand it.

Praise *Gott* for Elsie's caring spirit, wanting this frolic to be perfect for Abigail.

Elsie's breathing slowed, evened out.

Praise *Gott* he was able to comfort her, even though he'd probably regret it in the morning.

She shifted in his arms and he caught a whiff of...

Praise *Gott* for peppermint...

Wait. Elsie didn't smell like peppermint. She smelled like green apples. How was that even possible?

And he still wanted to kiss her.

CHAPTER 15

Elsie would always cherish the memory of these moments, even if she couldn't take them seriously. Levi was reverting back to his old ways, calling her Elle, honey, and sweetheart, and he didn't mean the endearments. Too bad, really, but it was unrealistic to believe his old feelings would flare to life with only two days—not even forty-eight full hours—in each other's presence. She wasn't counting Thursday since he was gone or avoided her all day.

He'd succeeded in calming her, though, so she needed to gather her frayed emotions together and find out if the eggnog ice cream truly was gag worthy with fruit punch or whether Gracie's overactive first-trimester pregnancy hormones had kicked in. Teen boys ate pretty much anything, and as a whole, the Amish were raised to eat what was put in front of them. But she didn't want Abigail to get a bad reputation as a hostess, especially since it was Elsie's fault.

Who knew that weird-flavored ice cream would have such a long-range negative effect?

Though, was eggnog truly weird flavored?

She pushed to her feet, extended her hand to Levi to help him up—not that he needed it—and gave him a quick hug. "*Danki* for listening. I really appreciate it. Especially since you really don't even want to be here."

He made a sound that might've been intended to be a chuckle, but it sounded rather rusty from nonuse. "*Jah.* My pleasure."

Elsie snorted. "Right. Should Abigail sign your note now that you made an appearance?"

"Ready to get rid of me so soon?" Levi almost sounded flirty.

The old Elsie would've flirted back. Instead, she stayed serious. "I know you really don't want to be here."

Levi shook his head. "It's very difficult for me to be here. You have no idea how hard it was for me to enter my own house tonight." His hand rose and cupped her cheek. His thumb brushed over it, coming to rest on the corner of her lips. "But I'm here now, and despite my deadline..." His fingers traced her lips. They tingled. His gaze dipped. "I might stay long enough for some refreshments." His voice was husky.

Elsie swallowed. Hard. "Levi, if I didn't know better, I'd say you were flirting."

He startled, jerking his hand back. Opened his mouth, shut it. Looked away. Opened his mouth again. Shut it again. Then looked at her again with something that might be shame in his expression. Remorse. Sadness. Pain. A whole mix of emotions. "Good thing you know better," he said quietly.

Jah. She didn't want to get her hopes up. Hope was deadly. Whenever she reached for it, it slipped right out of her grasp.

"I'm sorry, Elsie. It's not you. It's me." He backed away, leaning against the opposite wall.

And there was that classic breakup line that meant nothing. How many guys had she heard that from? So many times it rang false. Never before from Levi, though. It hurt. She'd thought Levi was above the clichéd.

"Levi Wyse, sometimes you're a real jerk." Her thoughts escaped. Unintended.

The pain in his eyes intensified. "I know. I am. I don't mean to be." He hung his head. "Someday, maybe, I'll attempt to explain."

"Why not now?" She steepled her fingers over her mouth. Answers, please?

"Now?" Levi frowned. "I haven't thought out what to say, yet."

"There is something to be said for spontaneity." Elsie looked up at him. "What do you want to say?"

Levi blinked. Opened his mouth and made a sound. "I—"

Gracie's brother Jon appeared in the doorway. He came into the room. "Okay, you two."

"We're on opposite sides of the room," Elsie said, waving her hand between them.

Jon smirked. "Now you are. When I peeked in before, you weren't."

Elsie's face heated.

"But I'm not here for that. Zeke is taking Gracie and Patience home, and the freezing rain has started, so I suggest we eat and go. Everyone can cut and wrap their candy at home. No one wants to be stranded when it gets bad, and we don't want a panic. My wife and your sister are setting the food out now." Jon pointed over his shoulder.

"Oh no!" Elsie pivoted and pushed past Jon into the kitchen. She had picked a bad evening for a youth frolic. She'd apologize to Abigail and Noah later for ruining their first date. "How can I help?" she asked Abigail. Without waiting for an answer, she grabbed the punch bowl and started assembling the drink. Noah moved to the mudroom where he divided chunks of pulled taffy so everyone could have an assortment of flavors.

"Leave the ice cream out of the punch," Abigail said. "Noah said some will eat it individually. Just set it open with a scoop and let them have at it. I put bowls and spoons on the table, near the spot for the punch bowl."

"*Danki*." Elsie stirred the mixture and set the bowl on the table as the youth lined up.

Jon and Levi came out of the mudroom. Levi quietly got into line for food as Jon headed back to the bedrooms or to the loft, maybe to round up a few missing couples.

Plates loaded with sandwiches, chips, raw vegetables, dips, fruit slices, and tons of cookies and brownies, along with several bowls of ice cream, passed by as she ladled punch into small plastic cups. Her stomach rumbled and she looked toward the window. She couldn't see anything, but some of the horses were getting restless. She could hear them stomping and whinnying.

She understood that Jon didn't want a panic, but did he have a plan?

Levi stood at the end of the line and said something

to a couple of guys as they passed by on the way to the trash can. They looked startled, glanced at the dark windows, then after throwing their plates away, went to whisper something to their dates, and the couples quietly headed back to the bedroom where maybe Jon waited. Then they exited through the mudroom door with a quiet click and a draft of frigid air that threatened to freeze Elsie's backside.

Jah, Jon had a plan. And Levi was just the guy to keep panic under control with a few quiet words. Noah was the one to hand out the candy, thank them for coming, and send them on their way, laughing.

Elsie glanced at Levi, awkwardly bouncing on his heels at the end of the line, looking as if he didn't have a care in the world. Which was so untrue. How could he appear so calm, quiet, and strong when the world was falling apart? She needed his strength.

Wait. Bouncing? Levi never bounced. That was a Noah trick. Noah must've suggested it.

Levi met her gaze.

And winked.

A wink that left her shivering with promise.

* * *

Levi continued to make the tricky move of bouncing on his heels like Noah suggested as he stood in line to get something to drink. He felt like a fool, but Noah said it would give him a carefree vibe, and Jon agreed. Whatever. It was making him thirsty. He wasn't sure what Abigail had planned for the beverage. Something with fresh strawberries, pineapple, Sprite, and ice cream, served in a big glass bowl with a ladle. He remembered those items because she'd asked for the money so Elsie could buy them for her. Of course, the ice cream wasn't added, but no matter. That would be eaten and enjoyed even if it was eggnog flavor.

What he wanted was one of Elsie's meatloaf sandwiches. He didn't know what she'd done different, but they were so good. Last night at supper, Abigail had told him only one and no more. Save some for the frolic.

Tell a man he couldn't eat something, and his stomach remembered it. And asked for it. Repeatedly.

Kind of like a girl. He wanted Elsie, especially now that he couldn't have her.

He whispered an ice storm alert to five other men and stepped closer to the table. The meatloaf sandwiches were all gone. And he'd had quite enough bouncing. He stilled. Had Noah suggested it just to make Levi look foolish? Payback for the alpha thing, perhaps? Though if that were the case, why did Jon agree?

Elsie handed him a cup of the strawberry-pineapple-Sprite-minus-the-ice-cream concoction. Levi took a sip of the tangy drink and struggled not to wrinkle his nose. He'd never been a huge fan of punch. It was tasty, but any of the ingredients on their own would've been just as good, if not better. He glanced at Elsie.

She smiled and pointed to the food he'd bypassed. "Aren't you going to eat?"

He glanced at Abigail, then shook his head. "Later." And it appeared as though everyone was leaving their leftover finger foods there in their hurry to leave before it got bad. So he could fill up with a nice healthy meal of sugar cookies and peanut-infused fudge, washed down with tangy punch and a spoonful of eggnog ice cream.

Except, Abigail hadn't eaten yet, either, so he'd have to share the bounty.

Jon came into the kitchen by way of the mudroom, surveyed the clueless remnant still talking and eating, and cleared his throat twice. "The ice storm has arrived." He sounded like he was introducing royalty.

That had every bit as much of a reaction as someone screaming, "Fire! Fire! Fire!" Plates were abandoned. Half-full cups of punch were bumped, knocked over, spilling onto the floor. And there was a mass exodus as people rushed for their outerwear.

Jon ushered his wife toward the mudroom. "I assume you're leaving right away?" He glanced at Elsie.

Noah carried out the remaining chunks of taffy to hand out at the door. "As soon as we can," he answered. "Our parents already know we might not come home tonight."

Jon nodded and they left.

"You need to go. I can finish passing out the candy." Levi looked out the door as a couple left, slipping and sliding down the steps.

"We're not leaving this mess for Abigail," Elsie said.

Noah nodded. "Our parents already know we might not be home. I called from the mudroom."

Levi nodded, though he was surprised Noah hadn't asked him first. It was bad, but not that bad—yet. By the time they got home…He was wise. "Are they okay with it?"

"*Daed* suggested it this morning before we left, if Noah felt we needed to. And I can't leave Abigail with this mess." Elsie joined them at the door. "Of course, *Daed* said a chaperone needed to stay, too."

"We have one," Noah said, but he didn't elaborate.

"We'll make room, right, Levi?" Abigail sounded anxious, as if she was afraid he'd refuse.

"*Jah*, we will." Levi reached for his coat to hide his reaction to the news that Elsie would be spending the night. He was pretty sure he lit up like flashing red fire engine lights. "I'll go to the stable and take care of your horse and close up the barn." He hoped he sounded calm, in control, and unaffected. He was anything but. He slipped his boots on.

And maybe the freezing rain would extinguish the blaze from his raging male hormones.

They'd have a chaperone, after all. Noah.

And with Levi's pressing deadline, maybe he could put Noah to work. And that way Levi would also be chaperoning Noah and Abigail.

He skated his way to the horse and buggy and led the unhappy animal to the barn. Except, there was another unhappy animal hitched outside the barn.

Who was still here?

He entered the barn cautiously but still found himself flung forward and landed hard on his hands and knees. "Oof." He took a moment to assess the damage. He'd live. But . . . seriously? Who strung a trip wire across the doorway of *his* barn? He glanced sideways from his position on the floor and found the lights on in his workshop.

He wanted to storm over there and give the invader what for, but the miserable animals had to come first.

He also needed to let his temper cool somewhat.

He took a deep breath, pushed up, unhooked the wire,

and led the first horse and buggy in. Another deep breath, and he got the second horse and buggy. Leaving the two horses in the buggy bay, he peeked into the shop. And was greeted by an old man wielding a walking stick.

George.

*   *   *

Noah went to work taking apart the church benches and tables borrowed without prior consent for the frolic while Abigail collected all the trash and Elsie swept the floor. They left the little remaining food on the table as well as the rest of the uncut taffy, since none of them had eaten yet, and the candy needed to be divided between the two families.

Elsie was hungry and she was sure Noah was as well, but Abigail wanted the house to look somewhat normal before Levi returned from caring for the animals. She was convinced it would cause him undue stress to find a mess. And she was probably right. This whole frolic had caused him stress. The pain in his eyes when he mentioned how hard it was for him to come in made her want to cry. Hopefully he would find the words to explain his emotions while Elsie was there. She really wanted to understand the man Levi had become.

Noah took the disassembled tables to the front porch and stacked them under the overhang while Abigail returned to the kitchen and Elsie went for the pail to scrub sticky spilled punch from the floor. With people wandering around in socks or slippers, that was kind of necessary.

Abigail emerged from the pantry clutching a one-pound box of elbow pasta. "There's not a lot left over from the frolic except sweets. Macaroni and cheese and green beans will be quick and easy."

Elsie wasn't going to argue. "I'll shred the cheese when I finish mopping the floor."

Noah came in from outside. "It's getting bad fast. I hope everyone makes it home okay. I'm going to see if I can help Levi in the barn, unless you have something else for me to do."

Abigail waved. "Go. Tell him he can work on his toys tomorrow. It's Saturday and he won't have to go out if the roads aren't clear."

"They won't be. Not if it gets as bad as they predict. I'll offer my help with whatever he's making. I'm a pretty good sander, if I say so myself."

"We can all help with something." Abigail filled a pot with water and set it on the stove, then turned the burner on. "Tell him to hurry, though. Macaroni and cheese won't take long."

"Will do. I'm going to get my coat." He headed down the hall to Levi's room.

As soon as the outside door shut behind Noah, Abigail turned her wheelchair around. "Okay. Spill. You and Levi…" She raised a brow.

Elsie ladled herself a glass of punch. "Um. Me and Levi, what?"

"You were alone in the mudroom forever." Abigail punctuated it with a little giggle. "Did you get any mileage from the mistletoe?" She waggled her brows.

Elsie pretend-scowled at her. "Stop being such a matchmaker. I already told you there is nothing between me and Levi. I'm not quizzing you about Noah." But there was something between her and Levi. History. A one-sided love that refused to die. Passion. She sighed.

So did Abigail.

Yelling came from somewhere outside.

The two women looked at each other.

The front door opened. And in staggered Noah and Levi with a shouting George supported between them.

CHAPTER 16

Levi held on to George's arm until the older man found his footing and hobbled, walking stick tapping, across the freshly mopped floor toward a chair. He clutched something in his left hand that he refused to let Levi see, something that seemed as important to him as the walking stick. Since George still seemed wobbly, Levi followed him across the room, hoping they weren't tracking mud or other messy farm stuff in, yet knowing—and sorry—they were because Elsie stood waiting, mop in hand as she sipped from a cup. He gave her an apologetic look.

George stopped midway to the chair.

"You okay, George?" Levi shouted.

"My cane was slipping on the ice," George bellowed to one of the girls, because Levi and Noah both knew that. "I was going to sleep in the barn and not put you ladies out, but he *insisted* I come in." He waved the hand holding the small item toward Levi. Hopefully, whatever he had wasn't dangerous.

Jah, George probably had planned to sleep in Levi's workshop—where they'd found him. But that explained why it was so impossibly complicated to get him out of the barn and into the house in the first place.

Abigail rolled toward him, stopped, and looked up at him. "You should be inside with us, George. The barn is much too cold for you or anyone." She didn't yell.

Levi gathered a breath to try and repeat all that loudly so George would understand.

George sat in a chair. "You're a sweet girl, Abigail. Your *mamm* would be so proud of you." He released the walking stick and patted Abigail's hand.

Levi blinked. George heard her? How was that possible? He'd have to ask Abigail her secret.

"Unlike that brother of yours," George continued. "He's such a man." That was said with a bit of disdain. As if that were a bad thing.

"One would hope." Noah chuckled where he stood by the door, waiting for Levi.

George didn't react to what Noah said. "Not a bit of sweetness to him at all."

Elsie coughed like she was choking.

Levi glanced at her.

She raised her cup. "Tried...to breathe...the punch," she gasped.

While also recalling how "sweet" Levi was?

He raised a brow.

She blushed as she glanced at the mudroom door and he felt a bit of something to know she was thinking the same thing he was...even if he shouldn't.

Still, Levi nodded. He wanted to go over and rub her back or something, but that would be forbidden with a chaperone present. His gaze returned to George and he expelled a frustrated breath. *Why?* Out of all possible chaperones to be stranded with, why did it have to be George? Since Levi couldn't touch Elsie, he needed something else to keep his hands—and thoughts—busy. He turned to Noah. "Let's finish up in the barn before it gets worse." And he went out the door.

This was turning into a major fiasco. The taffy pull combined with an ice storm and a possible blizzard later…Levi slipped on the steps, groped for the ice-coated railing, but missed and skidded down, arms flailing. Somehow he landed on his feet.

"Too late—it's worse," Noah quipped.

He didn't need to sound so cheerful.

A tree branch snapped, sounding like a rifle shot.

Levi took a step forward and slid again. He had to unhitch the horses, feed and water them, and close up the barn for the night. "You stay in," he said to Noah. "No sense in both of us being out in this." He slowed and carefully picked his way across the beginning of that icy patch. Except, it continued nonstop between the house and the barn.

Noah chuckled as if something was funny. "*Daed* made me memorize a passage. He gives us one every Sunday. The one he gave me this past Sunday—he said it's something you need to know."

"You as in me?" Levi asked. How would Stephen even know Noah and Levi would see each other?

"*Jah*. You. The verse is Ecclesiastes 4:9–11: 'Two are better than one; because they have a good reward for their labour. For if they fall, the one will lift up his fellow: but woe to him that is alone when he falleth; for he hath not another to help him up. Again, if two lie together, then they have heat: but how can one be warm alone?' " Noah quoted.

Levi's face burned.

"*Daed* wanted me to remind you of that if I had a chance." Noah somehow made it down the steps without falling. "Maybe in case you fall. I could help you up. And we helped George. And he fought us every step of the way."

Jah, but Stephen had to know that the sleeping alone part of the verse would wake not exactly dormant feelings.

Levi grunted. He needed to turn the tables on Noah the know-it-all by pointing out the sleeping instead of falling part of the verse. "You are *not* sleeping with my sister, but you're welcome to sleep with George if you want." Hopefully, Noah wouldn't taunt him with the idea of sleeping with Elsie.

Noah laughed. "*Danki*, but no. However, it's very telling which portion of the scripture you focused on."

Levi's face burned hotter. "*Jah*, well. Whatever." And that was a great comeback. Not.

But that brought up another problem. Levi carefully made his way across the ice. He wasn't sure where they were going to put everybody. Abigail had a full-size bed in her room, so she and Elsie could share. He also had a full-size bed, but George would get it. Neither he nor Noah wanted to sleep with George. He and Noah could crash on the living room floor, but they didn't have enough pillows. Why hadn't anyone suggested he'd need two or three fully furnished bedrooms when he'd rebuilt after the explosion?

He wouldn't have listened. With no family, who would visit?

"Elsie has blankets in her buggy." Noah seemed to read his mind. "Thick ones. They could be used as a pallet."

Or pillows, Levi silently amended. But his focus was on navigating the icy driveway, so he didn't answer. It seemed as if *Gott* was providing for his unexpected guests. If only *Gott* would provide for him and Abigail.

But then He had. With an impossible deadline. And with Elsie. Could he trust Him with the rest?

If only he could.

Lord, I want to believe. Help my unbelief.

Two are better than one . . . Noah's words replayed in his mind. If only Levi had someone he could trust to listen, to guide, to provide mental and emotional support. But he didn't. He was alone. All alone.

By choice. A still, quiet voice taunted him. Correctly. Because he'd made the choice to turn his back on the community. To reject offers of help, overtures of friendship, and everything. If they knew he'd killed his family, they would've rejected him. An unofficial shunning. This way, he'd walked away first. He attended church every other Sunday—and only because it was expected—but that was it.

He didn't know how to reverse the process. Wasn't sure he wanted to. Because that meant letting someone else get close. And when the truth came out, he'd still be shunned.

He and Noah entered the barn to the sound of whinnies and nickers. And a tiny bark. What?

"Did you bring a dog with you?" Levi asked.

"Puppy." Noah pointed to a black-and-white pup that appeared to be a border collie hiding partially behind the Millers' front buggy wheel. "No, I didn't. I'd suggest George did, but he collects cats, not dogs."

No collar. And the pup was skin and bones. Half-starved, poor thing. Probably dumped. But he didn't have anything to feed a pup. Nor did he have time for the training and care.

He could pawn it off on Noah and Elsie—they had a dog and, therefore, dog food—but that didn't solve the problem for tonight or for however long they were stranded.

"Abigail said she wanted a dog." Noah crouched down and held out his fingers. The puppy sniffed them, licked them, and wagged her tail.

Levi cringed. Abigail wanted . . . and if she asked, he'd be a jerk if he said no, but he couldn't feed it, and the training and care were an issue. She couldn't take care of it—that was for certain. How could she take it for a walk? Though maybe there was a way. If there was, she'd find it. But until he found out, he'd have to be the jerk and say no. Still, he bent to pet the dog. She leaned into his touch.

"I'd say you got yourself a dog." Noah gave the dog a final pat, then straightened.

"I'd say that's a negative," Levi muttered. He straightened, too.

"Why do you say that?" Noah turned. Something in Levi's expression must've clued him in because he held out his hands. "Okay. I'll take it home with me and just bring her to visit Abby."

That worked. Levi nodded.

"Or Elsie can, if I can't come."

That didn't work so well.

Levi tried to come up with a valid reason why not, but his brain was mush from exhaustion and stress.

Not to mention the worry about what George had been doing in his workshop—in addition to stringing tripwires to catch unsuspecting couples sneaking out for a little hanky-panky. How many couples had George caught that way?

And the havoc Elsie caused with his thought process.

Basically, he was a mess.

He eyed his workshop door, tempted to let Noah take care of the horses—and dog—so he could check the damage to his workshop, but it'd still be there after the animals were cared for. Besides, the responsible thing was to take care of the miserable animals first.

Others first. He was pretty sure that was in the Bible somewhere, but he couldn't quote it. He unhitched George's horse while Noah led Elsie's mare back to an empty stall.

Of course, he still didn't have anything to feed Half-Starved Dog. He was pretty sure sugar cookies and fudge wouldn't be good for it.

Levi led George's horse back to another empty stall. In the one next to him, Noah talked softly to Elsie's mare. Levi heard the low rise and fall of his voice but couldn't understand what he was saying. Noah wouldn't have that problem if Levi were to talk to George's horse. Since Levi would be venting his frustration with this entire situation, it might get a little loud.

But there was one thing maybe Noah could answer.

"Why the mistletoe?" Levi raised his voice so Noah could hear him.

Silence fell.

George's horse bared his teeth. Levi wasn't sure if the horse was laughing at him or threatening him. Either way, he picked up the pace and almost tripped over a cat that appeared out of nowhere and wrapped herself around his ankles. Where did that come from? Since the cat appeared well-fed and in the family way, it probably had stowed away with George. Hopefully, it'd return home with George, too. Though if it didn't, it might help with the mice population.

As Levi turned from filling the trough with water, movement in his peripheral vision caught his attention. He turned.

"The mistletoe." Noah leaned his arms over the half door, apparently done with Elsie's horse. "Elsie told me to shoot some down." He shrugged. "I think maybe it was a start of Christmas decorating, though it might just be an attempt to drive the males mad with the thought of kissing a cute girl under the mistletoe."

Jah, there was that.

"I won't hold it against you if you won't hold it against me." Noah's voice held a touch of humor, but he looked serious.

Levi's stomach churned. Noah was thinking about kissing Abigail? She was only seventeen. But who was Levi to complain? Elsie was sixteen when he first kissed her.

But still, this was his sister they were talking about!

Elsie was Noah's sister.

At least Noah's intentions were probably pure. Levi loved Elsie, but there was no hope of a happily ever after.

And if Noah knew Levi had no intentions of following through...

With that in mind...

"There'll be no kissing." He might have growled.

Noah shrugged. "Suit yourself. But the rules go both ways."

"We have a chaperone."

"George." Noah smirked.

It wasn't funny. Levi knew what George was capable of. His knees hurt just thinking of it. "And each other."

"Are you finished?" Noah grabbed a trash bag and two smaller bags from the buggy and glanced around.

"*Jah*, except I need to turn the heat and lights off in my workshop." Levi would sneak out later to work. He needed to be alone. To think. To pray. And hope that *Gott* heard him. But even if He didn't hear and didn't care, praying was too ingrained in him to just quit. It was nice to imagine that Someone out there heard and cared. That maybe Levi wasn't all alone, after all.

Two are better than one...

Noah stepped back to allow Levi out of the stall, then followed him to the workshop. The heaters were on high, blasting their pitiful heat into the large room. All the lights were on. The toys were scattered as if a child—or one elderly man—had been driving partially completed trains and marching the animals two by two.

Except, the lioness was missing. The lioness, which looked like a cat.

George had been clutching something in his hand. Something that might comfort him, being stranded here without a feline companion—except the one in the barn, which would not be entering the house.

Levi would have to make a new lioness since prying it away from George would be impossible.

At least the tools hadn't been disturbed.

Levi turned off the heaters and lights. Exiting the room, he shut the door.

"You got quite the layout there," Noah said. He sounded back to his normal friendly self.

Levi nodded, stepped out of the barn, turned to shut the doors, and his legs went in two different directions. He flailed his arms. This was going to hurt.

Noah dropped the three bags he was carrying and reached out and grabbed Levi's arms, keeping him from falling. He waited until Levi was steady on his feet, then released him with a chuckle. "Two are better than one...For if they fall, the one will lift up his fellow," he quoted.

Levi nodded. "*Danki.*" He swallowed. "One kiss, on the forehead, if she agrees." And Abigail would be over-the-moon excited for that.

Noah smiled. "*Danki.* Likewise." He picked up the bags.

Levi shook his head. "No, I can't."

"Why not? Because you already have?" Noah might've been mocking him. Levi wasn't sure. It was said with a pleasant tone and expression, but the words could be taken as being a bit snide.

Levi shrugged. He wasn't going to dump his internal drama on his little sister's boyfriend. Besides, since he hired Elsie as his elf, the community would be matching him and Elsie as a couple again. He'd alluded to it with his remarks about gossips the day he'd hired her but hadn't taken it seriously himself. Until now.

He supposed he could expect a visit from the bishop as soon as the gossip reached him, querying about whether it was wise to hire his girlfriend to "play house" for him. In fact, Levi was surprised the bishop hadn't already come. And what would Levi say? It *wasn't* wise, because now he wanted to take the "playing" to the next level. Kissing and more—*jah*, that'd go over real well.

He took a cautious step forward. And another. And another. Then found a semisteady pace.

A branch cracked under the weight of the ice. And still the freezing rain fell.

Half-Starved Dog appeared at his side, looked up, then settled in to walk beside him.

Slightly behind him, Noah said something that Levi didn't catch because another branch cracked.

Someone had spread warm stove ashes on the steps, so Levi and Noah climbed up without mishap. They entered the house, cold and wet from the freezing rain.

Abigail squealed. A happy sound.

Levi stared at her, puzzled.

Noah nudged him. "Two kisses. Not on the lips," he murmured.

Levi glanced at him. Noah wanted to kiss Abigail twice? Did that mean Levi could kiss Elsie twice? Never mind that he already had.

And never mind that he shouldn't.

Movement on the floor caught his attention.

And that was when Levi realized Half-Starved Dog had followed him in.

He had a dog.

* * *

Elsie turned from putting the bucket and mop away when the door opened and Abigail squealed. Oh, she hadn't thought about the men tracking ashes and icy water in again when she dumped the mop water. She'd just have to redo it later. Cleaning was a never-ending job on an Amish farm, especially during winter weather, but right now they might want something warm to eat, drink, and dry to wear more than a clean floor.

She left the mudroom and went into the kitchen where even George was rendered speechless. Levi and Noah shivered as they removed their sopping-wet outerwear, and Abigail cooed baby words at a black-and-white puppy snuggling in her lap.

A puppy?

It was up to Elsie to take charge. She pointed to the two plastic grocery store bags by Noah's feet containing their overnight things and a change of clothes—just in case they were stranded. The larger one held the blankets she kept in the buggy. "You need dry clothes and a hot shower. Now. George already had his. Dinner is in the oven."

"You first." Levi motioned to Noah.

Noah picked up both of the smaller bags, tossed one to Elsie, and headed toward the bathroom as Abigail peeked up. "What's her name?"

"Half-Starved Dog," Levi said.

"I called her Poor Thing," Noah said as he glanced over his shoulder. "She was dumped, I think."

Levi shrugged, then nodded.

George was uncommonly silent. He just watched with a half smile.

"You guys are pathetic with naming animals. I'll call

her Stormy," Abigail announced. She wheeled backward and twisted around to show George.

Elsie left her plastic "overnight bag" on the counter, swung around, and went back into the mudroom to get a large rag to dry the puppy. She lifted a ripped towel from the stack and turned to find Levi approaching, an intentional look in his eyes, his finger pointing to something above her head.

She looked up at a sprig of mistletoe. Her face heated. "I didn't know where Abigail asked Noah to hang them. You can ignore them, all things considered."

"Your brother said two kisses, no lips."

Elsie wrinkled her brow. "You talked to my brother about kissing me?" She felt a bit offended. Hurt. It was none of Noah's business.

"No. He asked permission to kiss Abigail. But if he gets to kiss my sister twice, if it's okay, I'd like to kiss you."

At least he was asking this time. "Okay." She offered her cheek. "Wait. You're cold. So, maybe not."

"Warm me. Please." At her nod, he reached for her, tugging her into his arms loosely. He was cold, but at least she would stay dry. He lowered his head.

She braced herself for a chaste peck on the cheek. For the emotional letdown that would accompany it. She and Levi had moved beyond cheek kisses years ago.

He bypassed it, heading straight for her ear.

His breath whispered across it. His tongue poked at it. Traced it.

She shivered violently. She might have moaned.

His teeth nibbled.

She dropped the old towel, wrapped her arms around

his neck, and clung. Never mind staying dry. He'd never kissed her like this before.

Her legs turned into quivering gelatin as his lips blazed a trail from her ear down her pulse line, leisurely exploring her neck. She arched against him, a groan coming from deep within her. She wanted him to kiss her again. The way he had last time.

Except, maybe not stopping.

At least not until the fire he'd lit inside her was extinguished.

* * *

Levi was losing control again. And he'd thought not lip kissing would be safe. Well, safer. It was far from it. Although, maybe it would've been if he'd stuck to her cheek or forehead, though he knew from past experience how unsatisfactory that was.

He trembled from the feeling of her soft body in his arms, or maybe because of his guilt when he said it wouldn't happen again and yet here he was.

One last time. Then no more even if he had to fire her. It'd be in her best interest to protect her from himself. He'd destroy her.

Alarm bells rang, but he smacked them down, instead finding her pounding pulse line and conducting a leisurely exploration, relishing her shivering in his arms, arching against him, and moaning quietly with pleasure.

Good thing George was half-deaf and Noah was in the shower...

Something hard smacked into the back of both legs,

knocking him and Elsie forward. Well, backward in her case. He barely kept them from falling.

"Of all people, Levi Wyse, I thought you had more self-control—"

George's bellows faded into background noise as the bathroom door jerked open, revealing Noah with a towel wrapped around his hips. Somewhere behind George, Abigail gasped when Noah appeared, and Elsie wrenched herself from Levi's arms and fled outside into the freezing rain.

Followed by a scream and a thud as she fell down the back stairs.

CHAPTER 17

Sharp pain radiated through Elsie's right hip as she lay on the patch of ice at the bottom of the Wyses' back stairs. She'd have a nice bruise there. She was pretty sure nothing was broken or sprained, but she might be stiff and sore for a day or two. Pellets of ice fell from the sky, stinging her skin as she struggled to a seated position. Abigail, George, and Noah all clustered around the open door as Levi cautiously made his way down the ice-covered steps. Abigail still cuddled the puppy while sneaking peeks at Noah, who was wrapped in a towel. George stood between them.

"Sheesh, Elsie. Couldn't you have enough common courtesy to fall when I'm dressed?" Noah grumbled with an exaggerated shiver and heightened color. He disappeared from the doorway, appearing moments later with a metal bucket containing a small shovel and the embers left over from sprinkling them—still glowing—

on the front steps. Elsie doubted they had enough heat left to melt all the ice coating the back stairs, but she hoped they had enough to make it slushy.

Levi dumped the ashes on the steps and took the small metal shovel to spread them out.

Noah turned away. "I'm going to get dressed just in case the klutz needs me. No sense in everyone getting a peep show."

Abigail blushed. Elsie laughed, but it shook her body and she gasped. Tears sprang to her eyes. Maybe she'd bruised her ribs, too. Not to mention her pride, since she embarrassed herself as a klutz again. And her brother parading around in a towel wasn't helping much in terms of pulling George's attention away from the fact he caught her and Levi kissing. But she appreciated the effort and apparently Abigail appreciated the view.

Levi shoved the empty metal pail and the shovel at George and turned. "Can you stand?" He didn't wait for an answer, bent, and scooped her into his arms.

"Don't drop me." She snuggled against his chest.

"I'd protect you with my life, Elle." His words warmed her heart. He carried her up the stairs. George and Abigail moved out of their way. Then he carried her through the bathroom—which Noah had exited—and into Abigail's room, where he set her on the bed. He knelt in front of her a bit slowly, awkwardly, as if his knees hurt. "I'm not sure if emergency crews can get through or not, but do I need to call for an ambulance? Or do you think it's a sprain?"

"I'm fine. Maybe I bruised my hip."

"So, you don't need to be in bed?" Levi glanced toward the door. Elsie followed his gaze. No one watched, but they might be lurking just out of sight. And probably were.

But oh, the temptation to pull him to her and let nature take its course...She swallowed. Hard. "Not outside of marriage, Levi Wyse." Her face flamed red. She hadn't meant to say that. Some of her *Englisch* friends would say they were two consenting adults, but they didn't understand the ways of the Amish most of the time. Though, most of her *Englisch* friends had moral values.

Levi blushed. "I didn't mean that, Elle. I meant bed rest, not...not..." The red brightened. "I wish you would marry me," he whispered; then something that might have been horror filled his eyes as if he hadn't intended to say that. "But of course, that is impossible." He sounded broken. "I can't marry."

And there was that *can't* word again. Mixed with the horror...Well, it spoke volumes about her chances. His feelings about her were plain. Wait. He wished she would marry him? Joy suddenly filled her but was quickly tamped down again by the *can't*.

She opened her mouth to ask why he couldn't marry, but George hobbled into the doorway with his walking stick raised.

Levi shot to his feet and moved out of swinging range. "We're just talking," he shouted.

"Eh? Speak up, boy," George yelled.

Elsie, slowly and painfully, pushed to her feet. She stood in front of George and repeated Levi's words quietly.

George frowned. "Talk around the others so we can chaperone, then."

Elsie nodded, but that meant the conversation was

over. There was no way Levi would discuss it now. He probably wouldn't have anyway.

"Come along, now. I do have another couple to keep an eye on, you know." George turned away.

"How did you do that?" Levi came up behind her. "He can hear you?"

"He lip-reads. But you have to make sure you have his attention," Elsie explained.

"Well, I'll be." Levi loosely wrapped his arms around her from behind. "How did I not know that?"

"You don't pay enough attention to others." Elsie didn't want to hurt him, but it was true. Still, she wanted to soften it a bit for his sake and let him a little off the hook to know that many others are equally ignorant when it comes to George. "But not many know that. I don't think Bishop Nathan even knows."

Levi's hug tightened. "I pay attention—"

"No, you don't."

He was quiet a moment. "I still love you."

She smiled, happiness bubbling over. He must've sensed it because he stiffened.

"It doesn't change anything, but I do." His voice hitched. "I know you wondered."

"Because I broke up with you? Because if I could undo it, I would." And that was a broad hint.

He rested his forehead against the back of her head. "No."

"Then why..." Elsie started, but then she stopped. That conversation still had to wait. She turned to give him a quick hug. "I still love you, too. But we need to get out there before George comes looking for us again." She also needed to tell Levi that she'd given Sam her word that she'd work for him, even if she couldn't mention she'd go with him to Chicago. The love between her and Levi was destined for doom. She'd be *Englisch*, and he couldn't marry.

"I'm going to shower; I'll be right there." He released her.

Her face heated more as she imagined Levi with a towel around his waist.

He chuckled, probably knowing exactly what she was thinking. He used to claim that he could read her expressions. Maybe he still could.

She swung away and slowly made her way to the kitchen. Abigail had already cleared the table and was pulling the baked macaroni and cheese out of the oven. Elsie went that way to help her, but she had it under control.

George already sat at the table, loudly proclaiming the benefits of bean soup to anyone listening. Elsie guessed it'd be on the menu for tomorrow. Maybe for the whole time they were iced in. Noah was belatedly rubbing Stormy dry with a rag. The puppy seemed to think it was a game and tried to fight the towel, growling as she grabbed it and shook it.

"Will you carry the food to the table for me, Elsie?" Without waiting for an answer, Abigail set the casserole dish on an empty burner on the stove top and shut the oven, then rolled over to where Noah and Stormy played. She giggled.

Elsie switched the gas to off—one of Levi's new-to-her quirks since the explosion that killed most of his family—then grabbed the pot holders and carried the hot dish over. She returned to the stove to drain the water off the green beans and put them in a serving dish.

Levi came into the room as she set it on the table.

George was ready from his end of the table. "Let's pray!" He bowed his head as everyone hurried to a place. Abigail between George and Elsie. Noah across the table, and Levi at the head, catty-corner from Elsie.

Elsie dipped her head. *Our Father, who art in*—Levi's hand closed around hers, stalling her prayer. Danki *that Levi still loves me. Help us to work our relationship out and*—

"Amen!" George shouted. "Let's eat!"

Levi's thumb slid over her skin, rekindling flames.

"And let go of that girl's hand!" George glared at Levi. "I'll take a switch to you, boy!"

"You mean walking stick?" Levi made eye contact with George.

George chortled.

And Levi released her hand with a sheepish look.

No wonder *Daed* laughed when Elsie called home and told him who they'd found to chaperone. She and Noah had thought he'd be worried. But George was far more observant than she and Noah thought he'd be.

* * *

After supper, Levi stared out the window at the darkness. Despite the heavy panes of glass, he could feel the chill in the air. He might not survive this ice storm. Well, physically he might if he exercised common sense, but not mentally or emotionally. As their late supper was finished and the kitchen cleaned up, the cracking of tree branches came more and more frequently. *Englisch* power lines were down—the neighbors' floodlights had gone out midmeal. Trees were likely falling.

And Levi was pretty confident he'd fall and die out there if he did attempt to escape to the barn to work on the trains after everyone else went to bed.

Two are better than one…Noah had rescued him earlier, and he'd rescued Elsie. He and Noah had both helped George.

How would the rest of the verse Noah had memorized come into play? For as long as Levi could remember, Stephen had never quoted scripture to Levi. His *daed* had, a lot. But Elsie's *daed*, never. And to make Noah memorize a portion of scripture to quote to Levi…It seemed almost prophetic.

Noah's laugh cut into Levi's thoughts. "I'll get it for you. Then we probably should get to work cutting and wrapping taffy."

Get what for who? Confused, Levi turned from the window. He instantly felt warmer. The woodstove would keep them warm enough and he had plenty of firewood stacked beside the back door under the overhang.

Noah took a cup from George and another from Abigail and filled them both with the last of the fruit punch. He glanced at Levi as he returned to the table. "Come join us. We'll get done a lot faster."

Levi swallowed, his thoughts heading to the barn and his pending Christmas Eve deadline. Finishing the trains in time was an impossibility.

Noah took a seat. "Abby told me about your train order. We will help you tomorrow. You, Elsie, and I can either work out there or bring stuff inside the house so George and Abby can help. We have to go out to take care of the horses anyway." He buttered the scissors, then started cutting the taffy ropes into one-inch pieces.

Elsie buttered her hands while Abigail started cutting the wax paper. George picked up the Amish newspaper, *The Budget*, and started reading.

Levi added another log to the fire, checked on the puppy asleep on the rag, then washed his hands and sat next to Elsie. He buttered his hands and helped her wrap the cut taffy. He didn't want Elsie out on this ice, so if she helped, he'd have to bring things in. Abigail wasn't really fond of him working inside the house—an understatement—but since Noah was there, she might make an exception.

He opened his mouth to ask but then realized Abigail was crying. And talking. And laughing. All at the same time. "My first sleepover since before the accident! This will be so fun!"

His, too, in like ever, but he wasn't going to laugh or cry about it.

He shut his mouth as Noah gave her a tender smile and Elsie gave her a quick side hug. There'd be time enough to discuss his ideas and plans in the morning. In the meantime, he should just relax—if he could figure out how—and enjoy their company.

Especially his strawberry-blond elf.

The love of his life.

Make that forbidden love. He sighed. Heavily.

Elsie.

* * *

The next morning, Elsie awoke to the wind howling. The doors to the woodstove squeaked as someone opened or closed it. She sat up in bed. Abigail and her wheelchair were already gone, the nightgown she'd slept in folded on her pillow. How had she slipped out without Elsie realizing? Though, it had taken a while for Elsie to relax enough to doze. Not to mention the pain in her hip had made it hard to get comfortable. And Abigail had talked and talked about the taffy pull and the weather until she fell asleep, midword.

George had been awake and bellowing about something in what seemed just a short time after they fell asleep. Elsie had popped a pillow over her head and ignored him. Abigail apparently hadn't.

Elsie crawled out of bed, shivering. They had shut the door for obvious reasons and the heat from the woodstove hadn't reached them. Besides, Elsie slept in shorts, her sports bra, and a tank top with her hair in a long braid. It wouldn't do for George or Levi to see her so indecent and her hair down.

She quickly made the bed, then opened the door to dash across the hall to the bathroom for a quick shower. Nobody was in sight. She crossed the space, shut the bathroom door, and locked it behind her, then turned as Levi came in the other door.

He caught his breath, his gaze skimming over her.

His gray eyes widened, then made the return trip, this time slowly, lingering. They rose to meet hers, the heat in them almost searing her.

His hands trembled. He gulped, his Adam's apple jumping.

Then he murmured something she couldn't understand, turned, and walked out, closing and locking the door behind him.

CHAPTER 18

Levi backed away from the *now*-locked bathroom door, his eyes, thoughts, body—well, everything—burning.

Elsie—his Elsie—was *hot*. Sizzling hot.

Don't kindle a fire you can't put out.

The conversation he'd initiated with Noah during the quiet of the postmidnight hours replayed in his mind. The same conversation he'd had with Elsie's *daed*, Stephen, when Levi and Elsie started getting serious over two years after dating three years before that. Even though the darkness should've made it easier, it was a difficult conversation to have with his sister's boyfriend, who also happened to be his girlfriend's brother. The same brother who'd caught him passionately kissing Elsie. Twice.

Kindling a fire he couldn't put out. The temptation seemed extra hard now for some reason.

Although self-defining Elsie as his girlfriend seemed

wrong. She wasn't his girlfriend. She was…what? She'd stepped right back into her former position of almost-fiancée in his heart and thoughts seemingly without effort. Probably in the eyes of the community, too. What should a fiancée who wasn't one be called? Make-believe? No. Pretend? That wasn't right, either. Faux fiancée? Maybe. She had him wishing he *could* marry her. Tomorrow wouldn't be soon enough.

Nevertheless, that was why he'd left the bathroom in such a rush. The flames were still roaring and he'd only looked.

If he'd touched, it would have been a raging inferno. As it was he could still remember the press of that body—those curves—against him when they kissed.

Love is a decision. A decision he made a long time ago and never wavered from. Not even when they parted ways. He'd coped by avoiding her.

Love is more than physical desire. That one was hard to remember, especially since he wanted her with every fiber of his body. It helped to remind himself that love was listening to her overreact or get dramatic. The last time she lashed out, he just let her leave. He should have explained his actions and tried to convince her that he did love her instead of letting her walk away.

Love was caring for her every need like he did with Abigail. In sickness and in health. For better and for worse.

Love honors and respects. And that was why he'd walked out of the bathroom when everything within him wanted to take that shower with her.

Even though Levi had initiated the conversation, Noah had ended it by reciting the "love chapter 1 Corinthians

13. The whole chapter. Noah had quoted the whole thing. Impressive. But a few phrases lingered.

"*Suffereth long.*" He'd obviously failed there. So obviously. That hurt. Him. And her.

"*Doth not behave unseemly.*" Massive fail there with his passionate kisses. The way he touched her, dreamed of her. Shame burned.

"*Hopeth all things.*" Could he? Ha.

Love never fails. He failed. In ever so many ways.

Faith, hope and charity. He had the faith, sorta; hope, not really; and charity? Gott, *I need help. I want to love like that.*

The wind howled louder and Levi turned away from the still-shut bathroom door to peer out the small window on the outside door. There was nothing but darkness. He never thought he'd miss the neighbors' floodlights. At least the loud cracking of tree branches had ended. He'd have to wait until daybreak to find out the extent of the ice storm damage. If he even could, because judging by the wind, the blizzard had arrived.

Movement in his peripheral vision caught his attention, and he turned.

George stood there, walking stick clutched in one hand and what must be the lioness clutched in the other. "Everyone accounted for but the redhead," he shouted.

Technically, strawberry blond, but that aside, it was much too early for George's loudness. This would be a very long day. And did Levi really need to announce in return that Elsie was in the bathroom? He didn't think so.

"At least she isn't in that boy's arms!" George yelled.

Levi's face heated. He caught George's attention. "*Danki* for adding that." He was being sarcastic.

"You're welcome." Apparently sarcasm wasn't picked up by lip-reading.

From somewhere in the kitchen Abigail giggled. Noah appeared behind George, chuckling—and probably checking for himself.

Levi's cheeks burned hotter, and he turned back toward the outside door, wishing he could escape to the barn.

The bathroom door lock clicked. Levi resisted the urge to turn. It was best not to see—again—what he couldn't unsee. However, he didn't hear George or Noah react, so maybe the door didn't open. She might've escaped out the other door. Still, to be safe, he'd knock.

He turned and waited until Noah and George left, then knocked. No answer. He opened the door a crack and peeked in. The room was empty, the other door wide open. Steam from the shower filled the small space, along with the scent of something fruity. Her shampoo, probably. Didn't they make peppermint-scented shampoo, or was she taking him seriously about not wearing it?

It wasn't helping. He still wanted to kiss her. Her. Not the peppermint. Her.

Besides, he missed the scent. It was uniquely Elsie, not just any woman.

He went into the bathroom, made his preparations for the day, and when he finished he returned to the kitchen as Elsie entered the room from the other side.

Their eyes made contact.

And the world around them faded away.

* * *

Elsie stared into Levi's beautiful gray eyes. She belatedly crossed her arms over her chest to hide herself, even though she was modestly dressed now in the same clothes she wore yesterday. Her hair was twisted and pinned in place, her *kapp* covering it. She should've thought to cover herself in the bathroom, but the idea never crossed her mind. What did Levi think when he saw her in her nightclothes? Was he horrified and worried about her being a bad influence to Abigail? She probably was. Abigail had commented about how much easier shorts and a tank top were to sleep in than a long nightgown that tangled around the knees or higher.

In fact, between her and Noah, both of the Wyse siblings had gotten eyefuls. If news got announced at top volume someplace like at church—she glanced at George—she and Noah could be in serious trouble.

Well, at least Noah would be. No one had seen her except Levi, and she was pretty sure he wouldn't tell.

George glanced at her, then sat at the table. "The redhead is here. Let's eat!" he shouted.

She wasn't a redhead. She was strawberry blond. But it wasn't worth trying to explain the differences to George. Elsie sighed.

Levi gave her a sympathetic look. He knew it was one of her pet peeves.

Abigail raised a wooden spoon from a kettle and turned her wheelchair with a frown. "The oatmeal is almost done, but not quite."

"That's what you get for oversleeping," George groused.

Elsie glanced at the battery-operated wall clock. "Overslept?" It was barely past four in the morning! And after staying awake talking most of the night...

Even Noah seemed draggy...as if he and Levi had had a gabfest. Did men do that?

"As the good book says, 'Early to bed and early to rise makes a man healthy, wealthy, and wise,'" George bellowed.

What? Elsie was pretty sure that was said by Benjamin Franklin, not in the Bible.

"And 'An apple a day keeps the doctor away'?" Noah quipped.

George pointed at him. "Exactly. And speaking of which, I want an apple cut up in my oatmeal."

"*Jah*, and we have no apples." Abigail glowered at no one in particular, yet everyone in general, and turned the wheelchair away, muttering something about bean soup and oatmeal under her breath. Even sweet Abigail was cranky in the wee hours of the morning.

"I'm going to let the puppy out before we eat," Noah said, right as George started beating his spoon on the table like an overgrown child.

Elsie smiled. George's wife had suggested George might be suffering from the beginning stages of dementia, but he refused to go to a doctor. All Elsie knew was George seemed to thrive on any type of attention.

Levi winced as he took the spoon away from him. "Behave yourself, George. Breakfast will be here in a minute." He glanced at Elsie and nodded toward Abigail right as Noah opened the door to a blast of cold air.

"Whoa. Would you look at this, Levi?" Noah called.

Elsie rushed to help Abigail when she almost dropped the hot kettle. Abigail's lap saved from the still-bubbling cereal, Elsie reached for the knob and turned the stove off as Abigail spun away and rolled over to Noah and the cowering puppy.

Levi walked over to the wide-open door as Noah picked up the puppy and carried it outside. Curiosity finally got the best of Elsie and she went to peek through the window. Darkness still covered the land, but what she saw from the inside lights were large flakes of blowing snow that had already accumulated so much the porch steps had vanished into an unidentifiable heap of white.

Noah put the puppy down, and the poor thing disappeared to her belly. Her tail curved down and in, and Stormy let out a pitiful howl.

"Aw." Abigail rolled a little closer to the porch. "Can you hold her above it?"

With a grin, Noah lifted Stormy above the snow and held her.

Elsie smiled. Her brother must really be in love to be willing to do this to keep Abigail happy. Hopefully, the wind wouldn't carry the puppy's "business" all over Noah's clothes.

Levi curved his arm around Elsie's waist, pressing her against his side.

She glanced up at him and smiled.

He glanced over his shoulder, then dropped a quick kiss on the tip of her nose.

A crash sounded behind her. Elsie jerked away from Levi and turned as George's feet tangled in his fallen chair, and he threw out his arms and lunged forward.

The walking stick went flying.

And with a savage roar, George hit the floor, rolled, grabbed his stick and...

Came up swinging.

* * *

Whoever thought George would make a good chaperone needed to have their head examined, but after three more painful whacks to his knees for simply side-hugging Elsie, Levi determined he didn't need to worry about anyone's virtue. Nothing—much—got past George.

Levi's legs would be black and blue. Who would've guessed that George would be so violent and cantankerous?

And if Levi survived this weekend, he owed the man a huge thank-you for keeping an eye on Elsie and Abigail.

Levi frowned. George hadn't attacked Noah with the walking stick. Which meant that Noah was behaving himself—a good thing—or that he was much better at sneaking around than Levi—a bad thing. Of course, it might simply mean that George liked Noah.

Everybody liked Noah.

Levi tamped down the green-eyed monster as Noah brought the puppy inside.

George pointed to his fallen chair, so Levi picked it up, hovered while George sat, then made his way to the other side of the table to his seat. Or at least his seat for now. George had claimed Levi's usual place at the head of the table.

Elsie hurried back to the stove and ladled out oatmeal while Noah put the puppy on Abigail's lap and handed her the rag to dry off the pup's feet. Elsie set a small bowl of oatmeal on the floor for Stormy.

"Let's pray!" George bellowed.

The wind howled louder in response.

Elsie bowed her head while standing at the stove—something generally frowned at, but George seemed disinclined to wait. Noah did move from where he crouched before Abigail and the puppy to an empty chair next to Levi. The one Elsie had sat in last night.

"Amen!" Another shout from George came before Levi even closed his eyes.

They ate in silence; then, in apparent mutual agreement, Levi and Noah bundled up to go out to the barn. The horses needed to be cared for. Not to mention the train orders needed to be worked on.

And Levi had forgotten to ask Abigail's permission to work in the house. He turned.

Abigail smiled. "Noah already asked. *Jah*, but nothing too messy."

"And obviously nothing requiring a generator to run," Noah added.

Obviously. "*Danki*. I will likely work out in the barn awhile, but call me if you need me." He wasn't looking forward to the chill, but he needed to get some serious work done. He also needed some alone time. Away from loud George and the major distraction Elsie caused.

"Me, too. I'll help him. I'm curious about it anyway," Noah added.

So much for alone time.

"We'll be in for dinner. Bean soup, I guess?" Noah bent to pick up Stormy.

"Supper will be bean soup. What was your first clue?" Elsie sounded a bit sarcastic as she dumped a bag of fifteen different kinds of dried beans into a large pot. But he could excuse a bit of snarkiness since it had been an early morning, even by Amish standards. And a late night, because even though he and Noah talked, he still heard the hum of the girls' voices coming from Abigail's room along with an occasional giggle.

George stood and trotted into the mudroom. A second later the bathroom door closed behind him. Levi hesitated, wanting to rush over and kiss his elf good morning.

But that would be a bad idea for more than one reason.

He settled for a wink and an unspoken promise to kiss her later.

And her sweet blush that threatened to highjack his thoughts.

CHAPTER 19

Usually, dry beans needed to be soaked overnight, but one could quick soak them for an hour or so after the water boils. Elsie set the pot full of beans on the woodstove to boil, and then chopped celery, carrots, onions, and ham to add later. The soup would mostly stay on the woodstove to cook all day, but George would have to be satisfied with whatever Abigail wanted to fix for the noon meal.

As soon as Levi and Noah left for the barn, Abigail disappeared, frowning and mumbling something about making beds—even though Elsie had already made one. Elsie cleaned up the kitchen from breakfast while George prowled and paced, muttering under his breath while eyeing the blizzard outside. The barn had disappeared in a sheet of white.

Realizing Abigail hadn't returned, Elsie went to check on Abigail and found her sound asleep on the bed. That ought to help improve her mood, providing George let her sleep. Elsie yawned, tempted to take a nap, too. But that would leave George unsupervised, and there were so many ways he could get into mischief.

Speaking of George, she should check on his elderly wife, Mildred. George wouldn't be able to talk with her, but Elsie could make sure she was safe and assure her that George was, too. They had to miss each other, being apart overnight after so many years of marriage.

Elsie grabbed her purse from the top of Abigail's dresser, quietly stepped out and shut the bedroom door, and while George continued pacing and muttering, she went up the ladder steps to Levi's loft office to work. She pulled her cell phone from the bottom of her purse and scrolled through her contacts for George's number.

Mildred cleared her voice twice after picking up the phone. "Hello, George's Buggy Repair, Mildred speaking." Despite clearing her throat, her voice still sounded a bit rusty from disuse.

"Mildred, this is Elsie Miller. George was chaperoning us *youngies* at the taffy pull last night as you know and he got iced in—"

"Oh, you just keep him as long as you need to, Elsie. Tell him his cats are fine and that I have plenty of bean soup prepared. Of course, there will remain plenty of soup because I won't touch it when he isn't here, but don't mention that part."

Elsie snorted. It must be awful to be forced to eat bean soup for every meal except breakfast. "I sure won't say a word—"

"Good. I'm feasting on a hamburger and French fries right now, but don't tell him that either or I'll get

a lecture on the many benefits of a bean soup diet."
Mildred cackled.

"We had that discussion last night." Elsie caught movement in her peripheral vision and she looked toward the
loft ladder. George's head and shoulders appeared. She
sighed. "I need to go, but I didn't want you to worry."

Though maybe she should be concerned about the
elderly man climbing ladders...

"Oh, I'm not worried a bit. Keep him as long as
you can. I'm overdue for a vacation. Bye now." And the
phone beeped.

Okay, then. Elsie could understand how the woman
might feel, and she'd only had to endure George's quirks
for a few hours instead of years. She dropped the phone
back into her purse and went to help George if he needed
it. He wobbled slightly on the top step but made it into
the loft without assistance.

"Give me a minute to catch my breath," George
huffed, bending over.

Of course, getting him down might be another story,
but at least he was leaving Abigail alone to rest. And
maybe Abigail would return the favor later and let Elsie
take a nap.

Although, George letting Abigail rest might have
more to do with George's distrust of Elsie and Levi than
kindness for Abigail. In which case, George would be
standing sentry outside the bedroom door if Elsie did
attempt to nap.

Not a bad thing with Levi's unexpected "friendliness"
and friskiness. Elsie liked it but wasn't quite sure what
to make of it. What was going through Levi's mind—
and how would he define their relationship? He'd said

that he still loved her. Did that mean he was implying they were back together as a dating couple? Or
were they unofficially almost-engaged again? Or did it
simply mean that he was a man and his basic caveman
tendencies were taking over? As in, any woman who
wasn't his sister would do? Except she'd seen him avoid
what's-her-name last night at the taffy pull, so maybe
"any woman" wouldn't do, but that still didn't mean he
really still loved her. That he wouldn't prey on her past
feelings to feed his ego and hormones. Maybe he was
simply saying what he thought she wanted to hear?

She did want to hear it, but she wanted him to mean
it. And if he didn't...

He didn't. He had no intentions to marry her. He just
wanted...

Her eyes burned.

Oh. That hurt. It was a good thing she was moving to
Chicago. She needed distance from Levi. His previous
method of avoidance worked best with their circumstances.

If it weren't for the blizzard, she'd quit her job and
demand that Noah take her home now.

After George sat, of course. He'd straightened and
begun to move. She eyed the distance between the shuffling, wobbly old man and the chair. George was slower
than brownie batter when walking without his support
stick. She offered him her arm but he waved her off. "I
got it!" he shouted.

Right.

Elsie pointed George to Levi's office chair, put him
to work helping her sort papers by vendor, then gave
him Mildred's message and a tissue when he started

crying about missing his cats. Though she might have to redo the paperwork later. Especially since when George started telling her about his cats and naming names, he began moving papers here and there and back again.

Elsie zoned out when he got to the nineteenth cat and was still going strong.

How many cats did the man have anyway?

Too many.

Not that she'd tell him that.

He droned on, his voice getting slower and lower; then he quieted.

She worked for a couple of hours, maybe three, making significant progress on the mess that was Levi's office. He should be pleased with the difference she made.

Even more pleased when he discovered that she found seven checks he'd never deposited. They weren't large, and together they totaled less than five hundred dollars, but still. Money was money. She paper-clipped the checks together and put them in an empty spot on the desk.

The blizzard winds howled, the fire in the stove crackled, and down below something thumped, bumped, and thudded as if the entire woodpile stacked outside the front door decided to tumble.

The puppy started barking. Well, yipping.

Elsie put her stack of papers down, glanced at George—his head bobbed over his chest as he slept—then went down the ladder.

Another crash.

Abigail came into the living room. "What's going on?"

Elsie shrugged. She flung the door open.

And in tumbled the Abominable Snow Monster.

* * *

As noon approached, Levi stretched and grabbed a couple of bottles of mostly frozen water from the shelf on the outside wall. He handed one to Noah. The two of them had accomplished more on the trains than Levi thought possible. Noah was a quick worker and once Levi explained what needed to be done, he went straight to work, first sanding and then assembling the train's cages as soon as Levi got the pieces measured and cut out.

Noah's cabinetmaking skills came in handy as he seemed to effortlessly fit pieces together. He took a sip of icy water. His eyes were wide as he looked around.

"You get paid for doing this? Really?"

The fourth time he'd said it that morning. With the same expression of wonder.

Levi had ignored him the first three times. Now he hesitated a moment. Noah hadn't asked an amount, but he—and his *daed*—probably wondered if Levi could support Elsie in the event they actually married. If Levi ever saw his way cleared from guilt. And hello, *jah*, he wanted to marry her with every fiber of his being. He cleared his throat, then mentioned how much the gift shop owner, Mark, had mentioned he sold the first train for. Levi hadn't been to town to collect the money yet.

Noah's eyes bugged. "Wow! Seriously?"

Jah, right now it paid much better than Levi's odds-and-ends "honeydo" construction business, but the construction job could be counted on to generate income year-round. Toymaking couldn't. Which was why *Daed* called it a hobby.

Would Noah expect a generous cut for helping out?

Levi studied Noah's work. He was good. He deserved some sort of honorarium, especially if Levi made his deadline, after all. In fact, if he married Abigail, maybe Noah could come to work for Levi as a cabinetmaker, because cabinet orders could be a year-round thing to fill in between toy orders, too.

And maybe Levi could find the courage to confess his sins to Bishop Nathan and find out if he was destined for hell or if *Gott* could somehow forgive him, extending enough grace and mercy for Levi to maybe someday marry Elsie.

If she'd have him.

She'd said she would take him back, but would she if she knew the truth?

Love never fails. The core of the "love chapter" Noah had quoted.

Did *Gott* love him like that?

Levi felt the sudden urge to bend his knees and pray— for forgiveness, for mercy, for him and Elsie, for so many other things. But would *Gott* hear him? And what would Noah think if Levi wept in agony and grief for no apparent reason? Noah would probably call the bishop— who didn't need to be out in this weather, and...Oh horrors, Levi would be excommunicated in front of Elsie and Abigail. His stomach cramped.

He turned away from Noah and forced his attention to what they'd accomplished.

The rest of the gluing and the clamping could be done in the house. Actually, that'd probably be best since they'd dry faster in a warm space. The painting could be done inside, too.

The heaters were still not even making a dent in the

frigid air. And now that Levi wasn't working, he felt the chill.

Or maybe it was the icy water freezing him from the inside out.

"How about we go in, get something to eat, and thaw out?" Noah apparently felt the same. Cold.

"If I find a box to load this stuff in, we could probably work on painting inside the house this afternoon. There's an old child's sled in storage. Up in the loft. There are probably boxes up there, too." He hadn't been up there for almost two years. His stomach cramped again, this time from grief. "We could use it to haul stuff to the house." His voice broke. The sled used to be his littlest brother's.

"I'll get the sled," Noah said quietly, "and find a big box, if you want to gather what you need together."

Like Levi's control over his emotions? He managed a nod. And gulped.

Noah left the workshop and Levi took the time to get down on his knees near the heaters. He bowed his head, words clamoring for release, but the jumbled mess of thoughts emerged as, *Oh,* Gott. *Oh,* Gott. *I'm so very sorry. If You could find Your way clear to forgive me*... Followed by a flood of tears that left him gasping for breath, as a refrain of *Oh,* Gott. *Oh,* Gott played over and over.

And he found a fragment of peace that maybe, somehow, it would all work out and he would find forgiveness.

He wiped his face dry with a rag that smelled of varnish, then rose to his feet and focused on collecting paints, brushes, toys, and whittling tools for the animals.

And glue and clamps and assorted pieces still to be assembled. As well as focusing on trying to gather himself together.

Noah reappeared, and though he gave Levi a long, assessing look, he didn't say a thing. They worked in silence as they loaded the box. Levi turned off the heaters and lights, and they tugged their outerwear on. After closing the barn, they trudged through the still-gusting blizzard and at least another foot of snow. Levi pulled the sled while Noah pushed. At least the snow provided traction, even though it was deeper than his boots and freezing his feet. Not to mention blowing into his unprotected collar. He needed a new scarf for Christmas. Maybe Abigail would make him one.

He couldn't wait to get inside and see Elsie again. How had the girls fared with George all morning? At least they kept him inside...

Maybe.

Or maybe not.

Levi stumbled to a stop when he neared the porch. The formerly neatly stacked woodpile was strewn all over, spilling into the yard. The church's benches were shoved over.

He glanced at Noah. "From the storm? Doesn't seem possible." Or had George done it, trying to be helpful?

Noah shrugged. Frowned. Whatever he said was caught by the howling wind and blown away.

They abandoned the sled in a semiprotected area on the side of the house, hoisted the box between them, and hurried around the corner to the back steps.

* * *

Despite the man wrecking the Wyses' living room, Elsie was terrified to take her focus from George—who now dangled by his fingers from the edge of the loft floor, having completely missed the ladder steps when he started to come down moments ago.

He might have been awakened by the Abominable Snow Monster's shouted tirade or maybe he'd simply sensed Elsie leaving the loft, since he bellowed something about staying out of that boy's arms.

"I'll sue you for everything you own for putting a mailbox and a drainage ditch so close to the road!" Abominable Snow Monster threatened, waving a shaking fist as she glanced over her shoulder. "That caused my accident, you..." He ended it with a string of foul words that made Elsie's face burn.

Never mind that the stranger's eyes were glazed over from driving under the influence of something—she had no idea what—during a blizzard with whiteout conditions.

"Help me! I'm going to die!" George shouted. His fingers slipped a degree.

"Hang on, George!" Elsie shouted, but it might as well have been quieter than a whisper for all the good it did. And she didn't know how to help either George or the snow monster.

"I'm going to fall and break every bone in my body," George bellowed.

Jah, he probably would.

Something crashed and Elsie jerked around. The kerosene lantern lay shattered next to the puppy, who left a puddle behind as she tucked her tail and ran.

The Abominable Snow Monster threw another kerosene lantern along with another string of bad words.

Abigail, dear sweet Abigail, screamed, "Stop!" crying at the same time, her hands shaking.

"HELP!" George shouted again. Sound barriers might have been broken.

Elsie was a serious failure as an elf. And this whole situation was totally out of sync with her upbringing as an Amish girl. What part of this was peaceful?

A door slammed open with an arctic blast.

What now? Elsie turned her head long enough to see Levi and Noah enter the fray from the mudroom entrance. They carried a box—and dropped it by the kitchen door.

"I'm going to fall!" George screamed.

"Scoot over, Elle." Levi crossed through the open rooms with giant steps, shoved past her, and climbed up the ladder steps to physically guide George's feet.

Why hadn't she thought of that?

"Abby, go to your room and shut the door." Noah's voice almost sounded like *Daed*'s and she glanced over to see him standing between Abigail and the stranger.

Abigail firmed her jaw, and sat there. But her eyes were wide and filled with fear. Apparently, it was an order she had no intention of following. Either that or she was too scared to move. Elsie understood that. She was terrified, too.

"Elsie, take Abigail to safety," Noah demanded.

Elsie twisted her hands in her apron. She tried to obey, really, but her legs wouldn't move.

Noah turned to the invader. "Sir, we can talk this out. Let's calm down a little."

The stranger took a swing at Noah, missed, then with a terrible scream rammed his head into Noah's stomach, knocking him backward. He fell on his behind, sliding backward on the broken glass and kerosene.

George's feet landed on the floor—due to Levi's help. He grabbed his walking stick...

And went to war.

CHAPTER 20

Levi had heard rumors that George was going crazy, but he wasn't convinced it was true. How much of his strange behavior was an on-purpose, free-to-be-me bravado, especially given the "selective" hearing with or without lip-reading? Because even crazy people generally knew not to pick a fight with a mean drunk sixty years younger while armed with only a walking stick.

He looked beyond George to where Elsie stood stock-still next to the loft ladder steps, eyes wide and her hand plastered across her mouth, as if physically holding in a scream.

Levi wanted to grab her and make her go to safety. Elle and Abig—

Something crashed. He jerked his head to the side to look. The drunk bumped into the end table and it wobbled. Tipped.

The stranger grabbed Levi's last surviving kerosene lamp from the collapsing table and bashed it against George's hard head as the table crashed.

"Stop! You're going to kill him!" Abigail shrieked, somehow crying at the same time.

Levi glanced at George. He wanted to grab the old man and stop this madness, but he had a feeling it'd be detrimental if he did. He wasn't going to hold George back to be killed, and he wasn't sure he could grab hold of the invader—who looked vaguely familiar. But he had to try. Despite being armed with his flailing walking stick, George wasn't winning the battle and Noah seemed distracted by something in his hand. Levi angled himself around the two men, trying to get behind the *Englisch* man. Gott, *if You're up there somewhere listening, help. I promise I'll confess to the bishop if You—*

"Elsie! Take Abby to her room *now!*" Soft-spoken Noah roared. He scrambled to his feet, tossed something at Elsie, and crouched, eyeing the two men.

Elsie caught whatever it was, glanced at it, then dropped it into her apron pocket and nodded. Oh, she was crying! Levi's heart broke. She hurried over to the wheelchair, swung it around, and ran. A door slammed.

The *Englischer* circled around in front of Levi in order to get at George, and Levi tackled the man from behind just as Noah grabbed George, almost throwing him out of the way.

George fell with a bellow and a scream and the stranger landed on top of Noah, Levi on both.

Noah oofed as the breath was knocked out of him.

Now what?

Years of wrestling in the barn with other boys never prepared him for what to do when he pinned a stranger. But the man was holding still. Too still.

Levi hesitantly straightened. Sat. The man didn't move.

Neither did George, who was sprawled next to the fallen end table. Except, he still screamed. Cried. Maybe both.

"I called for help," Elsie said quietly, appearing unexpectedly in Levi's line of sight. She bent, picking up the puppy. Her voice broke. "She wanted the puppy safe, too. I'll be right back after I give it to her." She turned away.

"No, stay back there." Levi wanted her out of harm's way.

But if Elsie heard, she ignored him.

"Let me up." Noah gasped.

Levi stood.

The unknown man didn't even wiggle. He was face down on Noah's shoulder. His snow-covered cowboy hat had fallen off at some point and he had a bloody handprint on his filthy tan coat.

"Did I kill him?" Levi hated the fear that gripped him. *Please, Lord, no.*

Noah pushed the invader off of him with his bloody hands. "No. He's still breathing."

Whew. Danki*, Lord.*

Noah sat, then winced as he wiped the blood on his pants. "Do you have anything to secure him?"

"Gardening twine." Levi grimaced. "Not sure how well it'll hold."

"I'll get it," Elsie said from the hallway. He looked up as she veered into the kitchen.

"I'm dying!" George bellowed, grasping at his chest. "My heart!"

"You check on George. I'll keep an eye on this guy," Noah said.

Levi limped over to George, the bruises on his legs from the walking stick probably aggravated by tackling the stranger and falling on him. Not exactly a soft landing, and compounded by those stiff cowboy boots the man wore...Noah was bound to feel even worse, having already landed on his rear on broken glass and then having two men fall on top of him.

Wait. Levi turned back and studied the man now that he was still. Could it be that wannabe cowboy who'd been hitting on Elsie in town on Monday? It was long enough ago that Levi wasn't sure, but he did look familiar.

He turned back to George just as the old man feebly waved the walking stick. Not hard enough to hurt if he connected, but thankfully he didn't, because Levi had enough bruises for one day.

"That man tried to kill me," George complained. "My heart is pounding!"

So, not a heart attack. Just excitement. And adrenaline. The same rush of sensation Levi currently felt that had started the moment he burst in the door and saw the lunatic throwing lanterns and cursing with his sister and Elsie just feet away.

Jah. Levi's pulse throbbed, too. "He probably was afraid you'd kill him." He lowered himself beside George and faced him.

"I wouldn't hurt a fly." There might have been a glint in George's eyes.

Levi disagreed, but then he had the bruises to prove

it. He caught movement from the corner of his eye and glanced that way.

Elsie reappeared with brown garden twine and gave it to Noah. She handed an aspirin bottle to Levi. "For George's heart. Chew it, George. I suppose I need to get busy cleaning up."

Noah held up a hand. "Not until the police come."

"You called the police?" A surge of panic worked through Levi. Would the police recognize him as the same man who'd killed his family? Would they arrest him this time? He glanced at the still-motionless cowboy and started praying the man didn't die or have permanent injuries like Abigail did.

"Noah told me to. And an ambulance. And the bishop." Elsie looked at him.

This was going from bad to worse. "Noah told you... Wait. What? When?" His voice was strangled. But he knew when. That thing Noah tossed at her was a cell phone. Had to have been.

Elsie's gaze was sympathetic. Did she sense his fear? "It's okay, Levi. They need to know. He"—she pointed at the stranger—"said he hit your mailbox and his car ended up in the ditch."

"And for that he destroyed your property? Tried to kill George?" Noah sounded incredulous. He knotted yet another string around the man's hands behind his back and down to his ankles so he couldn't get up or move should he regain consciousness.

A dented mailbox and broken household furnishings were a small price to pay for Levi's continued freedom. But if the police came and he was arrested... Abigail. Who would take care of her?

He tried to tamp the panic down.

He promised he'd confess. *Gott* was holding him to it. *Lord, help.*

* * *

Elsie didn't know what to do. Cleaning something seemed obvious, but Noah told her to wait. She didn't want to be hidden back in the bedroom, even though making sure Abigail stayed calm was important, too. But Abigail had the dog to comfort her and Elsie needed firsthand knowledge.

Maybe she should bake more Christmas cookies. They'd eaten all the earlier treats at the taffy pull. EMTs and police would need to be served coffee and cookies, right?

"You trying to poison me?" George shouted. He made spitting noises.

Huh? Elsie looked at him. Oh. The aspirin.

"Now, George, Elle said you need to take it for your heart." Levi somehow stayed calm.

"Heart attack," George corrected. "It's pounding."

"Right," Levi agreed. "Heart attack."

Elsie was pretty sure it was just excitement causing George's heart to race. Hers was, too. But she poured a glass of water and gave it to Levi so he could help George.

Levi drank it. "*Danki.*" But he looked confused. And scared.

Elsie swatted at his shoulder, then took the glass to refill it. "The water was for George."

"Oh. Sure," Levi muttered. "Of course it was." But his face was pasty white.

The stranger groaned but didn't wake. Elsie glanced at him then back at Levi. "Are you okay?"

He shook his head and opened his mouth as a loud vehicle rumbled into the driveway.

A door slammed. "First responder," someone yelled, but she barely heard him above the howling wind.

She patted Levi's shoulder, then moved to open the door.

She and Levi really needed to talk.

Sooner rather than later.

* * *

Levi pressed a hand against his roiling stomach. Hopefully, he wouldn't embarrass himself by getting physically sick.

"I'm having a heart attack!" George yelled as a man carrying a big black bag entered the house. "That boy tried to kill me!"

The man's gaze skittered over the scene. Levi scooted out of the way so the man could help George as the first responder neared. He wished he could hide in the bedroom until after the drama ended. While he was prepared—not exactly—to confess to the bishop and maybe even Elle, he was nowhere near ready to be dragged off in handcuffs. The shame consumed him.

The first responder stopped by the fallen invader. He knelt, apparently deciding George's heart attack was not an actual heart attack.

"It's that redhead's fault, you know. She let him in. They're probably in cahoots!" George loudly volunteered.

Levi's gaze shot to Elsie. She still stood in the entryway even though the door was shut. She'd been staring out the window but turned at George's words.

"I did," she said, glancing at Levi, then away and down. "But I didn't know he was there. I heard the woodpile fall over and opened the door. To see what happened. I didn't know—" She swiped at something under her eye and sniffled. "I'm sorry." She gave Levi a look that broke his heart. Pain. Guilt.

He stumbled to his feet and crossed the room. Tugged her into his arms. "It's okay, Elle. All's well that ends well." Except, he didn't know how this would end. Maybe this memory right here of holding her in his arms would have to be enough for a lifetime.

"She tried to kill me so she could be in that boy's arms. Hired an assassin! And look at her. Can't even wait for me to die," George shouted.

Someone snorted, but Levi didn't turn to see who. Instead, new vehicles arrived with snow chains and flashing red-and-blue lights that dimly lit the blizzard-colored world outside, catching his attention. It reminded him of the gas explosion almost two years prior and the aftermath. The bile rushed up his throat.

CHAPTER 21

Elsie swayed when Levi jerked out of her arms. He turned and almost sprinted down the hall, slamming the door to the bathroom. The poor man. He probably wasn't used to so much excitement, with both an invader and George's drama. She started to move toward the kitchen, needing to do something, even if it was to bake Christmas cookies or fix dinner. As if on cue, her stomach rumbled. She probably needed to fix coffee in addition to food. Lots of coffee. She glanced toward the wall clock, but something flashed outside, drawing her attention.

The police were there, two vehicles. One was parked out by the mailbox, probably where the guy's car went into the ditch. The other one pulled to a stop in front of the porch next to the first responder's diesel truck. This scene probably reminded Levi of the tragic night most of his family died. Elsie opened the door as an officer exited the vehicle, one hand resting casually on his gun holster.

"You called about a domestic dispute," the officer said, scanning the mess on and around the porch that the stranger had made before his impassive stare landed on Elsie.

Apparently, the message she'd given the 911 operator wasn't very clear if the police thought there was a domestic disturbance. "Um, I called because the stranger hit the mailbox, landed in the ditch, and then went berserk and tried to kill George. My brother and, um, boyfr—Levi managed to subdue him. He's tied up inside."

The officer pulled a notebook and pen out of his chest pocket. He frowned. "Your brother and boyfriend tried to kill George?"

"No, the stranger," Elsie corrected. "And he's not my boyfriend. Not anymore, but—"

The officer wrote something down. "George tried to kill your ex-boyfriend."

That was probably a little closer but still very wrong. "He's unconscious and tied up with gardening twine." She shivered, teeth chattering, both from the bitter cold and the adrenaline crashing now that help had arrived.

The officer's eyebrows rose. "George or the ex-boyfriend?"

This was going from bad to worse. Not to mention cold and snow blew into the house. Elsie stepped backward. "Come in, please. The first responder is here, trying to take care of him. I hope he doesn't die."

The officer opened his mouth and shut it. He pocketed the notepad and pen and returned his hand to his holster as he climbed the stairs to the porch.

Elsie held the door wide and the officer came inside as George started yelling again. "Not enough to give me a heart attack and hire an assassin, you have to give me hypothermia!"

"Assassin . . ." The officer's hand twitched. He shifted, yanked a flashlight out, and leveled it on Noah. "Everybody put your hands up!"

Noah raised his arms. Nobody else did.

"Now, Tony," the first responder said.

"Plotting murder, every last one of them," George shouted.

The bathroom door opened, and Levi came out. The officer swung to face him, leveling the flashlight on him.

"Murderers!" George bellowed.

"Hands up! Get down!" the officer shouted, and Levi raised his hands.

The officer clicked the flashlight on as Levi hit the floor.

Elsie caught her breath. She fought to keep from laughing, but someone snorted.

Then she realized it was her.

The situation wasn't funny. It was terrifying, except for the flashlight.

The adrenaline rush faded. She fought a wave of dizziness.

And the world went black.

* * *

Levi raised his head to look at Elsie just as she collapsed not so gracefully on the floor behind the flashlight-happy officer. He wanted to rush to her side but was afraid to move with the officer still holding the large flashlight. Except, now he looked at it as if he expected the object to bite him.

"Rookie," the first responder grumbled as he approached. "They sent you in alone? Really?"

"I thought I could handle it." The officer clicked the switch on the light, his face flaming a blotchy red.

George shouted something about dying.

"Didn't they warn you about Amish George? He tends to overreact. Now, put the light away, Tony." He patted the policeman's shoulder then lowered himself next to Elsie. "The perp is passed out on the floor but clearly on something." He glanced at Levi. "Are you hurt?"

"That was—is—Amish George?" The officer looked somewhat impressed. He slipped the flashlight back into the holder then pointed at George.

"I'm fine," Levi said, and started to motion toward Elsie but then noticed his sister's wheelchair in his side vision. "May I get up now?"

"Yes. You'd best check on that sweet sister of yours," the first responder said.

They knew Abigail? Levi cautiously moved to a sitting position and looked up at his sister. Her face was red and tearstained, but she beamed at the first responder.

"Thanks, Riley," she murmured. "I wondered if you'd come. I'm fine, but my friend, and Levi's girlfriend..." She pointed.

"Not my girlfriend," Levi muttered, but his gaze shot to dear Elsie, who struggled to sit.

She stared at him, hurt and rejection filling her beautiful green eyes that already glittered with unshed tears.

The policeman chuckled. "She said the same thing about you."

Oh. Ouch. *Jah*, the rejection hurt. But at least they were on the same page.

The officer grabbed his notebook and pen and turned away. "I'm going to get Amish George's autograph. He's practically a celebrity."

And that explained so much about George's foolish acts of bravado. He thrived on attention, positive or negative.

The first responder, who Abigail called Riley, crossed to Elsie and knelt beside her. "Hi, Miss Elsie. You had quite the scare there."

"I did, Riley. Thanks for caring." She smiled at him.

Elsie knew him, too? Levi battled the unfamiliar feelings of jealousy. Make that too familiar, ever since they broke up. He gulped. Stood. And limped on his sore, bruised legs into the other room.

Where George was all smiles as he signed the officer's notebook.

Levi took a seat off to the side, out of the way. Since he wasn't needed for a statement yet, and since it appeared that he'd remain free—*Danki, Gott*—he needed to plan out his confessions to Bishop Nathan and Elsie.

It'd be nice if he could talk to both at the same time.

Both separately was double the trouble.

* * *

Elsie swayed dizzily, her world briefly fading to black again before she blinked it into focus. She scooted back enough to lean against the wall and adjusted her dress over her legs; then Riley checked her blood pressure.

"I sure hate to ask this, Miss Elsie, but there's no chance you're in the family way, is there?" His face turned as red as hers probably flamed, judging by the burn.

She dipped her head to hide the embarrassment. "No, that isn't possible," she whispered. She'd never actually fainted before, but then she'd never actually witnessed someone she loved being told to "get down" by the police. She gulped back a wail. Her emotions were all over the place. A mess. She tried to briefly explain what she was feeling.

"Tony's a rookie," Riley said when she was finished, wincing. "He'll learn, and as soon as he finishes fawning over Amish George, he'll need to get statements." Something dinged and he glanced at a square banded on his left wrist. "Ambulance is two minutes out."

"I'm fine," Elsie insisted, though she still felt woozy.

"Have a glass of juice," Riley suggested. "That'll perk you right up." He stood. "I'll go check on your brother and Amish George." He walked off.

"I'll get you a glass of juice and start lunch." Abigail wheeled past.

A few minutes later, Levi—not Abigail—handed Elsie a juice glass. He lowered himself next to her.

She tried to smile, because she craved his comfort like that of the hug by the door and his current care of her, but she could still hear him saying she wasn't his girlfriend when she really wanted to be...And yet she thought it was probably her own words to the officer that set him up to yell at Levi. A mixture of hope and guilt and betrayal and relief. She moved her hand toward his.

He ignored it. "We need to talk about why I can't marry."

Finally, she'd get the truth and know what was going on in his mind so she could start convincing him otherwise. Unless he had a valid reason.

The front door opened with another frigid blast of air, and the bishop appeared, following the EMTs carrying a stretcher.

"Later." He squeezed her hand. "Pray for me. I also need to talk to the bishop."

CHAPTER 22

Levi pressed a hand to his still-roiling stomach as he started to approach the bishop. The older man seemed focused on a mission, though, so Levi stopped and stood quietly off to the side near George's head. Bishop Nathan made a wide swath past the unconscious stranger and the EMTs starting to work on him, past Riley, who knelt beside Noah on the floor and looked at his bloody hands, to George, still lying where he'd landed and loudly telling his tall tale to the spellbound officer who just sat and stared, mouth agape.

Bishop Nathan stopped a few feet from George and looked around. He glanced at Levi, raised an eyebrow, then approached. Dread built inside Levi with every measured step. "I overheard George's conversation with the officer. I'm assuming there were no assassins hired to murder George so Elsie and you could make out in the laundry room." His brows quirked with humor as he said the words *make out*.

The man got points for identifying "that redhead" as Elsie and "that boy" as Levi. And Levi was thankful for a bit of humor to break the tension and start the conversation. This was better than his original opening thought of "I killed my family" or "I'm a murderer."

"No assassins were hired," Levi said.

The bishop nodded, waited a beat, then a slight grin tipped his lips. "I notice there's no denying the charges of making out in the laundry room." His brow quirked again.

Hopefully, Elsie wouldn't get in trouble for Levi's laundry room hormones. His face heated. "I'm not a liar." Not a liar, but he was a murderer...just not in a plot aimed at George.

"Commendable." Bishop Nathan shifted to open their cluster at the base of the ladder steps, allowing Riley to join them.

"I'm recommending that Noah go to the ER to get the glass picked out of his hands, but he's refusing. Says either his sister or his girlfriend will do it."

Levi looked at Elsie's brother and Abigail's boyfriend. Glass in his hands? Right. He'd fallen into the broken glass from the lantern, then jumped right up to help tackle the intruder and tie him up. That had to be painful.

Riley glanced at George on the floor almost at their feet. "Amish George will be transferred on the next ambulance for his 'heart issues.' That ambulance is about ten minutes out."

Levi's gaze skittered to George. He was fairly certain George didn't have any heart problems, and from his attitude, Riley didn't think so, either, but there was no denying George would thrive on the attention.

It'd also ease the tension and stress level if Levi didn't have to worry about George and his walking stick. His eardrums would also appreciate the break from the screamed conversations. Wouldn't miss a thing if they took George.

"And on that note, I need to go." Riley nudged Levi. "My wife wasn't happy I went out in this blizzard, but we both care for Abigail and were concerned about what happened when we heard it on the scanner. My wife is Abby's physical therapist, and I might or might not have picked Abby up a few times after a fall."

Levi gave him a sharp look. "She fell? And no one told me?"

"Not recently, and she wasn't hurt. She didn't want you to know, but that's part of the reason she wanted you to hire a companion for her. Changing the subject, I should've known Amish George would be involved today. The dispatcher did mention a George." Riley winked at Levi. "However, you might want to stay out of the laundry room when Amish George is here."

Levi's face burned. The whole community would be aware of his behavior at this rate. George would no doubt announce it at church and give the gossips plenty of fuel to push for a wedding, but... It changed nothing.

"I'll say goodbye to Abby and make my way home," Riley said, then he walked off.

Bishop Nathan frowned. "I'll be taking George's place as chaperone, so there will be *no* hanky-panky." His frown deepened. "I hate that the *Englisch* call him Amish George as if that's his name. It makes me feel as though they are lumping all the Amish in the same category. Nothing I can do about it, though. George will be George."

Levi shifted, not sure what to say during the awkward silence. George had his walking stick, but the bishop was a more formidable chaperone. And Levi never was any good at small talk. But there was talking in his future. After all, he'd prayed before tackling the intruder and would hold up his end of the bargain. At least he could put "the talk" off for a bit more since the bishop would be staying the rest of the day.

"Later, after everyone else leaves, I need to have a talk with you. And with Elsie." There'd be less chances of her overreacting if the bishop witnessed the conversation.

However, it also would make it more uncomfortable for her if the bishop heard Levi's rejection of her.

Love is kind.

Levi gulped. If he loved Elsie—and he did—he would try to talk to her privately. Probably now would be a good time while they were still waiting to give their statement to the rookie cop.

The EMTs lifted the intruder onto the stretcher and hoisted it up. Noah picked up the guy's Stetson and dropped it on his chest. *Jah*, that needed to go with him.

The officer wrote down something George said, then looked at him. "It was a real pleasure to meet you, Amish George. I need to get statements now." He sounded a little shell-shocked. He stood.

"Don't know why you need statements. I told you all you need to know." George squirmed, started to sit up straighter, and groaned as he fell back. "I think I broke something!"

Good thing another ambulance was en route.

Levi turned away as another blast of blizzard winds blew in with the exit of the EMTs and intruder and the entrance of another policeman. This one looked familiar. Levi strode over to the woodstove to check the fire. Sort of. Mostly to hide just in case the officer was one who'd responded almost two years ago and recognized Levi as the screaming, panicking *youngie* who'd just accidentally murdered his whole family and outright admitted to it.

Wait. Why hadn't they arrested him back then? He'd *admitted* to it! Instead, they took him aside and told him to breathe. Someone prayed with him. Both the Amish and the *Englisch* members of the community had reached out in love, compassion, and understanding, not condemnation. He'd pushed them away. He'd been so foolish.

Levi added a log to the fire, closed the stove, gathered the tattered remnants of his courage, and straightened. He turned from the stove and scanned the room.

The newcomer cop talked to Noah at the dining room table. Bishop Nathan lowered himself down beside George, who was still yelling about broken bones and something about a cat. Abigail puttered in the kitchen, probably starting something for their midday meal. It was an hour past noon. The rich aroma of coffee filled the room. The rookie officer stood nearby, drawing a sketch and writing something. Levi walked a few feet, looking for Elsie. She sat alone, drinking the orange juice he'd brought her and leaning against the wall where he left her. She was still very pale.

Wait. George wanted a cat. Could he be referring to the one he stole from the workshop? Or the pregnant one in the barn? He could keep the carved one if it'd comfort him. Well, he could keep them both, but the living one wouldn't be allowed to go to the hospital with George.

Levi crossed the living room to George and caught his attention. "Where did you leave the cat?"

George's skin flushed. "Mudroom. On the washer."

Levi nodded. "I'll get it." He retrieved the carved animal—a small price to pay for George being peaceful, if that was even possible—and handed it to the elderly man.

George clutched it and cried. It was heartbreaking, really.

Levi patted George's shoulder and for a brief moment considered hugging the old man. But that would likely earn him a swat. He'd talk to Elsie while they waited.

He turned away from George, but now the rookie policeman sat too close to Elsie at the entrance to the hallway, grinning at her. Were police allowed to smile? It seemed unprofessional. But then blinding unsuspecting men leaving the bathroom with a high-powered flashlight was unprofessional, too.

His gaze lowered to the beautiful woman sitting on the floor mere feet away.

She might not be his girlfriend anymore, but he stood there, watching them.

Watching her.

Wishing things were different and that he was free to declare his intentions.

* * *

It seemed that hours went by before things quieted down and everyone left except the bishop and George, but really it was only a quarter hour longer. The bishop was seated next to George on the floor at the foot of the loft's ladder. At least George had quieted down about assassins.

Delicious scents filled the air as Elsie grabbed a pair of pot holders and pulled the quick tuna casserole from the oven that Abigail had tossed together while Elsie was recovering from her faint. Elsie'd felt helpless as the wheelchair-bound Abigail had moved from meals to nursing when she went for tweezers and removed the glass fragments from Noah's hands.

All Elsie had done was take the dish out of the oven.

Elsie carried the rectangular clear-glass dish to the table where Abigail finished up now, Noah's hand tenderly cradled in hers, his green eyes locked on her so trustingly even though what she did had to hurt. It almost was enough to make Elsie cry. Levi never looked at her that way. Though she never had to remove glass from Levi's hands. And if she ever tried to extract glass shards from Noah's hands, he wouldn't gaze at her with love and trust. He'd be howling in pain and complaining that she was killing him.

Speaking of which, where was Levi? He'd vanished. But the puppy was gone, too.

"You go wash your hands with soap and water. Pat it dry gently," Abigail directed Noah. "I'll get the antibiotic ointment and bandage it for you."

Noah carefully lifted Abigail's hand and brushed a kiss across the palm. Elsie teared up. So sweet. Abigail blushed but gave Noah a wobbly smile before she rolled backward out of his way. Her face flamed brighter when she caught Elsie watching her.

Elsie quickly looked away. "I'll get the plates and set the table."

"There are flashing lights outside again." Abigail pointed. "Do you think they're here for George?"

"Probably," Elsie said, changing directions and going to open the door.

It seemed the wind had picked up even more than earlier. Big flakes of snow blew sideways, leaving huge drifts in spots and almost bare ground in others.

The EMTs approached. "We had a call about a heart patient."

Elsie pointed in the general vicinity of George and stepped out of the way. It wouldn't do any good to tell them what she thought about his heart, because George did need some kind of medical attention, even if it wasn't heart related.

Once the EMTs had entered, Elsie stepped out into the blowing snow and looked around. A dark figure crouched beside the barn, holding something that wiggled. That had to be Levi and the puppy. Should she ring the dinner bell or . . . ? No, because he wouldn't be wasting his time out here in the bitter cold unless he needed to be and they wouldn't eat until after George left for the hospital. Maybe she should put the casserole back into the oven to stay warm.

She stomped the snow from her borrowed slippers as best as she could, but considering they had a mess in the house, thanks to the drunk, what was one more thing? At least she knew what she'd do that afternoon. Especially since with the bishop chaperoning, sneaking off for a nap wouldn't happen.

Work, for the night is coming . . .

She wasn't sure if that was scripture or not, but either way, it was often quoted among the Amish.

Abigail and Noah were back at the table, but now Abigail dabbed ointment on the wounds. It must hurt. He didn't say anything, but he pressed his lips together, and a muscle jumped in his jaw.

The EMTs talked quietly in the living room area, but George was bellowing again, so Elsie couldn't hear what they said. The bishop slowly pushed to his feet and approached the dining room table right as the outside door in the mudroom blew open with a crash. The puppy yipped, and Elsie glanced in there as Levi set the pup down.

"Grab her and hold on until I get the door shut. I need to dry her feet and underbelly," Levi said.

Elsie stepped into the room and knelt, her hands full of wriggling puppy covered in snow and icy water while Levi shoved the door shut against the wind.

"That redhead is in the mudroom!" George yelled from wherever he was. "Bishop Nathan, I tell you that you need to keep a close eye on them two. My walking stick is somewhere if they didn't steal it! Spare the rod and spoil the child!"

Someone chuckled. Elsie couldn't see who because it was somewhere behind and because she was busy with the wriggling, sopping-wet puppy that needed to calm down before she made another puddle inside.

"Since that boy has no father, it's up to us," George shouted.

Levi swallowed hard enough that a muscle jumped in his throat, and he scowled, but pain filled his eyes. "That explains why my own walking stick was employed against me," he said quietly. He slipped off his black gloves and laid them on the washer.

"You're hardly a child." Elsie peeked up at him.

His mouth opened, but a shadow appeared in Elsie's peripheral vision, and he shut it.

Elsie turned her head and looked up at Bishop Nathan. His eyes twinkled. "You just can't stay out of the mudroom, can you?"

"What can I say? It's a happening place," Levi quipped. His coat joined the gloves. "I'll take care of the dog now." He bent to take her from Elsie.

His rough and calloused fingers grazed the back of her hands as he grabbed the pup, sending delicious tingles up her arms. She pulled away, not wanting the bishop to witness them flirting. "I'll get the table set." Her voice might have been strangled.

"I ate at home, so if you give me a chore, I'll get busy. I notice you brought in a boxful of some type of woodworking project. Let me help. I used to enjoy that kind of work back in the day. After the prayer, explain what you're doing and how I can help." Bishop Nathan started to turn away, then stopped. "Working together is the best time to hold conversations, I've found."

Except, Elsie and Levi wouldn't be alone for a private conversation. She sighed as she entered the kitchen and met Noah's eyes. He snickered. "Sneaking off to be with 'that boy' again, ain't so?"

"She's going to marry that boy someday," Abigail sighed with a smile.

If only. But no. He couldn't marry, and she was going to leave the Amish to move to Chicago with her oldest brother.

"Careful, now," George shouted as an EMT parked the stretcher next to him. "I'm an old man. Don't want to break my back—Whoa!"

The two EMTs had George secured on the stretcher as Elsie watched. They covered him with a blanket as she rushed to grab his coat and hat.

She laid them on his lap. George grasped her hand with his free one that wasn't clutching the carved cat. "*Danki* for asking me to chaperone. Best fun I had in ages. I'll do it anytime."

Tears burned Elsie's eyes and she gulped, giving George a quick hug. "You've been a chaperone like none other."

George beamed, but that was the truth.

"I'll call your wife," she said.

George hissed. "Don't bother her. I don't want her out in this weather, and someone needs to stay with my cats."

But still, his wife needed to know.

"What about the walking stick?" She pointed to it.

"Borrowed it from Levi. I have more canes at home and the hospital lets me ride in a wheelchair. Great fun. Especially when they leave me unattended and I can race. Besides, the bishop might need the walking stick to whomp that boy with."

Okay, then.

She stepped back and the EMTs rolled the stretcher—and George, clutching the carved cat—out.

Despite the wind howling outside, the crackle of the fire, and Levi's low crooning to the pup in the mudroom, the house instantly seemed silent. Elsie took a deep breath and let the quiet seep in. The tension level dropped at least ten degrees even though the bishop was still there.

Then Abigail burst into tears.

Elsie took one look at her and decided they were happy

tears, since she was smiling. But all three men stopped what they were doing, turned toward her, and stared.

"Should I start screaming like George?" Noah teased.

Abigail sniffled. "I'm just so happy! We have food, heat, and the people I love most are here with me. And not only that, but Elsie and I get to start cleaning."

Levi snorted. "*Jah*, I can see where that'd make you cry."

Elsie glanced at the mess the drunk and the puppy had left in the main living area. It was a disaster, but it would be ever so satisfying to get it whipped back into shape for Levi and Abigail. And it could be done quickly with both of them working together.

Just in time for the woodworking the men were going to do on Levi's train project and for all the Christmas baking Abigail wanted to do. But the baking wouldn't be done today or tomorrow, since that would be Sunday.

And she and Noah might be home by then anyway.

She wasn't ready to leave.

"How long is the blizzard supposed to last anyway?" she blurted.

The bishop frowned. "Word is late tonight, but there's another one close on this one's tail. I told my wife that I might be gone several days since the windchill is supposed to reach dangerously low levels between storms. However, if you're anxious to get home, you could listen for the blizzard to end tonight and then start out."

Elsie glanced at Noah. He hesitated a moment before he shook his head. "If Levi doesn't mind, I'd like to stay here and help with his project."

Everyone turned to Levi. He looked down. "But...I'd miss peppermint."

Elsie's face heated.

Abigail giggled.

Levi blushed. "I mean, I'm...I don't know what to say. Or why I said that." He buried his red face in the puppy's fur.

"How about *jah*?" Abigail asked. "If I make sure peppermint is included."

"If peppermint's included, then..." Levi raised his eyes and gazed at Elsie with an undecipherable expression. It might have included acute longing. "*Jah*."

Elsie's whole body warmed. Would she and Levi be able to arrange any bishop-free alone time?

Did she want to, with only passion and no commitment?

* * *

Levi was pretty certain he needed either a cold shower or about five minutes outside without a coat to control the sudden heat that burned his entire body, both from the desire he felt for Elsie and from shame for blurting that out in front of witnesses. And judging from the low chuckles from Noah and Bishop Nathan and Abigail's giggle, everybody there was very aware of what those words had implied.

Implied? Ha! He might as well have shouted it. He *wanted* Elsie Miller. Even now, with a cream-colored shawl over her green dress helping to conceal her assets.

He gulped. If he were able to marry, he'd beg Bishop Nathan to approve a quick wedding—and he'd cite how long they'd courted before they broke up as a reason. Not to mention that he and Elsie still loved each other.

But if Noah eventually married Abigail and if Levi wasn't granted permission to marry, then he was destined to be alone forever. He wore the "mark of Cain," invisible though it might be. Not only did he kill his brother—two of them—he also killed a sister, his parents, and his *grossdaadi*. George's best friend.

Which was probably why George called him "that boy"—he was named after his *daadi*—and also why George took too much pleasure in whacking him with a walking stick.

Levi had earned every bruise. And then some.

His throat burned and his appetite fled.

But not eating wasn't an option. It would hurt Abigail and cause questions from the bishop. And speaking of whom, would they be able to find privacy for their conversation, or should Levi prepare for a public confession, in front of the bishop, his sister, and the two Millers?

There was time enough to think about that later. First, he had to appear natural with the meal the women had prepared. He motioned Bishop Nathan toward the head of the table and took his position at the foot. Noah still sat beside Abigail, his bandaged hands resting on the table. Elsie slipped into the seat Noah had used that morning as the bishop bowed his head. "Let's pray."

Levi bowed his head, but words wouldn't come. Instead, the pending confession weighed heavy on his mind. He dreaded it, but at the same time he wanted it over and done with so he could move on with what remained of his life. Would he be shunned? Forgiveness was too much to hope for.

Oh, Gott. *Oh,* Gott, he groaned again, hopefully not out loud, right as the bishop murmured, "Amen."

Elsie slid the casserole dish a smidgen closer to him, and just to be polite, he took the equivalent of a couple of forkfuls and passed it to Noah as Elsie popped out of her chair. "I forgot. Abigail made coffee. Who wants some?"

"I could use a cup while Levi explains the details of his project. Rumors have him building a train so he can leave town." Bishop Nathan chuckled.

Levi supposed George might've been the one who started that one. He had said almost the same thing when he came to "fix" Levi's buggy.

"It's amazing, that's all," Noah said. "I was seriously wowed when I saw his workshop and heard the details."

"Details I'm still waiting on." The bishop accepted a mug of black coffee from Elsie. He smiled at her. "*Danki.*"

Levi swallowed a mouthful of pasta and tuna, then quickly explained the circus train he'd spent months laboring over and the impossible deadline for two more that'd landed in his lap almost a week ago on Tuesday. "So now I have about a week and a half to two weeks to finish two trains, depending on when Christmas Eve is." He hadn't actually looked at the calendar to see. Ignorance was bliss. "Though Noah and I got a lot done this morning before the intruder came."

And that bothered him more than a little. Why was that man driving the back roads of an Amish community during a blizzard? Was he lost? Was he looking for trouble? Or...His gaze slid to Elsie as she set a mug of coffee in front of him. Or had he vaguely remembered the hot "babe" he'd seen in town Monday and gone looking for her? Levi would probably never know.

"I can't wait to see. I did notice the carved 'cat' that George had. Amazing craftsmanship. If the rest is as high quality, then no wonder you've got orders for two more." He paused a beat. "And I'm curious about our conversation you mentioned. Is it private"—Bishop Nathan looked toward Elsie and raised his eyebrows—"or is it a family affair?"

Levi clenched his hands. If only he were asking permission to marry Elsie, or setting the date with the minister. But no. That would be never. He drew in a deep breath. "I need to settle my fate and confess something. It'd be easier for me to do it all at once so I don't have to explain my sin and the punishment multiple times, but either way will be hard on Abigail and Elsie."

"We'll hear it all at once." Abigail put her fork down. "After we eat." She frowned at Levi as if daring him to ruin the meal. "You guys can work and talk and Elsie and I will work and listen."

Elsie opened her mouth, then shut it, apparently remembering her position as paid "elf." Abigail was her boss. To a lesser degree, so was Levi. But as Elsie's eyes filled with tears and her trembling hand lightly touched his shoulder in unspoken support, he vowed to find some way to let her say her piece.

CHAPTER 23

Elsie pushed a noodle around on her plate as she struggled to appear quiet and docile in front of the bishop. Everyone else knew she was opinionated...Well, truthfully, Bishop Nathan probably knew it, too, but she didn't want to get scolded in front of everyone. Not when she wanted—no, needed—answers. She just wanted them privately so she could argue her point and maybe, *Gott* willing, get her way.

Daed would tell her she struggled with faith, that she could trust *Gott* to know what was best for her. And he was right. She did struggle with faith. What if *Gott*'s plan and hers didn't mesh?

That was why she had a backup plan. Chicago with Sam. Though they'd made their decision to go before she reconnected with the Wyses, so maybe Levi was the backup plan.

On the other hand, did she truly want Levi if he was all wrong for her? What if they ended up hating each other? Although she couldn't see that happening. Not on her side. Levi was just plain nice. Quiet. Easygoing. She was the one who tended to rush in where angels feared to tread.

She pushed away from the table, noting that most of their meal was untouched. She hadn't been hungry—too much excitement, maybe. Only Noah had cleaned his plate—nobody else had really done justice to Abigail's tuna casserole, and between that and the bean soup they'd made for George, they had enough food prepared for several days.

"I'll do dishes and clean the kitchen while you start cleaning the living room." Abigail pointed to the room in question. Its mostly open floor plan layout allowed her to get around with ease and see from one room to another without a wall getting in the way.

Elsie nodded, but Abigail's plan put her farther away from the men. If they talked quietly as Levi tended to do, Elsie wouldn't be able to hear. But maybe that was Abigail's motive.

Levi spread old newspapers over the table, while Noah and Bishop Nathan emptied the box of small paintbrushes, paints, glue, and other things Elsie couldn't see as she retreated to the mudroom for a broom and dustpan.

"Abigail gave us special permission to work in the house." Levi nodded toward his sister as Elsie made the return trip. "She doesn't like the mess or the stench in here."

"Understandable. Not many women would." Bishop

Nathan picked up a carved elephant. "I just can't get over the quality of your work. This is amazing."

"You should see his workshop. It's no wonder the *Englischers* call him Santa." Noah flexed his hands and winced. "I'm not going to be much help, but I'll do what I can. I can paint maybe. Bright colors?"

"For the train. The animals should be true to life." Levi pulled the tall kitchen trash can over to the table. At least that gave her a valid reason to approach the table where the men worked.

"A friend of mine said she'd set up a website for Levi," Elsie blurted.

Conversation paused. Attention swung to her. Levi and the bishop wore matching frowns.

Oh. Oops. She sort of forgot to tell Levi so he could get permission.

"Elsie." Abigail pointed to the living room and the mess.

Elsie tried not to huff as she reached the living room. Why couldn't they start by talking about what she wanted to eavesdrop on instead of only talking shop? Although a website would be considered shoptalk.

She leaned the broom and dustpan against the wall, then bent to set up the end table, which the intruder had knocked over. It wasn't broken, but there might be a few additional nicks on the edges. Levi's Bible had fallen, too. It'd landed open, the pages bent and a little torn from being stepped on. That saddened her. She picked up the Bible, smoothed the pages as best as she could, and carried it up the ladder steps to the loft office. Levi had a tape dispenser on his desk.

Carefully, she patched the tiny tears, trying not to catch

wrinkles in the tape. She ran her fingers over the small print of Proverbs 3:5–6: *Trust in the Lord with all thine heart; and lean not unto thine own understanding. In all thy ways acknowledge him, and he shall direct thy paths.*

She wasn't very good at any of that. Shame filled her. She didn't trust in the Lord with all her heart. She leaned heavily on her own understanding. She didn't acknowledge Him in all her ways...

No wonder her path was so confusing and filled with false starts and failed dreams.

She glanced toward the loft entrance to make sure no one was coming before dropping to her knees.

Lord Gott, *I want You to direct my paths. Please help me to trust You. Help me not to rely on my own understanding and to acknowledge You always.*

The unrest that'd filled her settled into a strange sort of peace that she wouldn't have been able to explain. Just that whatever happened, *Gott* had this. He had Levi and whatever his confession involved. *Gott* had her and Sam and Sammy.

Oh. Instantly the unrest and fear stirred to life—for both Levi and her plans to join the *Englisch*.

Surrendering her paths to the Lord had to be a constant decision.

"*Gott* has this," she whispered. "Trust Him."

She put those thoughts on repeat in her head and went downstairs. Without the Bible. But she could get it later.

The men were talking quietly as she grabbed the broom and tried to sweep up all the glass. It was hard to do with everything soaked in kerosene. She'd need to mop it at least once before she could get more glass up. No wonder Abigail assigned Elsie to clean the living room. Abigail wouldn't have been able to do this job easily. It wasn't personal; it was common sense.

The stench burned her eyes and nose and clung to her clothes to the point she wanted to open a window to air out the house, but it was way too cold.

The bishop said something Elsie couldn't hear.

Levi answered, a low rumble.

Trust in the Lord...

Elsie picked up the dustpan full of broken glass and carried it over to the trash can. Levi sat with the trash can between his legs and used a knife of some sort to cut pieces from a chunk of wood.

Abigail scraped table scraps into a dish for the pup.

Levi glanced up at Elsie with a tortured expression. His hands shook and as Elsie dumped the glass into the trash, Levi placed the knife and the wood on the table, then snagged her free hand with both of his.

"Sit a moment. Beside me."

She gulped, glanced at the bishop for permission and, at his nod, tugged her hand free from Levi's grip and pulled a chair around to face him.

He scooted the trash can away, adjusted the chair so it was closer to his, and motioned her to sit.

His tortured expression didn't ease.

Her worry sprang to life.

Trust in the Lord...Gott, help.

She dropped into the chair, and Levi took the dustpan from her and set it beside whatever it was he had been working on.

Noah laid the paintbrush down and rested his hands, palms up, on the table.

Bishop Nathan continued gluing a circus train cage as if he didn't have a care in the world.

Abigail delivered a bowl piled full of taffy to the table since they hadn't made more cookies yet. And she lingered.

And Elsie's stomach was churning, and she braced herself for the coming talk and wondered why she'd even wanted to hear this in the first place.

Levi grasped Elsie's hands again. He gulped. And gazed into her eyes as if she were his sole source of strength. Of comfort.

Trust in the Lord...

He opened his mouth. Worked it. And nothing emerged. Except a strangled moan.

Bishop Nathan cleared his throat. "An Amish proverb goes, 'You can spare yourself many problems...' It doesn't say how, but I like to think that it's 'if you start with prayer.' With that said, let's pray. I'm going to break with tradition and pray out loud."

A muscle jumped in Levi's jaw, but he dipped his head.

Trust Gott... *acknowledge Him...* Gott, *lead this conversation. Help me to trust.*

The bishop bowed his head and Elsie quickly closed her eyes. "Heavenly Father, this conversation might be difficult for Levi. Please, go before us, guide this conversation, and let Your will be done in this conversation as well as in Levi's life. Give me wisdom on how to respond. Amen."

Elsie opened her eyes, and once again Levi gazed into hers. This time there were tears pooling on his lashes. And maybe a smidgen of hope glimmering in his expression.

"I killed my entire family," he blurted.

What? Elsie blinked. That wasn't what she had expected. How could Levi have done that?

That simply wasn't possible.

* * *

Levi latched his attention on Elsie, focusing on the trust reflected in her eyes. Her belief in him might spare him many problems. Although her tempting curves and peppermint caused their own problems. All he knew was that even if she overreacted, she was the one he needed to cling to. He wasn't convinced that *Gott* heard his cries for forgiveness, even if the police ignored his multiple confessions of guilt that terrible day.

Somebody gasped. Levi didn't look, but he thought it was Abigail.

"What do you mean, you killed your family?" The bishop's voice came through a thick fog.

Elsie's hands tightened around his.

He swallowed his fear. The confession had begun and that was the hardest part. Or it should be, anyway. "I was going out to my workshop to finish a gift I planned to make for Elsie." A still-unfinished gift, buried at the back of the highest shelf in his shop. "We were courting at that time. As I passed the propane tank, I noticed a gas smell, but I didn't take the time to go back into the house to tell *Daed*. I didn't turn off the supply. I did nothing. And then the world exploded and everyone was gone except for Abigail, and she wasn't expected to survive."

"*Daed* knew," Abigail whispered.

Levi gulped. Even though he heard the words, they didn't make any sense to him.

"I murdered my family. I'm condemned. And that's why I can't marry."

*   *   *

Elsie wanted to cry. What terrible lies Levi believed. Words of denial danced on the edge of her tongue, but she fought to keep them contained. She sensed the words needed to come from someone else. So all she did was squeeze his hands to show her support. Prayed, *Gott, help him know the truth.* And gazed into his tear-filled eyes, finally seeing the love shining in them, the exact same look in his eyes that Noah had when he looked at Abigail—absolute trust and faith that while this "surgery" might hurt, she wouldn't deliberately cause him pain. Mixed with them was a liberal helping of love—as if she alone mattered to him. Or that she was the center of his world. Or something that she wasn't able to find the words for. All she could do was stare back, offer her support and love, and pray.

The tears beading on his lashes spilled, running down his cheeks in rivers. And despite the presence of the bishop and that couples even touching was frowned upon—though really, that was unrealistic—she opened her arms wide. Levi fell against her shoulder and sobbed out years of pent-up grief.

She wrapped her arms around him, rubbed his back, and prayed.

Bishop Nathan went for…something. Shuffling sounds came from the living room followed by "Hmm."

"What are you looking for?" Abigail rolled in that direction.

"I thought Levi kept his Bible in here."

"I took it up to the loft," Elsie said.

"I'll get it." Noah stood.

Elsie gathered Levi closer.

He turned his wet face into her neck. "I'm sorry. I'm so sorry. I regret my mistakes. Every single one of them. Including you."

Wait. She was a mistake?

CHAPTER 24

Levi wanted to pull Elsie closer and kiss her for listening, but that would be highly inappropriate and, after crying like a baby, probably a turnoff. He'd noticed her stiffening there at the end. A man who cried on a woman's shoulder shouldn't expect said woman to be moved with passion, especially in front of an audience that included their throat-clearing bishop and their siblings.

He rather reluctantly disengaged himself from her arms and mopped his face with his sleeve. He looked around, surprised to find himself alone with Elsie at the dining room table. Abigail set three unlit taper candles on the end table in the main room while the bishop stood at the foot of the ladder, watching Noah climb down carrying something black. A book. Levi's Bible? What was it doing upstairs?

Noah handed the Bible to the bishop, who thumbed through it while returning to the kitchen.

He opened the Bible and handed it to Levi, then sat, followed by Noah.

Levi glanced down. 1 Timothy 1.

"Read verses nine and fifteen. Out loud, please." Bishop Nathan picked up an unpainted circus train cage. He ran his fingers along the edges. Levi hoped they were sanded smooth. Though honestly, that paled considering the harsh judgment about to be passed down straight from *Gott*'s mouth. He braced himself, then winced as he realized Elsie would hear the punishment. And not only her, but also Noah and Abigail. However, now that he'd brought up the topic, it was best to get it over with.

Elsie shifted her chair farther away as Abigail wheeled into the room.

Levi looked down at the passages. He cleared his throat, running his fingertip over the words. "Knowing this, that the law is not made for a righteous man, but for the lawless and disobedient, for the ungodly and for sinners, for unholy and profane, for murderers of fathers and murderers of mothers, for manslayers..." He stumbled to a stop, his voice breaking. Even if he did blame himself for letting it happen... He glanced at Abigail to see tears running down her cheeks. *And injuring sisters*... "It was an accident!"

Noah nodded.

It hurt too much to look at Elsie, despite being very aware of her skirt brushing against his pant leg.

"I know. Read verse fifteen."

Levi stared at the bishop for a long moment; then he cleared his throat again. "This is a faithful saying, and worthy of all acceptation, that Christ Jesus came into the world to save sinners; of whom I am chief."

"Remind me what Paul did." Bishop Nathan raised his bushy gray eyebrows.

Levi closed the Bible on his fingers, keeping the location. "He, um, when he didn't know Jesus, he killed Christians."

"On purpose. Not accidentally."

Levi nodded. Paul had done much worse than Levi ever had. If anyone deserved to be arrested, it was—

"And he was forgiven. Now read Ephesians 1:6." Bishop Nathan picked up a piece of sandpaper.

Levi thumbed through the Bible to find the verse. "To the praise of the glory of his grace, wherein he hath made us accepted in the beloved."

Accepted? Was it possible? He looked up.

Bishop Nathan speared him with a glance. "If He can forgive Paul, can He forgive you?"

Levi's gaze skittered from the bishop to Elsie, still sitting in front of him, head bowed. His throat threatened to close. He swallowed and managed a mute nod. *Lord Gott, forgive me. Help me to forgive myself.*

"Think on this: The Lord knows us through and through. Despite our sin, He loves us. Because of our sin, He came and died to save us." Bishop Nathan rubbed a spot on the circus train car with the sandpaper. "Now Abigail has something to share."

Levi glanced at his sister. She had said something earlier. What was it? He tried to remember. Something about *Daed*...

Noah reached for her hand, a silent show of support.

"*Daed* knew." Abigail stated it as absolute fact. "He was going to call the company on Monday, but we used propane for everything back then and we were cooking and showering for church the next day and *Daed* reasoned that it should be okay for another day or two. And maybe it would have been, except our sister Susan got into an argument with *Mamm* about her bad choices. Susan snuck out for a forbidden cigarette; I saw her from the back window, and the lit match and the fumes..." She shook her head. "For months, I was so angry at Susan for doing this to me." She waved at the wheelchair. "But her must-have cigarette cost her own life. Forgive yourself, Levi. You aren't to blame."

"Daed knew? Susan smoked?" Levi stared at Abigail. How could he have missed knowing that? Then again, he'd been consumed with thoughts of Elsie and their hoped-for upcoming wedding...

He vaguely remembered Susan storming into the kitchen that Saturday evening. He'd turned his back on her drama, grabbed a cinnamon roll that *Mamm* was making for breakfast, and hurried out to the workshop...

"I had no idea you blamed yourself. I would've told you sooner," Abigail whispered.

"Your *daed* would've left the propane on, for the necessities," the bishop said. "If Susan hadn't lit a match, it might have been fine. You are not guilty of murdering your family. Forgive yourself."

Levi tried to absorb the truth. To let the truth of the situation fully sink in and the burden roll off his shoulders. It was Susan's fault. And instead of paying penance with extra work for the past years, he'd been the man of the house and caring for the household that remained. He sat straighter, a lightness around his heart.

"And forget that nonsense you said earlier. You *can* marry..." His gaze slid to Elsie. Lingered. Then returned to Levi with a furrow in his brow.

Levi embraced the gift of forgiveness. Of hope mixed with a desire for Elsie. Of a sudden craving for peppermint…

"But you need to explain to Elsie why she is a mistake," Bishop Nathan continued.

"What? She's not." Levi blinked. Looked at Elsie. Pain radiated across her expression, darkened her eyes. "Did I say she was?"

"Mind that I couldn't hear clearly, but I believe you said, 'All my mistakes. Including you,' to Elsie," the bishop said.

"I didn't mean that the way it sounded," Levi whispered, grasping her hand again. Time for damage control. He couldn't let her get away again.

"I'll give you and Elsie ten minutes of unchaperoned time alone to talk. But you might want to stay out of the mudroom." Bishop Nathan winked.

"The bedroom's okay, then?" Levi raised a brow.

* * *

Elsie didn't quite know what to think as she looked into Levi's twinkling eyes. He made a joke? It'd been far too long since he'd made a joke. Since there had been a twinkle in his eyes. She was glad he found freedom in the truth even though she wasn't sure what he meant about her being a mistake. Or what he could do to undo the pain of his words.

The bishop spluttered.

Noah chuckled. "It's not often you find a rabbit in the middle of a field."

Daed quoted that sometimes, crediting a rather quirky

Michigan bishop who visited Hidden Springs as a guest speaker once. It meant to "grab an opportunity when you can" as near as Elsie could figure. Now she had an opportunity to demand and get the truth about how he really felt about her.

"The bedroom!" Bishop Nathan's face flamed red. "Not before marriage, young man. Just for that, you can talk outside or have your moment of privacy in the living room."

Which wouldn't be very private, with it being open to the dining room and kitchen.

And outside meant talking quickly so they wouldn't get frostbite.

Levi smiled, but it wasn't big and bright. It was more of a smirk. He stood, pulled Elsie from her chair, and led her to the loft ladder steps. Open to below, yet more private than the main area. They'd be able to talk quietly—the blizzard winds would block most of the conversation, if not all. She wouldn't ask for more.

If he didn't mean she was a mistake, though, why'd he say it? And what did he really mean to say? That breaking up was a mistake? That leaving her behind at his third cousin's wedding was a mistake? That letting her walk away and avoiding her were mistakes? Or that even if he could marry, she wasn't his first choice now?

She scampered up the ladder steps behind him and looked for a clear spot on the floor to sit. Levi would get the chair, of course. But he shoved everything off half of the desk, undoing hours of her work—no wonder he had such a mess—and motioned for her to sit. On the desk.

Okay, then. She perched on the edge, leaning against it, because really, who sat on a desk? Other than schoolteachers. But who cared about that right now? She was alone with Levi.

He swirled the office chair around to face her.

He hesitated. Frowned. "This will be awkward. I had no time to plan out what to say." He inhaled. Exhaled with a puff. "You are *not* a mistake. How I treated you was."

Oh. Well, she could definitely agree with that. Not that she was completely innocent. "I'm the one who lashed out irra—"

He rolled forward, reached up, and touched his finger to her lips just as his cell phone buzzed. He didn't let his finger linger but pulled away. He picked up his phone, glanced at it, then frowned and set it down, focusing on Elsie again. "I was wrong to accuse you of that. I was the one who left you alone at a distant family wedding and forgot you when Abigail had a setback and nearly died. I didn't pay for your bus ticket. And I didn't even bother to explain when you confronted me."

"I didn't give you a chance." Guilt over her own actions filled her, overriding the relief at hearing him admit to his mistakes. "I'm sorry." Maybe once they got past this they could start healing their relationship. A sliver of hope flared to life.

He hung his head. "Then I avoided you for over a year, and when you brought me a huge check I needed but had lost, I acted immature, hiding like a child in the weeds behind the barn, then saying some unkind things, followed by hot-and-heavy kissing that I shouldn't have done. Using you at the frolic to keep other girls away and, quite honestly, guys away from yo—"

The cell phone buzzed again. Insistently. The interruption

irritated her, but at least it gave her a few moments to process his words and let them settle in her heart.

Levi picked it up again. Glanced at the screen. "I don't recognize the number." He swiped it. "Wyse Construction. Levi speaking."

* * *

"Hi." The female voice sounded vaguely familiar. "Levi, this is Jane Turner, Elsie's friend. I mentioned that I was going to be building your website, but in the meantime I listed your handcrafted toys on—"

Oh. He'd forgotten about that and he needed to discuss it with Elsie. He pulled the phone away from his ear and pressed the speaker option. Elsie—as his elf—would be able to hear, then, and they could discuss it rationally. He also needed to get permission from the bishop if he decided he needed a website to pursue his hobby as a job.

"Anyway, we have a slight issue," Jane continued. "A man wants to order several items for Christmas gifts for his grandchildren. He's willing to pay double and for expedited shipping. I know you said you're booked until after Christmas, but Elsie said you needed the money for medical bills, and with that in mind, I accepted on your behalf."

Levi saw red. "I haven't even discussed the website with the bishop yet, and—"

The woman made some sound of dismissal. "Elsie always says that it's easier to ask forgiveness than to get permission. I'll email you the details."

Really? She said that? Levi looked at Elsie. The

color drained from her face, leaving her eyes wide, her cheeks pale.

He counted to ten multiple times.

Jane apparently took his silence as agreement, gave a cheery goodbye, and disconnected.

Levi placed his phone back on the desk. Sighed. "Elsie…"

"She's a bit pushy."

That was an understatement. But then so was his elf. "Elsie." He took a deep breath.

"You know, I'll just give you some space." Elsie's smile wobbled.

That was probably wise.

Not that he was mad at her. It was more that her flippant impulsiveness had put him in an impossible situation both with the bishop and with meeting the new order deadline.

He wanted to shake her…

No. He wanted to kiss her. To thank her for her support and belief in him and then gently suggest clearing things with him first.

She straightened. Grabbing a small pile of papers, she handed it to him. "I know this won't change anything, but I found these." Her voice broke. "Uncashed checks." Then she turned and almost dashed for the ladder steps.

He glanced at them. "*Danki*." He exhaled. "Elsie…"

She didn't pause.

Levi bowed his head. Clasped his hands. How would he explain this to the bishop? Gott, *help*.

CHAPTER 25

Elsie was so fired. She didn't need to hear the words to know the truth. Why was she such a mess-up? And Jane quoting her words about it being easier to ask forgiveness than permission back to Levi...She could only imagine what he must think, but the flash of anger, the clenched jaw, and the jumping muscle on his face spoke volumes without him saying a word.

Once at the bottom of the steep stairway, Elsie brushed away the stubborn tears that'd escaped her burning eyes. She didn't want anyone witnessing her return to know that her discussion with Levi hadn't gone so well.

It'd gone terribly.

She would be getting fired! Again!

She bit back a wail that wanted to emerge, averted her eyes from the men working at the table and Abigail doing something at the sink, and even though Elsie hadn't finished the living room, she slid her feet into her shoes.

She needed space, too.

But not for the same reason.

No, her temper wasn't about to explode, but rather the waterworks were going to gush with the force of a collapsing dam.

Elsie grabbed her outerwear off the hook near the door. She put them on as she yanked the door open, shoved through the screen, and went outside.

The logs and the church's benches were still scattered on the porch and driveway. She went to work restacking the firewood. It would give both her and Levi time to cool down and regain control of their emotions—she brushed at the tears still spilling—before they calmly discussed her discontinued employment as an elf.

Though he might not fire her while Bishop Nathan was there.

Then again, he might. He'd have a witness to testify that she'd behaved unseemly by hiring a web designer without permission. Or not hiring. It was free because Jane had owed Elsie a favor.

She'd meant to tell Levi about it, planned to chalk it up as a benefit of having her for an elf, but every time she'd thought of it, he'd kissed her and she'd forgotten her own name.

At least she was still working at the moment, saving Levi the job of restacking the woodpile.

Not to mention she was burning off steam. Amazing how she could still do that while crying up a storm to rival the one outside.

The tears froze to her face while the wind howled, the snow blew, and heavy gray clouds still hung low over the earth, filled with the promise of things to come.

More snow. Actually, the bishop had said another blizzard.

The road crews were probably working overtime trying to keep the busy interstate highway cleared.

She'd just finished restacking all the fallen logs when the rumble of a very noisy vehicle filled the air. She turned toward the road and peered through the snow.

A mustard-colored older-model Jeep boomed down the street. Her brothers would call it a 4x4 and joke about off-roading, but Elsie wasn't sure what that meant. Other than the obvious.

The Jeep paused at the end of the driveway, next to the intruder's vehicle—which was still in the ditch and waiting on a tow truck—and Levi's now very crooked mailbox. The pole was at an approximate forty-five-degree angle.

Sam stuck his head out the open window on the passenger's side of the Jeep and yelled something that got blown away in the wind.

The Jeep pulled into the driveway and roared up to the house.

Elsie brushed the wood chips off her gloves and waded through the almost knee-deep snow to the vehicle.

Sam must've seen something in her expression because he frowned. "What's wrong?"

Little Sammy babbled something from his car seat in the back and kicked, reaching for her. She needed a snuggly cuddle from the sweet toddler.

Elsie gulped. "Levi's going to fire me."

Sam laughed. Laughed! "Is that all? You're an old pro at that. A master at getting fired."

"Wow. *Danki* for your overwhelming sympathy." *Jah*, she was sarcastic.

Sam laughed again. "Come on. Get in. The apartment opened up. We're moving to Chicago now before the next blizzard hits."

Now? She wasn't sure she wanted to go ever. Especially with the talk she and Levi had been having before Jane called. Hope had bloomed...only to be plucked and crushed.

And Levi's probable firing of her had sounded the death knell for anyone else in the community ever hiring her.

Elsie glanced at the driver. Sam's *Englisch* friend, Ryan. She forced something that she hoped resembled a smile. "Hey, Ry."

"Hey, beautiful." Ryan winked. "Wanna go out sometime?"

Not even. "In your dreams."

Ryan groaned.

"Leave your stuff here. Noah can take it home. You won't need any of your Amish clothes in Chicago." Sam twisted to make sure the back seat door was unlocked.

True. But... "Bishop Nathan is here." She glanced back at the house. A shadow moved in front of the window. Was it Levi? Coming to make the firing official?

"Then get in quick. You know our way. We just leave. No time for apologies, no time for delays, no time for goodbyes."

Still, Elsie hesitated. It was their way, though. It was just that she wanted to say goodbye to Noah and Abigail. To ask them to keep in touch. To explain why. And Levi—oh, her heart. Would the bishop shun her for this? Was she burning bridges forever?

Ryan revved the engine.

"Elsie, you will never get a job and keep it here. Sorry, but it's true. Get in!" Sam yelled the last word.

Elsie sniffed. More tears escaped. Her brother's words echoed her thoughts. She was worthless. Worthless!

The Jeep rolled forward an inch. Maybe two.

"Last chance. I need you. And you know none of the Amish will hire you now." Sam gave her a pointed look.

Sammy reached for her again. "Ellie come." His lower lip trembled.

Elsie's heart lurched.

Sam was right. Her future here was doomed. She flung the back door open and tumbled in next to Sammy. She straightened just as the house door opened and Levi stepped out.

His mouth moved. He extended a hand toward the Jeep.

Ryan hit the gas.

The door blew shut.

And they roared out to the road.

* * *

Levi watched the Jeep race down the drifted drive as it carried his Elsie away. Snow flew from the tires as if it were mud. Whoever was driving definitely went too fast for the conditions.

He'd recognized Elsie's older brother, but it seemed odd that Sam would pick up Elsie and not Noah. It was an even bigger mystery that Elsie left without saying goodbye. Without warning. She hadn't finished the job Abigail had asked her to do, which left his sister in the lurch. Why hadn't she said something? Unless it had been an emergency—and in that case, they would've picked up Noah, too. So he was back to square one.

Wait. She'd said she was giving him space. Surely she hadn't decided to step out of his life. The air was sucked out of his lungs. No. No, no, no.

The Jeep fishtailed as it reached the ice-covered main road. They must not have the four-wheel drive on. Levi whispered a prayer for Elsie's safety and tried to figure out what he'd done wrong.

Had she seen the flash of temper when he bit his tongue to keep from growling at Jane? He hadn't been angry at Elle. Mildly irritated, perhaps. He knew a good thing when he saw it, and Elsie was a good thing. A hard worker, she'd already made a significant difference in his loft office. It was still a mess but ever so much less cluttered. And the fact she'd found a stack of uncashed checks more than paid for her wages.

No, he'd been upset at pushy Jane and only irritated at Elsie for putting the cart before the horse. She should've asked him, given him time to consider it, and then he would've asked the bishop himself. Of course, he still could. And he would. But that wasn't the issue now.

The door opened behind him. "Where's Elsie?" Noah asked. "Abigail said she left in that noisy vehicle?" As in an unsaid but implied *Did she? Why?* and maybe a *What did you do now?* tacked on the end.

"*Jah.*" Levi swallowed a lump in his throat. He didn't know what else to say. He shut his eyes, then remembered Sam was in the front seat. He opened his eyes, turned, and looked at Noah. "Your brother Sam was in the front seat. I thought maybe it was an emergency. But if it was, they would've called for you."

Noah frowned. "Sam. Figures. He's been sneaking around lately. *Daed* fears he's planning to jump the fence. And, of course, he'd convince Elsie to go with him. She's so vulnerable, what with being fired so often and unable to find a beau. All she ever wanted was a home, a loving husband, and children, like any other normal Amish girl. Like Abigail wants."

Jah. That would be important to her. A dream he'd destroyed so many times and in so many ways. His throat hurt. His eyes burned. And there was nothing he could do. Except pray. He balled his fists to try to keep his emotions under control and attempted to look Noah in the eyes. He failed. His gaze rested somewhere near Noah's left cheek. "Abigail will get there." Just in case Noah harbored the same dreams about Abigail that Levi did about Elsie.

"She's there now," Noah said quietly. "She's not as helpless as you think."

"No, she isn't." But maybe Levi had needed to pretend that she needed him as much as he needed her.

Noah's mouth flexed and he pulled his cell phone from his pocket. He pushed something and put the phone to his ear. Then he grimaced. "Voicemail. Hey, Elsie, it's Noah. Call me." He touched something else and returned the phone to his ear. "Sam. Noah here. What's going— Hello? Hello?" He looked at Levi. "We got disconnected. Either that or he hung up on me."

It was probably the latter, especially since Noah's next two attempts went straight to voicemail.

Noah sighed. "I don't have a good feeling about this."

Neither did Levi. He looked toward the road again, but even though he could hear the roar of the engine in the distance, the Jeep was no longer in sight.

The wind and the snow picked up, obliterating the mailbox and the beat-up car still in the ditch. Levi shivered. He and Noah had both come out without a coat. Without shoes. And there was nothing they could do except pray. *Lord, keep her safe, and if it's Your will, please bring Elsie back to us.*

Levi cast another glance in the direction of the road. But the Jeep didn't magically reappear.

He turned to the door and noticed the now-stacked wood and still unstacked benches. Elsie had done something—been doing something—when the Jeep arrived. She'd been outside because of her anger and hurt and had therefore been easy pickings for Sam to convince to go with him.

If Levi hadn't lost his temper, then she'd still be here, because Sam would have had to go inside to talk to her... and the sight of the bishop would have sent him running without Elsie.

With a sigh, he returned inside.

Abigail sat at the kitchen table, twisting her hands together. "You let her leave."

It wasn't like Levi had a choice. Wait. His anger had hurt her feelings and put her in that position? He'd had a choice upstairs to not let her go. A choice to answer or ignore that phone call.

Bishop Nathan's head was bowed, but at Abigail's words, he raised it. His brow was furrowed. He opened his mouth and shut it a couple of times, then shook his head and returned his attention to the train car he held. Seconds ticked by. They felt like an eternity. The silence grew stifling.

Elsie weighed heavy on Levi's mind, but that reminded

him—it was time for that website conversation. Levi cleared his throat. "How do you feel about a business web page?"

The bishop didn't look up. "For the construction business, or for the toys?"

Levi cringed, almost afraid to admit it would be for his toy "hobby," like *Daed* had called it. What if the bishop felt the same? Silence stretched as Levi tried to find a little more courage.

Noah heaved a sigh and turned away from the open door. He shut it. "Sorry, Abby." He didn't say more, but Levi guessed he was referring to Elsie.

Abigail sniffled.

"Ask and it shall be given," Bishop Nathan said, paraphrasing part of a verse.

"Toys," Levi mumbled.

"If you're planning to make this"—he held up the toy he was sanding—"into a business, I'd say a website was needed."

Levi caught his breath. "Could I?" Good news, that. He grinned. Sort of. It probably resembled more of a grimace.

Bishop Nathan shrugged. "May not support a wife and children, especially at first, but it has definite possibilities."

Wife and children?

And with that the joy faded. Because the one he wanted to start a family with was in a mustard-colored Jeep going who knew where.

"Now faith is the substance of things hoped for, the evidence of things not seen," Noah quoted.

Levi stared down at his cold, wet, sock-covered feet. *Lord, give me faith.*

* * *

The Jeep hit an icy patch on the road and slid into the oncoming traffic lane. Nobody was near, though, and Elsie clenched her fists, trying not to scream as Ryan fought the wheel. He steered into the skid, which seemed wrong to Elsie, but it worked as he quickly got it under control. He said something about four-wheel drive and did something.

Sammy babbled about playing in the snow in Pennsylvania Dutch, waving his little hands in the air as he talked and kicked his feet. He was hard to understand unless she focused on him. She wasn't focused. One of his tiny tennis shoes flew off, landing on the opposite side of the back seat from Elsie. Sammy chortled.

Elsie patted his hand and peered up front. The roads were ice covered, and snow was still falling. It seemed heavier to Elsie. Her stomach cramped. She leaned forward as far as the seat belt allowed. "Shouldn't you maybe slow down?" Even in a horse and buggy there was such a thing as driving recklessly.

Ryan laughed. "This ain't nothing, beautiful. Let me find an almost empty parking lot and I'll show you fun."

Something about the sound of his laugh told her it wouldn't be fun. Not for her. She kept quiet because both agreeing and disagreeing would egg Ryan on. She had enough experience with him to know that. And she still didn't understand how Sam could be his friend. But then again, a free ride to their destination meant more money in their pockets. Money—she'd left her purse back at Levi and Abigail's house. No ID on her. No phone, so she couldn't call and apologize.

"I need practice driving," Sam said. He sounded a bit nervous, as if Ryan's driving bothered him, too.

Elsie's stomach cramped again. As far as she knew, Sam didn't know how to drive and now wasn't the time to learn. She bit her lip to keep the words unsaid.

"You got your permit?" Ryan glanced at Sam.

Sam had a permit? Bile rose in Elsie's throat. But then again, Sam would be careful since he had little Sammy in the vehicle.

Sam shifted in his seat and a moment later he flashed something in his worn brown wallet in Ryan's direction. Elsie couldn't see what it was, but Ryan nodded. "Cool. We'll give you highway time. The interstate should be clearer than these backroads." He looked over his shoulder at Elsie. "Do you got your permit, beautiful?"

She'd never even thought about her need for one in the *Englisch* world. But then again, Chicago had other transportation options. She wouldn't need to drive.

Sam laughed. "I'd hate to see what she'd do behind the wheel of a car."

Jah, there was that. But, "Hey." If they weren't in a moving vehicle, she'd swat him.

Ryan pulled off at a fast-food restaurant by the interstate for hot drinks. Despite being plowed, the parking lot was covered in snow. The wind caused drifting and Elsie wondered if visibility was affected for drivers. They shivered and hurried inside.

Sam paid for Elsie's drink since she forgot her purse. After bathroom breaks, they went back outside and Ryan paused at the door and motioned for Sam to get behind the wheel. "Make sure you get up to speed on the on-ramp. Some of those trucks come fast."

Sam grinned. "This is going to be so fun! Sammy, pay attention to your *daed*. Someday you're going to do this."

Elsie's stomach cramped again. This was not a great idea. She hesitated, hot drink in one hand, Sammy's hand clutched tightly in the other. "Maybe you should leave Sammy and me here. We could call for a ride home and join you later." Except, she didn't have a phone with her so she'd have to convince Sam to let her use his...

"Get in." Sam glared at her. "We'll stick together. Besides, most people would prefer to stay home in this."

True. She could have been warm and safe at Levi's house, even if she was fired. And with that thought, her eyes burned again. She blinked the tears away. She shouldn't have allowed Sam to talk her into this.

"Besides, what would you go home to? You can't get a job or a beau. You need a fresh start as much as I do."

Also true. It just hurt. Elsie sighed, put her drink in the cup holder, then buckled Sammy into his car seat and buckled herself in next to him. Sammy kicked one of his shoes off again. He looked at her and laughed.

Elsie closed her eyes a second. Gott, *if you don't want us to go, please stop us.*

Ryan got into the front passenger seat as Sam climbed in and started the engine. He backed out of the parking place, turned right toward the highway, got onto the on-ramp, and hit the gas.

Sam knew how to drive. Amazing.

An air horn blew.

Elsie turned.

A semitruck grill seemed to fill the back window.

Someone screamed. It took her a second to figure

out it was her. Ryan shouted something she couldn't understand over the screams. Sam jerked the wheel to the left.

The world changed to slow motion.

There was already a vehicle in the other lane. It swerved and lost control.

There was a brief moment before the Jeep hit the other car.

Then a hard shove as the semi rammed into the back of the Jeep.

The world went black.

CHAPTER 26

Something was wrong. Levi could feel it. Sense it. He could almost taste it. His thoughts were fixated on Elsie as the wind picked up and the falling snow turned into another blizzard. He tried to focus on the toy trains, but while he worked on making a new lioness to replace the one he'd given to George, his mind was a jumble. He wanted to fix the Elsie problem, not pretend to feel creative. He missed her.

Noah coaxed the puppy outdoors to take care of business while Abigail set pretzel dough near the wood-stove to rise. Normally, that would set Levi's mouth to watering.

This time it didn't.

Abigail hadn't finished the cleaning she'd asked Elsie to do, though he assumed it would be next on her to-do list. She wouldn't save it for Elsie even though she was convinced Elsie would return.

Especially since Noah seemed to have that verse on repeat. "Now faith is the substance of things hoped for, the evidence of things not seen." He quoted it what seemed like every five minutes.

Bishop Nathan was strangely silent, his attention seemingly fixed on the part of the train he was working on. But he got his cell phone out of his pocket and set it on the table where he'd notice if it lit up, as if he were expecting a phone call. And he might well have been.

Levi was tempted to do the same. But did Elsie even have his phone number anymore? She did have Noah's, though, so if she wanted to reach him, she could.

Abigail went to the back part of the house and returned minutes later with Elsie's purse. Abigail opened it and took out Elsie's cell phone. Abigail laid it on the table. "Elsie left it."

Levi stared at it numbly. Unless Sam or someone else let Elsie borrow a phone, and she used it to call him, there'd be no contact.

Noah came in with the puppy. He held up his phone. "There's been an accident just on the interstate. A police officer called on Sam's phone to the last call received. They are taking them to the nearest hospital in—"

Levi put his whittling knife on the table and stood. "I'm going." The hero racing to the heroine's side, just like in one of Abigail's romance books.

The bishop gave him a look. "Of course you are. You and every other Amish person brave enough to navigate a blizzard. It wouldn't be a hospital stay without an Amish field trip to visit the victims." He quirked a quick—and fleeting—grin. "Of course, you're the only one with a romantic interest in one of them."

"With plans to marry her in the not-so-distant future," Levi amended with an equally pointed look at the bishop, since he hadn't exactly asked permission yet. The declaration was followed with resolve and a prayer for her healing and safety. But even so, he'd take care of her no matter what injuries she'd sustained, just to have her in his life.

"I'll call for a driver," the bishop said.

Noah pushed a button on his phone. "I'll activate the Amish grapevine."

* * *

Elsie reclined on the hospital bed in the room she was taken to. The doctor made the decision to admit her for observation since she was unconscious when the ambulance arrived. Other than a few cuts from shattered glass and a stiff neck, she felt fine. But the doctor said she was a living miracle.

A mix of emotions filled her. Relief that *Gott* had saved her warred with fear and worry for her brother and nephew. The nurses she'd asked about them either didn't know anything or refused to tell her.

Down the hall, someone bellowed. George. Elsie smiled. Some normality in the situation.

Someone tapped on the open door, and she carefully turned her head toward the sound.

Levi approached, his hands behind his back. As he neared, he pulled one hand out, revealing a bouquet of red roses. "For you," he said. "I'm so sorry, Elsie. I never meant to make you go away—"

She barked a short laugh. But oh, she was ever so glad to see him. "You fired me!"

He frowned as he pulled up a chair and sat. "I don't think I did; I didn't mean to anyway. I'm sorry. I want to keep you as my elf and—"

"I didn't want to go with Sam, but he said...I mean, I thought..." Though Levi had never actually said that she was fired. She'd jumped to conclusions again.

"Elsie, I—"

"I saw that boy, Bishop!" George bellowed from somewhere down the hall. "Is that redhead here?"

Forget this. They could go on all day talking about their mistakes. The point was the lessons were learned. Elsie slowly and painfully slid out of the hospital bed and sat on Levi's lap.

He caught his breath, his hands automatically going to the curve of her hips to steady her and draw her nearer. "Elle, please forg—"

She snuggled closer, turning her head into his neck and kissing him the way he did that last time. "I forgive you. I love you. I'm sorry for my mistakes, too." She found his pounding pulse with her lips.

He groaned. His hands found her waist. "Elle..."

She trailed kisses up his neck, the strong curve of his jaw, and teased the corner of his lips.

He groaned again. Pulled her tight against him, caught her chin, and brushed his lips over hers.

Brushed! That was so not good enough. She twisted in his arms, caught his head in her hands, and took control, kissing him with every molecule of pent-up desire she had in her.

He moaned deep in his throat. "Elle, if you don't stop, this isn't going to be G-rated."

She squirmed, kissed him again. "Marry me."

The breath left him in a whoosh. "I think"—kiss—
"that was supposed"—kiss, kiss—"to be my line..."

His hands slid up just a smidgen. She tangled her
fingers in his hair, arching against him, a whimper
escaping.

"Yes," he might have growled. "I'll...marry...you."

"I think marriage is a good idea," the bishop said from
somewhere right behind her.

* * *

Levi froze.

Elsie launched herself off his lap so fast she tumbled
awkwardly onto the bed. Good thing she was fully
clothed and not in a hospital gown.

She buried her face in her hands. Shaking. He wasn't
sure if she was laughing or crying.

He looked over his shoulder at the bishop, who was
halfway into the room. The man smiled indulgently and
was probably semiproud of the fact that he had only
given them five minutes instead of the ten he'd promised
earlier. But oh, they'd made the most of that time.

Levi's cheeks burned.

"Since *she* proposed and you accepted..." The bishop
paused a beat. "We'll start marriage counseling tomorrow.
And as for the wedding, I have next Thursday free."

CHAPTER 27

Elsie's embarrassed laughter died. She peeked through her fingers at the bishop, who stared semisternly at Levi.

"George wasn't kidding when he warned me about you two." The bishop had a twinkle in his eyes.

Levi muttered something that might have been "Sorry." Except Elsie wasn't sorry at all. They'd worked things out.

"I hope you talked—uh, communicated verbally— before it got physical."

Her cheeks burned. At least they weren't in the bedroom—oh, wait. They were. The hospital "bedroom."

"We did—Wait. Thursday? This Thursday? As in before Christmas Thursday?" Panic filled Levi's voice.

Come to think of it, she started to panic a bit, too, at the thought of a dress and the other things that go into a wedding and how her family didn't have the money to feed that big of a crowd on such short notice.

"Is that a problem?" Both of Bishop Nathan's eyebrows shot up.

"No. I mean, *jah*. I mean, the impossible deadline, which will be even more impossible if I have to stop work and get married."

Elsie recalled the bare pantry at his house just a week ago. He did need every hour to work. And Amish weddings took forever. Sure, he loved her. But he couldn't afford to miss a complete day of work unless he wanted to offend and lose a well-paying customer.

"*Have* to? Which is more important? Elsie or the deadline?"

"Elsie," Levi said. He glanced at her and smiled.

"The deadline," Elsie choked out. "He needs the money for Abigail."

Bishop Nathan fixed his gaze on Levi, ignoring her. "Right. And since I know the quality of your work, and since you have made yourself available to others such as Luke for a pittance, and since you have been so kind to George and gave him the carved cat, I've taken the liberty of talking to Elsie's *daed* in the waiting room. After the blizzard, the men of the community will gather at your home for a work frolic. With your permission, we'll have an assembly line process, and if all goes as planned, your circus trains will be done, or mostly done, that evening."

Daed and the other men would help?

She had nothing to worry about. Trust *Gott*. If He had the circus trains, He could handle a wedding.

CHAPTER 28

Monday morning, after the blizzard ended, men who were able to came on foot and by horse and buggy. The community outpouring of love and compassion rocked Levi to his core, both at the hospital the previous evening and day and that morning. Abigail had thrived on the attention she received. She had insisted she be able to go visit Elsie, and Levi had allowed Noah to assist her in and out of the van that'd come to take them to the hospital Saturday evening.

Elsie arrived a couple of hours later with her *daed* and two *grossdaadi*s bringing good news. Sammy had been discharged—with minor cuts—to his *daadi*'s care. Sam was still alive, in intensive care due to internal injuries. No word on Ryan, but Levi didn't know him. He was Sam's friend.

Elsie helped Abigail prepare sandwiches, pretzels, and plenty of cookies to keep the men well-fed.

The coffee flowed while the bishop preached a mini-sermon on the verse Noah had quoted about two being better than one. And looking around the room at the men working, talking, and laughing made Levi realize it was true. He would've been so much wiser and stronger if he hadn't shut others out. He'd denied himself—and Abigail—the blessing of having friends, advice, and support. And he'd denied others the opportunity to be blessed by giving of their time, skills, and wisdom.

When Levi paused work for a short break to stretch his legs, he glanced outside at Abigail and Elsie putting the final touches on a family of snowmen. Four of them, maybe to represent the families they would become. Hopefully. Levi and Elsie and Abigail and Noah.

By the time evening fell, the trains and animals were finished, except for letting the paint dry, in time for them to be delivered—early—the next day. They also had the online orders completed and ready to be shipped.

By *Gott*'s grace they'd met Levi's impossible deadline, and he learned that it was okay to lean on others.

The next day, Bishop Nathan gave Elsie and Levi a comprehensive marriage counseling based on 1 Corinthians 13.

* * *

Thursday morning Elsie sat on a bench sneaking peeks at Levi during the looong wedding sermon. Abigail sat in her wheelchair beside her, probably daydreaming of her own someday wedding.

Sam was somewhere in the crowd in his own temporary wheelchair while he recovered from the accident.

Finally the bishop made the man-and-wife pronouncement while George—who hadn't broken any bones—wildly rang sleigh bells and shouted something about being a matchmaker, much to the amusement of the entire community and the embarrassment of his wife.

And then after the long day filled with meals, family, friends, and conversation, Elsie and Levi were—at last—alone. They'd arranged for Abigail to spend the night at Elsie's house.

Levi pulled out a wrapped gift. "I started this two years ago, but I can't think of a better wedding gift." With a grin, he handed her the red-and-white package and sat on the bed, covered with her hope chest quilt, watching as she opened it.

Her fingers fumbled a bit with the tape. She removed the paper to reveal a hand-carved recipe box. "Oh, it's beautiful." Elsie opened it, and inside was an envelope of recipes. She recognized the handwriting and looked up with a pounding heart. "Your *mamm*'s? These were her prized recipes only shared with family?"

He nodded with heat in his eyes. Tears pricked hers.

"*Danki*. I couldn't think of a better gift. I was afraid these got lost in the explosion." She thumbed through them.

"They did, but she had copied them out as a wedding gift before, when we were getting serious." Levi's gaze was filled with something that made her want to snuggle him on the bed.

She put the recipe box down on the dresser and sat beside him. "I'll treasure them always, but they pale in comparison to the gift I've waited for. You."

A grin tilted his mouth. "You're the only gift I really wanted."

She giggled as she slid a bit closer. "Santa knew exactly what I wanted this Christmas."

He chuckled and pulled her into his lap. "And me. An elf."

And then he kissed her.

RECIPES

Amish Baked Oatmeal

This recipe was my Amish grandmother's. She never measured, using a pinch of this and a pinch of that, so I played with it to get approximate measurements. It tastes like an oatmeal cookie. It stores well in the refrigerator and can be reheated in the microwave and served with milk. This has to sit overnight, so plan accordingly. It is well worth the wait, however!

Serves 6

- ⅓ cup butter
- 2 large eggs
- ¾ cup brown sugar
- 1½ teaspoons baking powder
- 1½ teaspoons vanilla
- 1 teaspoon nutmeg or 1 teaspoon cinnamon
- ¼ teaspoon salt
- 1 cup plus 2 Tablespoons milk
- 3 cups oatmeal (regular or quick)

1. Grease 1½-quart baking dish and drop in eggs and beat well.
2. Add brown sugar, baking powder, vanilla, nutmeg or cinnamon, and salt. Mix well until there are no lumps.
3. Whisk in butter and both measures of milk, then add oats.
4. Stir well and refrigerate overnight.
5. Preheat oven to 350°F.
6. Bake, uncovered, for 35–45 minutes, or until set in the middle.
7. Serve hot with warm milk poured over it.

I like to sprinkle this with walnuts and fruit—usually bananas, but other fruit works well, too.

SALTWATER TAFFY

Saltwater taffy is a candy and an upper-body workout all in one. To give it its light but chewy texture, you'll be pulling it, and pulling it, and pulling it for up to 15 minutes. Still want to make it? One of my sons and my three daughters all took a day to make some. They had a blast! Here's a recipe.

Makes about 50 1-inch pieces

- 2 cups sugar
- 3 Tablespoons cornstarch
- 1 cup light corn syrup
- ¾ cup water
- 2 Tablespoons butter

- 1 teaspoon salt
- ¼ to 1 teaspoon flavoring of choice (i.e., vanilla, lemon, maple, mint, etc.)
- 3 drops food coloring

1. Mix together sugar and cornstarch in a saucepan.
2. Use a wooden spoon to stir in the corn syrup, water, butter, and salt. Place the saucepan over medium heat and stir until the sugar dissolves.
3. Continue stirring until mixture begins to boil, then let cook, undisturbed, until it reaches about 270°F, or the soft-crack stage. Wash down the sides of the pan with a pastry brush dipped in warm water while the syrup cooks.
4. Remove the saucepan from the heat and add food coloring and flavoring. Stir gently, then pour onto a greased marble slab or into a shallow greased cookie sheet to cool.
5. When the taffy is cool enough to handle, grease your hands with oil or butter and pull the taffy until it's light in color and has a satiny gloss. You can have a friend help with this step, which should take about 10 to 15 minutes.
6. Roll the pulled taffy into a long rope, about half an inch in diameter, and cut it with greased scissors or a butter knife into 1-inch-long pieces. Let the pieces sit for at least a half an hour before wrapping them in wax paper or plastic wrap and twisting the ends of the wrapper.

Are you loving the Hidden Springs series?
Don't miss Kiah and Hallie's story in
The Amish Secret Wish.

Available in Spring 2021.

ABOUT THE AUTHOR

Laura V. Hilton is an award-winning author of more than twenty Amish, contemporary, and historical romances. When she's not writing, she reviews books for her blogs and writes devotionals for the *Seriously Write* blog.

Laura and her pastor-husband have five children and a hyper dog named Skye. They currently live in Arkansas. Laura enjoys reading and visiting lighthouses and waterfalls. Her favorite season is winter, and her favorite holiday is Christmas.

You can learn more at:

Twitter: @Laura_V_Hilton
Facebook.com/AuthorLauraVHilton

Fall in love with these charming contemporary romances!

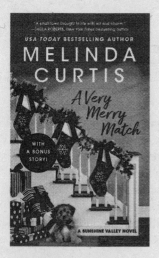

A VERY MERRY MATCH
by Melinda Curtis

Mary Margaret Sneed usually spends her holiday baking and caroling with her students. But this year, she's swapped shortbread and sleigh bells to take a second job—one she can never admit to when the town mayor starts courting her. Only the town's meddling matchmakers have determined there's nothing a little mistletoe can't fix . . . and if the Widows Club has its way, Mary Margaret and the mayor may just get the best Christmas gift of all this year. Includes a bonus story by Hope Ramsay!

THE TWELVE DOGS OF CHRISTMAS
by Lizzie Shane

Ally Gilmore has only four weeks to find homes for a dozen dogs in her family's rescue shelter. But when she confronts the Scroogey councilman who pulled their funding, Ally finds he's far more reasonable—and handsome—than she ever expected . . . especially after he promises to help her. As they spend more time together, the Pine Hollow gossip mill is convinced that the Grinch might show Ally that Pine Hollow is her home for more than just the holidays.

CHRISTMAS ON REINDEER ROAD
by Debbie Mason

After his wife died, Gabriel Buchanan left his job as a New York City homicide detective to focus on raising his three sons. But back in Highland Falls, he doesn't have to go looking for trouble. It finds him—in the form of Mallory Maitland, a beautiful neighbor struggling to raise her misbehaving stepsons. When they must work together to give their boys the Christmas their hearts desire, they may find that the best gift they can give them is a family together.

SEASON OF JOY
by Annie Rains

For single father Granger Fields, Christmas is his busiest—and most profitable—time of the year. But when a fire devastates his tree farm, Granger convinces free spirit Joy Benson to care for his daughters while he focuses on saving his business. Soon Joy's festive ideas and merrymaking convince Granger he needs a business partner. As crowds return to the farm, life with Joy begins to feel like home. Can Granger convince Joy that this is where she belongs? Includes a bonus story by Melinda Curtis!

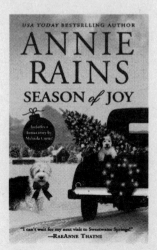

HER AMISH WEDDING QUILT
by Winnie Griggs

When the man she thought she would wed chooses another woman, Greta Eicher pours her energy into crafting beautiful quilts at her shop and helping widower Noah Stoll care for his adorable young children. But when her feelings for Noah grow into something even deeper, will she be able to convince him to have enough faith to give love another chance?

**THE AMISH
MIDWIFE'S HOPE**
by Barbara Cameron

Widow Rebecca Zook adores her work, but the young midwife secretly wonders if she'll ever find love again or have a family of her own. When she meets handsome newcomer Samuel Miller, her connection with the single father is immediate—Rebecca even bonds with his sweet little girl. It feels like a perfect match, and Rebecca is ready to embrace the future...if only Samuel can open his heart once more.

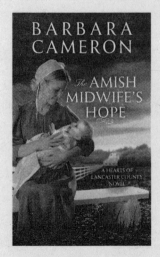

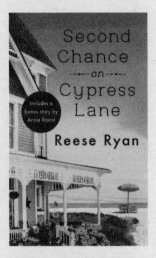

SECOND CHANCE ON CYPRESS LANE
by **Reese Ryan**

Rising-star reporter Dakota Jones is used to breaking the news, not making it. When a scandal costs her her job, there's only one place she can go to regroup. But her small South Carolina hometown comes with a major catch: Dexter Roberts. The first man to break Dakota's heart is suddenly back in her life. She won't give him another chance to hurt her, but she can't help wondering what might have been. Includes a bonus story by Annie Rains!

FOREVER WITH YOU
by **Barb Curtis**

Leyna Milan knows family legacies come with strings attached, but she's determined to prove that she can run her family's restaurant. Of course, Leyna never expected that honoring her grandfather's wishes meant opening a second location on her ex's winery—or having to ignore Jay's sexy grin and guard the heart he shattered years before. But as they work closely together, she begins to discover that maybe first love deserves a second chance...